# THEOAS FORGE

## BY SCOTT EDWARD BLADES

Rædld
Press™

Theoas Forge
Published by Rædld Press
Wichita, KS

If there be words
on these pages that
bring Him glory
I pray it be done.

Amoda

— SEB —

# Contents

Special thanks to my
loving wife, Kelly, for her
enduring encouragement.


Many thanks to my editor:
Victoria Kovacs
a.k.a.
The Magnificent Pen

 PROLOGUE 

The enmity between the Varruns and Darkrruns had started seasons prior, beginning with a sage named Stolt who had rebelled against his brothers. His peers oft wondered why Stolt had chosen the life of a sage, as he displayed no characteristics of one pursuing self-sacrifice. He was, by the accounts of his fellow sages, both arrogant and proud. Leaving his cloister island, he began a pilgrimage of sanctuary to the jagged peaks of the Varrun homeland.

Stolt was a student of folklore and legend, obsessed with the story of the Ehkkahn, a dark entity who according to age old myths resided in the recesses of a long forgotten pit among the gorges of the far shore. Accounts of the Ehkkahn had passed from generation to generation as far back as any Varrun could remember. The legends chronicle a massive black swirling pillar, rising from the depths during certain celestial phases, with the Ehkkahn birthing arms that extended out for lenads-even as far as the Sea of Chime. The Ehkkahn's arms scoured the surface world seeking out willing souls to join to it. The reward for the submissive soul was a power said to enable one to fulfill the whole of their desires. However, in this case, the fable proved to be a reality.

Stolt discovered the lair of the Ehkkahn and built a hut that faced its entrance. He stayed for many phases, continually calling out for the Ehkkahn to ascend. He poured through the ancestral parchments he had brought with him, seeking some incantation to arouse the entity. All his efforts were too no avail. Cursing Patayros, the god of his brothers, he began summoning the Ehkkahn even more fervently. Above all else, Stolt sought to fulfill his own will, rejecting that of the one who gave him life. Whether by Stolt's pleading, or the Ehkkahn's volition, it eventually rose to the surface. The Ehkkahn enveloped Stolt, causing the darkness of his own soul to permeate the flesh and bone of his body, with his skin and garments taking on the color of death. The essence of his being given over completely to his inner nature, Stolt became a vessel for the Ehkkahn and was rewarded according to the desires of his heart. He had achieved influence over the souls of other language beings. What he could not find in the faith of his brothers, he found in submission to the Ehkkahn.

The Ehkkahn had a loyal servant in Stolt, who set about seeking converts, beginning with his own brotherhood, finding those weak in the faith and willing to follow. Varrunas also provided another field for harvest. Being aware of the reputation of the Varrun war forces with their incessant lust for conquest, he reckoned them to be of kindred mind and made them a prime target of his efforts-with much success. With many followers at his beck and call, he directed an altar be constructed to Ehkkahn and a low wall, interspersed with open alcoves, was built around the expansive pit. Willing souls would come to stand in the alcoves, waiting for the Ehkkahn to consume their spirits. The transformed beings came to be known by some as the "Darkrruns." Each being that joined to the Ehkkahn made it stronger, allowing its arms to reach out even farther into the Sea of Chime.

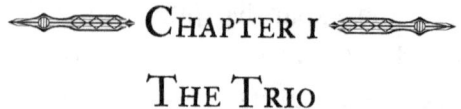

# CHAPTER I

## THE TRIO

They were born into the same tribe of Yonduts, attended the same school, and their family hutches were within shouting distance of one another. Jeddok was the undeclared leader of the trio; his two companions would follow his lead with little debate, whether it be into mischief or marvel. As children, the three would spend countless hours with Lohjji's grandpap, listening to him recount the stories of the tribes. It was these stories which impressed adventurous ideas upon Jeddok's young mind. He was inquisitive by nature and would bring the old Yondut to the point of exhaustion with endless questions. Lohjji respectfully listened and on occasion would ask a question, but his questions were directed toward entirely different discussions and caused great frustration for his grandpap, who would whack poor Lohjji over the head with a small sheaf of grain stalks he used as a bug swatter.

Then there is little Poodwah, the gentle, introspective scholar. He spent much time pouring through copies of the tribal belief books. It was as though the books gave the little Yondut strength beyond his size. As Poodwah matured, he spoke publicly in the hutch Commons. Though small of stature, his bold and eloquent discourses on the faith would put the fear of Theoas into the hearts of all those within hearing distance of his voice.

Quite a trio they were, but though from different families, the three bonded as close as brothers.

"Hey Jeddok!" shouted Lohjji as he ran towards the doorway of his neighbor's hutch.

Jeddok stepped outside and gently closed the door behind him, "Can you hold it down? My wife is trying to rest. What is all the noise about?"

With great exuberance Lohjji continued. "Do you remember all the stories my grandpap used to tell us? Look at this! Before his passing, GrandPap wrote down everything. This is only one of the dozens I found in some wax sealed leather pouches under GrandPap's old bed."

Jeddok's mind was immediately flooded with memories of his childhood. At first he had no words, but then roused himself back into the present. "Lohjji, have you told Poodwah about this?" Jeddok asked.

"No, he is not home and I haven't been able to find him. I think he went off to visit his grandmum, but I'm not sure."

"Well," Jeddok replied, "Let's go find that little Yondut. Let's start at his pap and mum's hutch."

The two started off before Jeddok realized he had not let his new bride know he was leaving. He didn't want his dear one to become distressed, and turned back toward his hutch.

Lohjji boomed, "Hey Jeddok! Where are you going?"

As Jeddok reached the door of his hutch, Lohjji continued his chides. Jeddok snatched a fruit from the taeris bush growing under the front window. The fruit traveled through the air as if it had been directed by another power and landed in Lohjji's still wide open mouth. The fruit splattered in a uniform pattern, covering both his hair and upper garment with juice and pulp. "If you don't hold down your voice, I'm going to give you seconds," Jeddok warned. Lohjji sighed and consumed what was left of the taeris fruit.

Jeddok slowly approached Seeanna as she slept and crouched down close to her. He took a moment to admire her beauty before whispering, "My dear one, Lohjji and I are off to find Poodwah. We have something we want to show him."

Seeanna slowly turned her head toward him and smiled sleepily. "Please don't be gone too long. Remember we are entertaining guests tonight, and you are roasting the bonabeast." Jeddok had forgotten about the dinner social they had planned for that evening and reluctantly assured his wife that he would be back in time for the preparations.

As Jeddok stepped back outside, Lohjji had just finished his fruit and was spitting the pit with explosive force at a child who was jeering him because he carried a small harp strapped to his back. After all, no self-respecting grown Yondut would carry such a prissy item around without shame. While Lohjji may have been the least gifted in other respects, he was truly skilled in the art of music.

Jeddok spoke up "All right, Lohjji, stop fooling around. We need to make good time in our search for Poodwah." The two jogged to Poodwah's folk's hutch and pounded on the front door. It was evident they had awakened Poodwah's pap from slumber. They inquired of Poodwah's whereabouts and were informed in a gruff tone that he had indeed gone to visit his grandmum. Off they went to the edge of the village, marching through the countryside and scattering a herd of bonabeasts before reaching their destination. They had not a chance to knock when the door opened and there stood GrandMum Erna with a wide and inviting smile.

"I haven't seen you boys in so long. Lohjji, you look as strong and healthy as ever. However, Jeddok I have to say that you are getting a bit pudgy around your midsection. I'm sorry I didn't make it to your wedding. I have been suffering spells of an ailment and have a very difficult time getting about. Soon I will have to move into the village."

Jeddok nodded. "GrandMum Erna, I understand, and I am greatly pleased to see you again!"

GrandMum Erna embraced both with a hug which could have broken ribs. "I'm guessing you boys are here looking for your Number Three? He is out on the patio repairing my handle cart. Go on back and make yourselves at home."

As they stepped out onto the patio, they were greeted with Poodwah's standard term of endearment. "Dearest chums! You've come at just the right moment. I've finished my task and my time is now yours. May I get you a drink or a snack of nuts and fruit?"

Lohjji excitedly gave Poodwah the news. "We are the ones who have a treat for you. Look at this!"

Poodwah took the parchment and studied it for a moment. His eyes sparkled with delight. "Where did you get this? I've so often longed to hear your GrandPap's stories again. This is wonderful. Are there any more?"

"That's the best part," Lohjji replied. "There are dozens of them." As was the trio's way, both Lohjji and Poodwah turned to Jeddok with a "What next?" look in their eyes. Jeddok, in his decisive manner, suggested that they return to the village and inventory all the parchments. They said their goodbyes to GrandMum Erna and were soon at the hutch Commons.

As Poodwah and Lohjji turned in the direction of Lohjji's hutch, Jeddok turned in the direction of his own home. "Sorry, friends. I'll have to meet up with you later. Seeanna has invited the in-laws over tonight, and I have bonabeast to cook."

Snickering, Lohjji whispered to Poodwah, "I think Jeddok isn't his own master anymore."

Poodwah laughed and shouted to Jeddok, "We'll see you later, my dear chum!"

The sun was setting, the fire pit had been stoked and the coals were glowing. The smell of the roasting bonabeast was a delight to the senses. Despite the pleasant atmosphere, Jeddok wished for the evening's events to be finished soon. Seeanna was puzzled by Jeddok's behavior as he carelessly slung slices of bonabeast on everyone's plates, and then rushed through the blessing of the meal. He ate like a ravenous wild animal and let loose with an embarrassing eructation. This was a side of Jeddok that Seeanna had never seen before. However, Jeddok was oblivious to Seeanna's confusion; he could only think about joining his friends. His in-laws shared their daughter's confusion and while remaining polite, they seemed unusually eager to leave. At the same moment they stepped out the door, Jeddok was mentally drafting a sentence or two which would somehow keep him out of trouble. He first had to excuse his behavior during dinner; then he had to explain why he was about to leave Seeanna alone again.

"Sweetest, please forgive me. I have been terribly preoccupied since Lohjji's visit earlier today. The parchments, the stories, his grandpap—"

Seeanna interrupted him. "You're not making any sense. What are you trying to say?"

"Well, Sweetest, I hoped to go to Lohjji's house tonight and reminisce about our childhood."

"It seems to me," she replied sourly, "that you reminisce every time you see one another."

Jeddok shook his head. "It's different this time. Lohjji has found his grandpap's old parchments. And —"

Once again she interrupted him. "Oh, all right, silly boy. You can go, but only because I love you." With that she planted a lingering kiss on his lips, as if to remind him why he would not want to stay out too late.

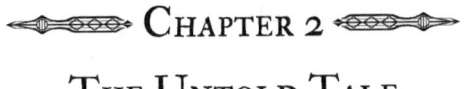

# CHAPTER 2

## THE UNTOLD TALE

As Jeddok entered Lohjji's main room, he found both his friends sitting on the floor surrounded by sheets of parchment.

Jeddok commented, "You fellows aren't exactly doing this in a methodical manner. Are you keeping track of anything?"

Poodwah blushed. "We have been a bit zealous in our, um, research. Please set down and join us, dear chum," he replied meekly. "I had nearly forgotten how intriguing these stories are. So much history and thoughtful insight-I'm very happy Lohjji found them."

Lohjji piped up. "Why haven't we found the story of the talking bonabeast?"

Jeddok and Poodwah looked at each other and burst into laughter. When Jeddok finally caught his breath he replied, "That wasn't one of the tribal stories. That is a bedtime tale your mum told you when you were a wee little one."

Lohjji looked confused, then annoyed. "You two think you are clever, don't you? And I suppose you are going to tell me the story of the giant shrilly birds is another bedtime tale?"

Jeddok and Poodwah made every attempt to maintain their composure to not offend their friend a second time. Their attempts proved futile and they erupted in a concert of chortles which made their bellies hurt.

When the laughter had subsided, Jeddok began again with his initial concern. "This is a wonderful treasure. We need to catalog and preserve these stories for Yonduts to come. Is there any order to these piles of parchment?"

"Actually there is," assured Poodwah, "We have eight piles for the eight tribes, except for one bundle that we have been unable to find a proper place for."

With great curiosity, Jeddok inquired, "What bundle? Why can't you find a place for it?"

Poodwah opened the bundle, "Listen as I read the first section of the parchment. Then you will understand."

*The Grhytans love to make things from rocks. In fact, it would be more accurate to say they are masters of stone. A mature Grhytan can gaze upon a stone no matter how large and peer into its depths to search for fractures and other weaknesses which would jeopardize its stability.*

*The land of the Grhytans is a spectacle of monuments erected over eons from all matter of colored stone. Each of the colored buildings in the elevated octagonal court at the center of the capital offers its pleasing iridescence to the skyline. Along the length of the capital city wall stand watchtowers decorated with ornate carvings depicting the important padymir tree.*

*Outside the city are the lowlands covered with symmetric fields interspersed with large groves of the trees.*

*The common Grhytan lives in a moderately sized dwelling composed of stone and timber with a sloping roof. Often their dwellings reach two or more levels underground. Here are kept food stores, including grains, large urns of padymir oil, roasted nuts, and dried taeris fruit. Each Grhytan family dedicates the first underground level of their home to the collected libraries of their ancestors. These hoards contain a wealth of artifacts and written knowledge dating back to time immemorial. The Grhytans live exceptionally long lives and many celestial seasons can pass without a Grhytan dying or having been born.*

Poodwah handed Jeddok the bundle, "This account does not appear to address any of the tribes. I've only reviewed the first few sections and I'm not familiar with any of it."

"Let me look at it," Lohjji chimed in. "Maybe I can help."

"Thanks, but no," said Jeddok, "Lohjji, do you mind if I take this bundle home with me and give it a thorough read? I'll get it back to you as quickly as possible."

"Of course not," Lohjji replied, "keep it as long as you need it. Let us know what you discover. I'm very interested in what it's about."

It was getting late and sleep was lying heavy on their eyes, so each went their way for the night. As Jeddok quietly stepped in through the door, he smiled as he saw the small lantern which Seeanna left burning for him. "She is such a sweet girl," he said. He placed the bundle on top of the dish cabinet and thought, "That can wait until morning," Changing into his robe, he blew out the lantern and tucked himself into bed next to his wife.

In the darkness of the early dawn Jeddok heard the birds and beasts awakening. Their morning sounds always brought joy to his heart. He arose and tossed a small chunk of rondra into the belly of the brew pot and lit it. He poured in the water and placed the beanbuds in the sift, and then the pot began to work its wonders. Jeddok so enjoyed a big hot stein of beanbud in the morning. He lit the table lantern, took the parchment bundle from the top of the cabinet, and proceeded to read its contents:

*These events occurred in the final seasons of the reign of King Therak of Grhytnod. For ages the Grhytans lived complacent lives, not desiring to seek any more than what they already understood. The geology and climate of their lands had provided the opportunity for a thoroughly self-sufficient culture. Their large, sturdy frames weathered the ages well and their life spans extended beyond anything a Yondut could comprehend.*

*The people of Grhytnod were very fond of their King, for he had thwarted many an attempted invasion from the Varrun Islands. Growing weary of the ages of war, he decided to take the offensive. The Varrun Islands lay in waters which were easily navigable. However, the Grhytans had never ventured far into the Sea of Chime. The King faced a great dilemma as he and the Council prepared an invasion strategy. For the Grhytans had no armada of war ships, only vessels designed for fishing along the coast. After much discussion among the members of the court, it was decided that an armada must be constructed if the Varrun threat was to be permanently defeated. An edict was circulated among the Grhytan population that within two moon phases all capable males were requested to congregate at the trade docks near the coast city of Osrall. Should they join the Armada project, they would be paid four hundred grollets a month until the project was completed.*

*At the end of the two phases, the city of Osrall was overwhelmed with eager Grhytans. The King's engineers developed a ship design combining the best of a Varrun sea ship and the Grhytan fishing vessel. While the Grhytans were known for their stone work, they proved to be worthy shipwrights. The construction brigades first worked on prototype designs which were rigorously tested and refined. Soon, the engineers and workers agreed upon a final design. Many season cycles passed and the brigades worked tirelessly. The project had taken so long that many of the brigade's family members relocated to Osrall to keep the families together during the project. Finally, the Armada was deemed seaworthy, the King and Council made their final plans. At the beginning of the next moon phase they would launch and conquer. On the day of the launch, all were in good spirits as the fleet sailed towards where the sun sets. The families of the soldiers and sailors stood upon the graveled beaches and watched until the ships disappeared beyond view. Never had such a thing been tried in the history of Grhytnod. "What would become of this?" they asked themselves.*

*Much time had passed and no word was heard of the Armada, then late one evening a single ship was seen silhouetted against the sun. As it grew closer it was evident it had sustained much damage, though by whether by storm or battle it could not be determined. The vessel set to anchor and a small boat dropped into the water. The rower's struggled against the waves and current until finally grounding upon the beach. In the boat were but four Grhytans badly injured and scarcely able to speak. They were hauled out of the boat and taken into the nearby home of a Council member. There they were cared for as best they could be, and it was hoped by all they would be able to recover. Upon the rising of the sun, the Grhytan boatmates looked to be improving. Despite their condition, they urgently insisted upon meeting with the Council. The oldest Grhytan spoke for them all, relaying a message from King Therak which he read from a piece of tortoise shell hidden inside his garment: "The inhabitants of our country must remain upon the land from which they come, never losing sight of their home. We have failed to reach the Varrun homeland. Well into our journey we encountered an enemy against which the might of the Grhytan's cannot stand. Your King has failed his loyal people and for that I bear great shame. These messengers have been sent by my order and by the time they arrive home they may be the only surviving members of the Armada. Be led by the Council and continue your lives. Farewell to all." The four boatmates, severely traumatized in mind and body, had great difficulty describing what had happened. Their stories were broken and inconsistent, but one thing was common between them all: they had faced some storm, entity or dark tempest. Whatever it was, it had not been seen by the Grhytans before.*

*The population was broken and grieved as one. In the ensuing phases, many monuments were built to the King and the others who were lost upon the*

*Sea of Chime. The Council was reorganized to more effectively lead the country and King Therak's last edict was made into a national law. All seafaring vessels were prohibited from venturing beyond the sight of the coast. Yet a Grhytan by the name of Rondur was not content to go about his business while the possibility remained that his King and fellow Grhytans may have survived, possibly by taking up residence among the many scattered islands of The Chime. The King's final edict forbade sailing beyond the view of land, but not other means of crossing the sea. At first he kept his idea to himself, thinking it foolish, until he gathered the courage to mention it to a friend who sat on the Council. The idea of a pier extending endlessly out into the sea seemed preposterous. Rondur had a simplistic answer for his friend. In Rondur's mind, all that was needed was time and stone, and the Grhytans had both in great abundance. The idea was presented to the Council, and much debate was had on both sides of the issue. Ultimately, grief and sentiment won out over reason and logic. The directive was passed; Rondur's Pier would be built.*

*Because the Grhytans had been exhausted by the building of the ships and the loss of the Armada, it proved extremely difficult for the Council to generate support for the pier among the populace. A conscript was decreed and all young male*

*Grhytans were required to work at the pier project for a lengthy span of time. They would be paid fairly and their families would be relocated to the coast if they so desired. So it began and so it has continued until this writing. The building of Rondur's Pier was accepted as an honorable civic duty and it became engrained as part of the culture. Though none thought it could truly happen, enough celestial phases had passed that the pier had extended beyond what was thought possible. It was very wide, with numerous spanned bridges, and a series of hamlets had sprung up along its length. The hamlets provided the workers and their families with comfortable dwelling places. The constant stream of immense barges hauling stone alongside the pier also carried supplies for the inhabitants of the hamlets.*

*Then something occurred one day which brought both blessing and dread. As a stone barge was being unloaded, a keen-sighted worker spied a small sailing boat coming from the direction of the setting sun. It was not the Varruns, for their ships were larger, and they sailed in a multitude. The work ceased and all anxiously waited to see what and who the vessel carried. As it grew closer, it was seen to carry no threat. One lone figure stood upon the tiny deck. It was a single Varrun but not of the warrior clan; he was dressed in the animal skin of a sage. A crowd quickly gathered as the vessel nudged into a crevice between stones. The sage, who was very old and sickly, stepped out of the boat and approached the crowd. He spoke softly but clearly: "I must speak with those who lead and protect your people. My words must not be delayed." A foreman of one of the crews volunteered to take the old Varrun to the Council. The small sailing ship that the sage had arrived in was waterlogged and barely afloat, so the trip back to the mainland was made in one of the returning barges. The sage spoke nary a word as they made the uneventful return trip to the coast. Once docked, a cart pulled by a single oolog was prepared to take the Varrun all the way to into Nernod.*

*The cart master urged the oolog along  and all the days of travel had no conversation with the old Varrun. After reaching the edge of the city, they passed through the main gate into the city court and on to the assembly building of the Council. A messenger had been sent ahead of the cart and the Council was already gathered as the cart master assisted the sage up the steps and into the chamber room.*

*The Varrun straightened and spoke: "Through the ages, our people have warred against one another. The only other Varruns who have* reached your shores came to take what was not theirs. I come alone, and I come for a different reason. First, as I sailed to your land, I passed through a group of islands which have not been named. In my haste to arrive here, I chose not to make landfall there and I did not contact those who walked the beaches. They were very large, and though I saw only a few, I recognized them as Grhytans."

There was a great uproar among the council members, and a new member in particular was singled out. Rondur had gained a seat on the council and heaps of praise was poured out upon him. For it was he who had kept hope alive that some from the Armada might still be rescued. The sage held up his hand and the crowd quieted.

"Let your rejoicing be short lived. For what I am about to say will bring fear to your hearts," the old Varrun continued. "In the soul of every living being that possesses language is a darkness. It is the essence of what is not seen in the living. It comes not from deeds that are done. It comes from the blood of forebearers. It merely is, and will remain until the soul has relinquished itself to Patayros." The time-weary sage paused for a breath, his mind searching for the words to continue. "Those in the land from where I come gave no thought to the darkness. They pursued their quests for things that breed lust in the soul.

*They came trampling upon the shores and cities of many like your own. All the while they became as the darkness they could not see, living and dying as wild beasts of the field. Yet, even in death, the darkness does not rest. And now you wonder why this old one speaks to you of such things. If you value your lives as they are, you will begin your journey in the direction where the sun sets. There you must confront what has become, but what is not." With his last sentence the Varruns eyes grew blank and distant. He stood in a wobbly stance, not speaking another word. The court bailiffs escorted the feeble sage out of the court through a side passageway. The Council members spent an awkward moment looking to one another for answers about what they had just heard. The Grhytans were generally not schooled in the disciplines of such abstract ideas.*

*Finally, Rondur spoke in a strong tone. "The Varrun is weak and tired from his voyage. He does not speak coherently. I move we wait until he has had his rest and healing time, then seek clarification of his words."*

*In rebuttal, Wallyon barked out, "Why should the Council pursue any more dialogue with this old one? We have pressing civil matters to contend with. Find the Varrun a nice place at the Gofals home and he can rest as long as he wishes." All in attendance came into an agreement with Wallyon's proposal and made the appropriate arrangements for the sage.*

*Though the Council was dismissed, Rondur sat on his bench alone, lost in thought and murmuring to himself. The words he had just heard brought great discontent to his heart. What did they mean? He knew he must converse with the Varrun and clear his mind of many questions.*

Jeddok flipped to the next page of parchment and was taken aback by what he saw. "What is this?" he exclaimed. "It can't be!"

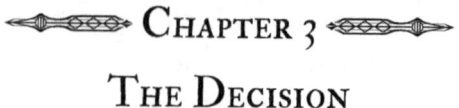

## CHAPTER 3

# THE DECISION

There it was: the unmistakable crude, bold strokes of a metal crafter's hands. He knew the writing well, yet it had been a long while since he had seen it. The words were penned by Jeddok's pap, Arunthal, who had abandoned him and his mother when Jeddok was a lad of seventeen seasons. The words were large and scribed with great intensity: "DARKNESS COMES." Underneath the words was a map partially detailing Yondusland and extending out to describe landmarks with which Jeddok was not familiar. On the right hand side of the map was the word "Grhytnod" and an arrow pointing off the edge of the sheet. "What is this?" Jeddok asked himself. "How did my pap's words come to be on this parchment? There isn't a land called Grhytnod-is there?"

In the world that Jeddok knew, there was no such thing as Grhytans. He knew of the Luurds who inhabited the coast of the Sea of Krell. Disgusting beings they were with oblong heads with huge bulging eyes and multiple folds of the brow drooping over their hideous orbs. There were the enormous drooping ears, always with tufts of hair poking out from them. They had only the whisper of lips, scrawny frames and a very unpleasant smell about them. The Luurds were a race of traders and gamblers. Only a fool would engage a Luurd in a game of cards. He also knew of the Untras who lived in the woodland areas. Nomads and the most skilled of hunters, they kept to themselves. He had never heard a soul speak of such beings as the Grhytans.

Jeddok felt a deep sadness as he remembered back to that awful day. He had just come home from school to find his mum kneeling and sobbing on the floor by her bed. On the bed lay one of his pap's swords and a partially rolled up parchment. The young Jeddok's heart was filled with anxiety as he knelt down beside his mother and wrapped his arms around her. He tried to hide the uneasiness he felt as he spoke. "Mum, what is going on? What happened?"

She turned her tear-stained face to him. "Your pap has gone away and I don't know if he will return. He has left a note which makes no sense at all. The sword is for you."

Her words made Jeddok's head spin. "My pap has left us? What have I done? Did I make him angry?" He turned toward the bed and grabbed the parchment, thinking he would discover that this was some kind of grievous misunderstanding. "My pap is a good man and he would never do such a thing." The parchment, he thought, would clear up the matter, but as he read the words, they made no sense:

*Dearest,*

*My love for you is great and I desire to protect you with all that I am. I love my son, I love my people. This simple warrior has been mustered and his life surely will be ended. Take the sword, my son. Take care of your mum; remember your teachings and honor Theoas.*
*Diodef Gwirion...*

With tears in his eyes, Jeddok had thought to himself, "A good man does not break the hearts of those he loves." The last two words of the sentence were in what was known as the "oldsay," an extinct Yondut dialect. The words meant, "Truth Endures."

Jeddok now thought to himself, "Arunthal, why do you haunt me now? This page has been hidden under an old Yondut's bed all these past seasons, and now by some providence my eyes are upon it." Jeddok grew frustrated and said to himself, "Enough of this! I'm a fool for reading this nonsense." He studied the map laid out before him and then gazed at the sword standing in the corner of the room. It was covered in dust, yet still a thing of beauty. The Yonduts had not engaged in war in many ages. However, the metal crafters of the Tribes still created swords. They were often used as legal tender in costly transactions. Even in the neighboring countries they held great value.

And then he thought of his dear mum. She lived in a hutch adjoined to the home of Jeddok and Seeanna.

A strong being she was, strong in heart, mind, and faith. She never stopped loving Arunthal and never gave up hope that he would return. She always said to her son, "We will not pass judgment upon your pap until we know what was in his heart. And the only way we can know that is to ask him." Jeddok began to ponder the idea that his pap was still alive and that reconciliation was still possible. He turned back to the map and studied it more closely.

The map depicted a mountain range in the direction of Grhytnod. This was intriguing to Jeddok as he had never seen a mountain. The Yonduts had always preferred the lowlands where the soil was rich and fertile. The Yonduts love to grow things and were never in want of food. There were also rough drawings of odd six-legged creatures with flowing manes on both ends of the animal. "I wonder if those are the fabled oologs I've heard stories of?" Jeddok mumbled to himself. Two large rivers were depicted as well as an area of what appeared to be small mounds or hills. It admittedly wasn't much of a map. Jeddok thought again of his pap and the possibility of seeing him again after the many seasons of separation. "I must find out more about this map and Grhytnod," Jeddok thought to himself. "Would it be possible to find this land, and find my pap? It sounds like a fool's quest. Or, could it be Mum's stubborn love and loyalty to Pap are not in vain." Then he reasoned that if he could research the issue and gather more information that he could possibly, maybe, embark upon a quest. "Would I be proven a fool?" he asked himself. "Do I tell Seeanna what I've found? Do I dare to tell her my thoughts on the matter? What would she think of my pondering?"

By now, the sun had fully risen and Jeddok had his fill of hot beanbud. Sending his thoughts upward, he asked, "Theoas, what would you have me do?" For it was Arunthal's desire for Jeddok that he 'remember his teachings, and honor Theoas.' Jeddok rose to his feet and went back to the bedroom. There Seeanna lay awake.

She sighed. "Your eyes are far away. Is your heart?"

Jeddok smiled. "No, my wife. My heart is with you always."

She sat up in the bed, looked at him directly in the eyes and said, "That is the correct answer, my husband. You have just earned a wonderful morning meal prepared by a wonderful wife." Jeddok sat on the edge of the bed, gave Seeanna a hug, thanked her, and headed out to the large garden patch behind their hutch. He began tending his crops, but his mind was reeling with questions.

Finishing his chores, he thought, "I must seek the counsel of my friends regarding this map and what I have found. However, I must first partake of the meal which beckons me through that window."

After his morning meal, he told Seeanna he was off to the Commons to conduct business. She offered him her blessing and proceeded with her tasks. Jeddok grabbed the parchment bundle and went directly to Lohjji's hutch. He pounded hard on the door with the intent of bringing Lohjji out of his unusually deep slumber. "That Yondut could sleep through an earthquake," he thought. Finally, the door slowly opened and there stood a very groggy Lohjji wearing his britches backwards and struggling to put his shirt on in the same manner. "You are a sight to behold so early in the morning!" chided Jeddok. "Should I fetch GrandMum Erna to help you dress?"

As usual, Lohjji took the remarks in stride and invited his friend to sit at the table. As Lohjji sat down, the very distinct sound of ripping fabric could be heard. Lohjji was oblivious to the tear in his britches and pulled the bowl on the table close to this chest, stuffing large pieces of taeris fruit into his mouth. With the juice dripping from the sides of his mouth, Lohjji asked, "Why are you here, Jeddok? Surely you did not just come over to watch me eat?"

Jeddok replied, "No, my friend, I am here for your counsel." Lohjji immediately stopped eating and looked at Jeddok with surprise and joy in his eyes. It was extremely rare that anyone sought advice from him. Jeddok explained the contents of the mysterious parchment which Lohjji and Poodwah had found. He then rolled out the parchment, removed the last page and put it on the table in front of Lohjji. His friend took a keen interest in what he saw. Jeddok pointed out the large words on the sheet and indicated that it was, without question, his pap's handwriting.

Lohjji exclaimed, "Your pap! Why, several times I saw Arunthal and my grandpap meeting together on the benches over in the Commons. I often wondered what they were discussing. Now I know."

Jeddok rolled it up and placed it back in its covering. "Lohjji, I have this foolish idea that my pap may still be alive in a place called Grhytnod. My heart is telling me to pursue, but my head is reining me back. What if he is alive and I don't seek him out? I want so much to know why he left Mum and me."

Lohjji replied, "My friend, I may be a bit slow in some matters, but this I know-there are times when the head should listen to the heart. You need to speak to Poodwah and seek spiritual counsel. He knows the faith of our people. He knows the words Theoas has given us."

Jeddok knew Lohjji's comments were true. "Then I am off to seek the advice of our little sage." Jeddok thanked his friend and went to Poodwah's home.

Poodwah lived in a hutch adjoined to his folk's hutch. This was common for unmarried Yondut males. Jeddok walked around the side of the dwelling and knocked. The door opened and there stood Poodwah with his always welcoming smile, "Come in, my dear chum!" he spoke in a chipper tone. "Please sit down and let me serve you a fresh stein of hot beanbud." Jeddok seated himself and waited for his beverage. Poodwah spoke up, "Jeddok, you are unusually quiet. Is everything well with you and your new bride?"

Jeddok replied, "Yes. I am greatly blessed with Seeanna, but there is something else which brings trouble to my heart." Jeddok told the tale of the Grhytans once again. And, as he had done with Lohjji, he presented the map to his friend.

Poodwah studied the sheet for a moment. "My grandmum once spoke of such things, but I did not take her seriously."

Jeddok replied, "That's not all. Those large words, 'DARKNESS COMES', are in my pap's handwriting."

Poodwah was filled with excitement. His eyes grew bright and his smile even wider. "This is absolutely wonderful news!"

Jeddok replied, "What brings my soul strife is the desire to seek out my pap in a land which seems nothing more than a bedtime tale. It is a foolish thing to ponder and I have been beating myself up for thinking it."

Poodwah looked his friend in the eyes. "You still love your pap and that is what compels your heart. Every effort that is taken to restore the bond of those separated is worth every bit of grief it might bring. The words of Theoas tell us such actions bring Him honor."

Jeddok answered, "Poodwah, your words were few, yet they give me much to ponder. I must spend time with Theoas and search these things out." With that Jeddok bid his friend farewell and took off down the creek path behind Poodwah's hutch.

Jeddok thought back to the note his pap had left with his mother on the day he left. The phrase, 'honor Theoas' kept running through his mind. Now he knew what to do, but how was he to present his plan to Seeanna? They had only been husband and wife for a short while and Jeddok was still unsure of himself in many respects. How would she react when he told her he was heading in the direction of the setting sun to find his long lost pap, and he didn't know when he would return? How did you tell anyone that? How would he explain all this to his mum?" Jeddok thought to himself, "Maybe, it will be more acceptable to them if I told her my friends were coming with me? However, I must see if Lohjji and Poodwah are even willing to take on such a foolhardy venture."

It had been a fruitful year for all Yondusland. The staple grains produced an unprecedented harvest. The storage silos were overflowing. All that was left was the minor tending of the late season crops. Jeddok had done well trading livestock and his smokehouse was filled to capacity. The rondra bins were full and the mines were producing heavily. Jeddok thought, "If I leave now, both Seeanna and Mum will be filled and warm. I will not need to worry about them. Neither

Lohjji nor Poodwah have anyone but themselves to provide for. Surely, this is the opportune time to travel."

# CHAPTER 4

## HAVE OOLOG WILL TRAVEL

Jeddok thought of the words he could offer his friends to entice them to travel with him. "Would I be leading them into harm?" he pondered.

He once again knocked on Lohjji's door. As it opened, he noticed Lohjji had changed britches and wore them correctly this time. His shirt also faced the right direction. It didn't take long to convince Lohjji that an adventure awaited and he needed to be a part of it. Lohjji and Jeddok made their way to Poodwah's hutch.

The door swung open and with a grand smile, Poodwah asked, "You two could not resist such an undertaking could you? Well, if we are going to embark upon a quest, we must first speak to GrandMum Erna. We can see if she knows any more of Grhytnod."

It was a great relief to Jeddok that his friends were so willing to accompany him. They made the short trek to GrandMum Erna's home, and, after her warm greeting, asked her to sit at the kitchen table with them. Jeddok took out the parchment and relayed the account of the Grhytans. He passed the map over to GrandMum Erna, pointing out his pap's handwriting on the parchment.

GrandMum Erna studied the sheet for a moment. "I haven't heard the tale of the Grhytan's since I was but a wee one. There were a few elders who visited my own pap and would tell of such stories. However, many of them spoke only the oldsay and I did not fully understand them." She paused for a moment. "What I do remember, is that they mentioned a crazed Yondut named Hurshon, who took off to the Farlands and he has not since been heard of. I suspect if anyone could give you answers about such things, it would be him-assuming he still lives."

Poodwah spoke up. "GrandMum, what are these Farlands?"

She replied, "As I understand, it is a hilly region in the direction where the sun sets. I suspect it is a journey of many phases to get there. Surely, you young ones are not thinking of heading out to the Farlands?"

Poodwah hesitated before answering. "Yes, GrandMum, we are. We must help our friend seek out his pap, if he lives."

GrandMum Erna just shook her head. "May Theoas protect you."

Poodwah nodded. "Yes, GrandMum. He will."

Hearing the story of Hurshon energized the trio and they discussed what would be needed for such a journey. Jeddok was caught up in the discussion, and then abruptly interrupted his friends, "I haven't said a word to Seeanna and Mum about this! What am I thinking? Will you two please go over to the market and gather whatever dried foodstuffs you can get your hands on? I have to run home and explain this to my family."

With great apprehension, Jeddok approached the door to his hutch. He slowly opened the door and there Seeanna sat at the table with her small grain mill completely disassembled. On the edge of the table was a screw clamp, and snugly in its grip was one of the internal metal parts. She was slowly and meticulously drawing a small file across the part. She glanced away from her work towards the door and greeted Jeddok, "Hello there! I take it your business went well?"

Jeddok sheepishly replied, "Yes, Seeanna. It went well. What are you doing with the grain mill?"

In a very matter of fact tone she answered, "I grew weary of the roughness in the crank and decided it was time to take care of the problem."

Jeddok grinned with pride at his industrious partner as he sat down at the table across from her. He carefully cleared away the parts of the grain mill which were strewn about, then withdrew the parchment bundle from his jacket. He unrolled the pages and laid them out facing Seeanna. By now, Seeanna had stopped filing and was attempting to figure out what her husband was doing. She asked, "What do you have here? This isn't anything I've ever seen before."

Jeddok quickly responded, "No, Seeanna, you've never seen this. And neither had I until the dark of this morn. This is one of the parchment bundles that Lohjji's grandpap had tucked away under his bed. Do you have a moment for me to relay its contents to you?" Seeanna nodded and Jeddok told her the story. As he finished, he pulled out the sheet with the map and handed it to her. "Seeanna, that is all there was of the tale. It was left unfinished. All that remained in the bundle was this map." He pointed out the handwriting on the sheet. "Seeanna, this is my pap's handwriting. There is the possibility that he may yet be alive in this land called Grhytnod. I sought counsel from my friends, yet I regret that I did not come to you first with this. You are my closest friend and I should have asked you before I spoke with Lohjji and Poodwah."

She looked at him with bewilderment. "Counsel? What do you mean? Counsel about what?"

Jeddok's stomach clenched as he continued. "GrandMum Erna heard of such tales as a small child and knows of an old Yondut who may answer questions about Grhytnod. Seeanna, I must know if my pap still lives."

Seeanna was slowly putting Jeddok's puzzle together. "Are you intending to go in search of him?" she asked.

Jeddok nodded. "Yes, Seeanna, Lohjji and Poodwah have agreed to be my traveling companions. Please understand. I must know if my pap is alive."

Seeanna grew quiet and introspective and then looked at him with worry in her eyes. "When will you return?"

This reply brought relief to Jeddok. "We would return before the planting and trading season begins. I have taken stock of our stores and both you and Mum will be taken care of. However, I don't know how to speak to Mum of this."

Seeanna sternly, but lovingly, replied, "You must promise to return when you say. And let me take care of this matter with your Mum."

Jeddok was overjoyed. He jumped off his seat and wrapped Seeanna in a big hug. "Never did a man have such a wonderful wife as you."

She turned to him, "And you shall not forget that. Do you understand?"

Still grinning widely, he nodded. "Without question."

Jeddok explained he had sent Lohjji and Poodwah to the market for supplies and that he must join them in the preparations. He bid her his love and took off toward the market. He found the two struggling under the weight of many large bags of foodstuffs. He suggested the two set the bags down and wait for him to return with a bonabeast and a cart. Jeddok returned shortly and they loaded up the provisions in the cart. The bonabeast wasn't the fastest animal to be found, but they were sturdy and dependable for such work as this. Jeddok, always one to be prepared, turned the animal around and led it back towards the market.

"Where are you going?" said Poodwah.

"I know Lohjji's appetite all too well and we will need to fill the cart even more," replied Jeddok. "We must also go back to my home for the smoked meat and fetch a second cart to carry tools, spare parts and other sundries. Furthermore, we cannot forget weapons, so get them if you have them."

Lohjji and Poodwah looked at each other as the reality of their task came to bear upon them. Until this moment, it had only been a fanciful notion, but now they fully understood the seriousness of it. After completing his rounds at the market stands, Jeddok led the beast back towards his hutch. He unhitched the cart and led the bonabeast to the haystack. Then he pulled out his spare cart from under its covering and moved it next to the stall fence. By then Jeddok's two friends arrived and they finished packing.

Jeddok bid them goodnight. "Sleep well. Tomorrow, the Farlands."

Seeanna prepared a meal and the two sat down together. The atmosphere was somber as Jeddok offered the thanksgiving prayer. "Theoas, we give you honor and praise for your faithful provision. May your blessing and protection be upon us and our loved ones. If I have found any favor in your eyes, I ask that you direct the steps of our journey, may they go the way that you lead. Amoda."

In a soft voice Seeanna echoed, "Amoda."

The thanksgiving lightened the load the two carried in their hearts and they began to converse. Much was discussed about tasks which needed completing while Jeddok was away. After the practicalities were finished, Seeanna took a deep breath. "I know your motives for this journey are noble, and I respect your decision. All I ask is that you keep yourself safe and return to me. Your mum and I will abide just fine, so do not weary your mind on our account."

Jeddok nodded. "I love you, Seeanna."

As was his way, Jeddok awoke with the birds and beasts and brewed his beanbud. "This is the day." he thought. After finishing his stein, he stepped out into the darkness of the morn and roused the two bonabeasts he had chosen for the journey. He led them to the carts and hitched them up. Poodwah arrived and assisted. The rigs were ready, but there was no sign of Lohjji. Jeddok and Poodwah made their way to Lohjji's hutch and both pounded on the door. Lohjji flung open the door and seemed more awake than usual. He grabbed his jacket and passed his friends with long strides. Jeddok and Poodwah were surprised they had not roused the grumpy Lohjji. This morning they were greeted by the pleasant Lohjji. Jeddok gave Poodwah a nod and they followed Lohjji all the way to the stalls.

Jeddok turned to his friends. "Now you two do understand I have to go back in and bid my wife goodbye? Please be patient, because this might take a few moments." Jeddok then stepped inside and closed the door. Lohjji and Poodwah busied themselves with tightening harnesses and battening down the provisions in the cart.

Soon Jeddok then emerged from his hutch. "To the Farlands, my friends!"

Poodwah chose the larger of the two bonabeasts, climbed up the side of the cart, and nestled himself comfortably on top of the covering.

Lohjji piped up, "What are you doing up there?"

Jeddok laughed. "His legs are short and so is his stride. Let's be gone."

They left the village as the sun was rising behind them, casting a warm glow upon their path. It was a beautiful morning. The small caravan settled into a healthy pace and they traveled most of the day, stopping only for a brief snack. As the evening drew near they selected a recessed grassy area to protect them from the cool night breeze. Arising early each morning, their travel proved uneventful. Each one was lost in thought and there was not much conversation between them.

After three moon phases, they began to wonder how far the Farlands really were. At the beginning of the fourth phase, they came to a large river. At last, they seem to have encountered one of the landmarks depicted on the map. The river was wide with a strong current.

Jeddok pulled out the map he carried close to his chest. "I estimate this is the first river shown on the map. If we follow its bank, we should meet the second river at some point."

Lohjji grinned, "Yes. We follow the right path."

Poodwah nodded in agreement. They led the animals along the river for a short while before coming upon an enormous area of matted grass.

"What do you think caused this?" asked Poodwah, "Do you think a storm could do such a thing?"

Jeddok shook his head. "Neither wind nor water. I don't know what this is. Just keep alert and be aware of what is going on around you."

They resumed the trek along the bank. After a few more days travel they came to the confluence of two rivers. It made a large expanse of water to cross.

Lohjji asked, "Do either of you know if bonabeasts can swim?"

Jeddok spoke first. "Well, Lohjji, that is something I've never considered. Poodwah, can a bonabeast swim?"

Poodwah shrugged. "Now why would I know such a thing?"

The three stood there gazing from the water to the beasts and back again. Finally, Lohjji piped up. "What would you say to settle down right here until morning? We could try to catch some fish and relax a bit."

Poodwah answered, "That's the best idea you've had in a long while."

The decision made, they began to make camp. Jeddok turned to Lohjji. "Wait for me before you run off with the fishing gear. I would like to try my skills along with you."

Poodwah started a fire, stoking it with driftwood he collected. Lohjji and Jeddok headed to the bank and took up position on a sand bar. Poodwah sat near the fire with his books, gazing toward the setting sun.

On the far horizon, just barely discernible, he saw outcroppings and hills. "The Farlands!" Poodwah thought. "But we must first traverse this water. Theoas, I ask that you make a way for us."

He dozed off and began snoring with loud reverberation. His two friends made their way back to the campsite with a full string of fish and proceeded to clean them. Then, off in the darkness, they heard a reply to Poodwah's snoring. They waited a moment for Poodwah to belt out another note, and sure enough there was a reply in kind from a distance.

"That can't be an echo," Jeddok said to Lohjji. They walked in the direction of the sound until they reached the edge of the campfire light and listened. Straining, they could pick up a chorus of snorts which responded to Poodwah's melody.

"That is something we must investigate in the morning." Jeddok whispered to Lohjji, "Let's finish up the fish, set them on the drying rack, and then rest our bones." Soon, they sunk into a deep slumber while the fire burned down to embers.

Just as the sun rose over the horizon, the trio awoke to sounds of thrashing in the water. They jumped from their sleeping pads and bolted through the tall grass to the river's edge. "What are those things!?" Jeddok shouted to his friends. Before them, plowing through the water towards the opposite side of the river, were large beasts the likes of which they had never laid eyes on. One of the animals emerged on the other bank and Poodwah shouted, "Six legs! They have six legs!"

The animals paid no mind to the Yonduts and continued across the river.

"I don't believe it," Jeddok said to his friends, "From the map-these things are oologs!"

Lohjji spoke, "If those things can cross the river, we need to trade our bonabeasts for oologs." Lohjji was definitely in rare form and his friends were impressed with the idea.

"Do you truly think we could catch one, let alone control one?" Jeddok asked.

Poodwah observed that the oologs did not seem to mind their presence and suggested they scout the area around their campsite to find another herd of the beasts.

"I guess nothing will be lost in trying. At least I hope so," said Jeddok, "But we should fill small packs and take water pouches. We don't know how far we will walk."

The three spread out in an evenly spaced line, not losing sight of one another. They proceeded in the direction that Lohjji and Jeddok had heard the snorts and noises just the night before. Poodwah came to a small rise closest to the riverbank. The grass was shorter there and much easier for his short legs to traverse. They walked until they reached a small branch creek which emptied into the river. The vegetation was thick but they were able to make their way to the other side. Snorts could be heard as they broke through the greenery. They slowed down and crept to the edge of a small lowland meadow. There they saw several oologs lying down in a semicircle, dozing in the tall grass.

"Now what?" Jeddok whispered.

Poodwah answered, "Let's approach them and see how they react."

Jeddok was the first to emerge from their hiding place, slowly walking toward the closest animal. It was almost impossible to tell which was the front end and which was the back. Each end of the animal had a protrusion covered by a thick, long flowing mane. He took a few more steps and one end of the animal lifted off the grass. It made a low rumbling sound, not one of aggression, but more like an inquisitive query.

Jeddok stepped closer and the oolog merely turned its 'head' toward him then laid it back down. Two more steps and Jeddok was right next to the oolog. He gently laid his hand upon the beast and began to stroke its back. Once again, he heard the low rumbling sound, and he could feel the vibrations coming from the animal's body. Jeddok turned back to look at his friends and waved them in closer.

In a low voice, he said to them, "You two try it."

Neither Lohjji nor Poodwah were enthused about the idea, but both chose an animal and approached cautiously. As they laid their hands on their chosen animals, they heard the low rumble and to their amazement, in moments the three oologs were in harmony with one another. The rumbling seemed to surround them.

"Hey Lohjji, do you still have some dried taeris fruit in your bag?" asked Jeddok.

Lohjji nodded and Jeddok continued, "Toss some of the fruit in front of it."

Lohjji dug out a large piece of taeris and placed it as close as he dared. There was the obvious sound of heavy sniffing and then a very long tongue appeared out from under one of the manes, wrapped itself around the fruit and withdrew. Lohjji could hear the sound of chewing and took great delight in his accomplishment. He looked at both of his friends with a wide smile.

Poodwah spoke up. "Maybe we could draw them back to our campsite using the fruit as bait?"

Jeddok and Lohjji agreed it was worth a try. They took inventory of the taeris in their bags and distributed it evenly among themselves. Each Yondut held the bait in front of their oolog and began backing up. The beasts arose from the ground and began slowly plodding towards the treats. They easily plowed through the thick vegetation near the creek. The animals continued to follow the Yonduts up to an area near the campsite.

Jeddok said, "Toss your fruit in the front of them and we'll run to the carts for a bit more."

The oologs consumed the fruit before lying down in the grass, seeming content with their situation. The trio returned and was pleased at what they saw.

"Well, my friends, now we must make an attempt to ride one of these beasts. Lohjji, you are the largest of us, and I think you would have the best chance of success.

Lohjji seemed eager to oblige, walked up to one of the oologs, and eased his leg up over the animal's back. When he shifted his full weight to the animal, the oolog responded by standing up. It seemed confused as to what was happening, then let loose with a forceful buck. The strong legs of the beast sent Lohjji high into the air. In a vain attempt to soften his landing, Lohjji flapped his arms like a bird. He landed in the grass next to the oolog with a thud and a "Yow!"

Jeddok and Poodwah ran towards him. "Are you injured? Are you okay?" asked Poodwah.

Jeddok helped Lohjji stand. It was clear by the look in Lohjji's eyes that he had taken this mishap personally. He spoke not a word to his friends but went directly to the oolog. He grabbed a handful of mane and swung himself back into position on the animal's back. The oolog began an undulating wave of bucks, its six limbs working in unison to remove the foreign object from its back. Lohjji pulled himself in close to the animal and squeezed hard with his legs. By now, the oolog was moving in a large circle. The other two oologs serenely stood up and moved away from the chaos. Round and round went Lohjji on the oolog until finally he was bounced off again. The oolog stood still. It seemed satisfied that things were as they should be.

Lohjji walked towards his friends as Jeddok spoke. "Apparently oologs are friendly by nature, but they don't like to be ridden."

Lohjji looked at Jeddok. "Indeed? When did you first notice?"

Jeddok grinned and offered an idea. "What if we wait until the oologs go to rest again, and then we can weave their manes into loops that go up and over their backs? We could use the loop as a bridle?" They agreed and when the animals settled back down into the grass, they went to work.

After finishing, Poodwah spoke, "We have given the oologs enough grief for today. I say we let them be and see if they remain here tomorrow. We could take watches through the night to keep an eye on them. Keep the taeris fruit handy to entice them to stay."

Jeddok and Lohjji were all too happy to give the oologs a rest. The three went back the short distance to their campsite and plopped down on their sleeping pads. Lohjji pulled the harp from his pack and began a melodious strum. Poodwah opened one of his ever-present books. Jeddok, still a bit restless, went to the carts and removed his awnaxe.

Though he had never mastered sword techniques, he had become very proficient at the awnaxe. As a lad he had spent much time behind his mum's hutch perfecting the throwing techniques which made him the participant to beat in the village competitions. After finding the sharpstone, he laid it out on the gate of the cart and began to sharpen the awnaxe. After achieving a satisfactory edge, he walked closer to the river bank and found a large piece of deadwood protruding from the soil. He took careful aim and followed through. The awnaxe struck the wood with a solid *thunk*.

As Jeddok continued his practice, his friends began to boil a stew of dried bonabeast meat and grain. It was standard Yondut fare and always pleased the appetite. The scent of the stew drew Jeddok back to the campsite. He sat down and Poodwah offered the blessing before they ate. With their bellies full and the sun now setting, they discussed the arrangement of the night watches. Poodwah was to go first, followed by Lohjji and then Jeddok.

The moon rose higher in the sky as Poodwah gazed. "Magnificent," he thought. He enjoyed the unified, soothing sound the oologs made as they slept. The moon continued its climb, and later Lohjji came bristling through the grass. They traded spots on the stump Poodwah was using for a stool and Lohjji began to strum his harp. The night proved uneventful and Lohjji was happy when Jeddok showed up for his watch.

As dawn approached, the oologs rustled and stood up. Two of them ambled towards Jeddok, giving him cause for concern, but he held his position on the stump to see what the oologs had in mind. With a beast on either side, they plopped down beside him in the grass, creating a small breeze in doing so. Each animal then lifted its head and their tongues extended to Jeddok's face. The oologs offered him what can only be described as a show of affection. They licked the side of his head, up one side and down the other. Jeddok jumped off the stump and stepped away from them. The offering was a bit too wet for Jeddok's liking. He decided it was time to wake up his friends and roused them from their pads. He prepared the morning meal while they awoke. The three sat together and ate in the quietness of the morning.

As the beanbud began to wake Lohjji's mind, he commented, "I just need more time with the oologs and I know they can be ridden."

Jeddok was quick to agree, "Yes. We should spend a day or two working the animals. Poodwah and I can assist in whatever way you need us to."

For the next three days they worked the oologs and progress was made. They oologs were now trained sufficiently to be used as transport animals. The final test was seeing how Poodwah could handle riding an oolog. All three mounted the beasts and headed towards the creek they had been to earlier. They crossed the creek and back again and Poodwah proved to be a natural oolog master, although, they would have to rig some kind of mounting ladder for the small Yondut.

The test ride was a success and Jeddok offered up the next task. "We need a way to carry our provisions on these animals. I believe the heavy coverings on the cart could be fashioned into pouch bags which can be draped over the oologs."

They had a good afternoon of work ahead of them as they stitched the pouch bags. Their hands cramped as they formed the heavy fabric. Finally, the stitching was done and all that was left to do was to drape the animals and fill the bags. That was something for the next day. The trio was exhausted and quickly fell asleep without even making a fire.

Morning dawned and Jeddok had failed to wake before the sun. The previous day's oolog exercises had taken much fire from him. In an unusual turn, Lohjji woke first and began brewing the beanbud. Outdoor life suited him well. After the other two had stirred themselves awake, it was decided to skip breakfast and outfit the oologs right away. They were pleased with their handiwork with the pouch bags, as they worked better than had been hoped for. The cart frames were dismantled just enough to be well-hidden in the grass. They thought maybe they would use them on the return trip.

They strapped what weapons they could on their heavy leather belts; Jeddok and Lohjji also strapped on their backs scabbards and swords. The bonabeasts were freed from their tethers. They would be fine on their own, for they were but tamed wild animals themselves.

Poodwah scurried up the fiber ladder he had designed to roll neatly up. Jeddok and Lohjji gave themselves a running start, grabbed the mane loop and hauled themselves up on their oologs. As the three looked at one another, it was evident that none of them were sure about what they were going to do next. Jeddok gave the mane loop a tug and gently nudged with his boots and the oolog went towards the river as his master desired. Jeddok did not hesitate when reaching the water's edge. The water was colder than he had anticipated and he yelled a quick warning to his friends. As the animal moved forward, Jeddok could feel the rhythm of the oologs muscles change as it left the river bed and began to swim. The oolog felt solid and sure underneath Jeddok. He turned to see his friends following confidently behind. In short order they made the other bank. The animals shook wildly, splattering water in all directions, and then stood still waiting for further instructions.

Lohjji spoke up, "Try that on a bonabeast!"

Jeddok, always the practical one, replied, "Yes, my friend, that was an ingenious idea. However, now we have work to do. We must replenish our foodstuffs. I see taeris bushes and greetroot plants in that marsh down the way."

Jeddok had not wanted to harvest one of their traveling bonabeasts, should they be able to round them up on the return journey. He had hopes they would find a wild prairie bonabeast on the way into the Farlands. The soggy work of harvesting in the marsh was completed; they traveled up the river to a dry area to make camp. They ate their fill of roasted greetroot as the fire dried their clothing. Then night came upon them and all slept well.

# CHAPTER 5

## HURSHON'S OUTPOST

The next day the trio put many lenads behind them. The geography and vegetation began to change. The prairie and grass gave way to hills and timber. The scent of the cone trees wafted through the air. The travelers enjoyed the change in their surroundings, when in the late afternoon a crashing noise was heard on the lee side of the hill they were traversing. The oologs became edgy and restless as a very deep, low growling could be heard just over the rise. The trees shook above them and dropped their needles.

The friends were horrified at what their eyes beheld. A creature of such stature that it made the oologs appear small. The head was almost square, with two large horns protruding just above the massive nostrils. Black hair rose on its back and fish-like scales on its tree trunk-size limbs flashed in the sunlight. The monster pounded its thick front claws on the ground and charged.

"Follow me!" yelled Jeddok. Eying a path through the trees, he kicked his oolog in the haunches. The animal responded without hesitation. The trio pressed their oologs hard down the path, through a ravine and up to a ridge on the other side. Jeddok turned his animal to follow the path along the crest of the ridge with his friends close behind. They passed between two large stone cairns and there came a sound like thunder. Pieces of stone rained down and a cloud of dust surrounded them as they heard the monster let out a hideous wail. The three ducked into a grove of trees and Jeddok turned his oolog back in the direction they had come from. The monster was gone, but standing there next to the rubble of the cairn was a very ragged looking old Yondut holding a smoldering twig and laughing hysterically. His clothing was in shreds and his hair sprang wildly in every direction.

"The hootchka near got ya', didn't it?" asked the old Yondut and continued laughing. Then his laughing abruptly stopped. "Greetings, visitors to the Farlands. How nice. How nice indeed! Please, please forgive my skrugins. A little experiment I've been working on. I have several of these along this hunting trail. They have proven very effective on those pesky hootchkas."

"*Pesky?*" the three responded in unison.

"You call those monsters pesky?" Jeddok added.

The old Yondut walked up next to Jeddok's oolog. He patted Jeddok on the leg and said, "Why, yes. I've been pestered by those things since I moved in many, many seasons back. Dear visitors, please forgive me, I believe introductions would be appropriate. My mum named me Hurshon."

The trio turned to one another in stunned silence. Jeddok stammered, "Hurshon? You are the one who brings us to the Farlands. May Theoas be praised! A monster has brought us to our destination."

Hurshon looked up at Jeddok with suspicion in his eyes. "Why would one come so far from home to find an old Yondut? The others say I'm crazy, you know."

Jeddok did not know where to begin. He took a deep breath. "Do you know of a land called Grhytnod?"

Hurshon stepped back away from the oolog, his face filled with surprise. "How do you know of Grhytnod? You aren't old enough to have heard those tales."

Jeddok's heart began to settle and he replied, "Hurshon, do you have a place we can sit and talk? Maybe share some hot beanbud?"

Hurshon's demeanor also calmed. "Yes, yes my young friends. Hoist me up on that animal and I will direct you."

The old Yondut guided them up a small creek, all the while swatting at nonexistent insects swarming about his head. They approached the rock face of a hill and there in front of them was the grandest hutch Jeddok had ever seen. It had two stories with a smelter and a metal crafter's shack off to the side. On the backside of the hutch was a tower made of heavy timbers. The group tethered the oologs in the small pasture in front of the hutch and made their way inside. The smell of smoked bonabeast filled the air, making their mouths water.

"Do sit down. How about a bowl of stew?" Hurshon inquired.

They were quick to thank him and devoured the stew almost as soon as the bowls touched the table. After the dishes were cleared, Jeddok pulled the parchment bundle from inside his jacket and laid the sheets on the table.

Hurshon gave the sheets an inquisitive glance. "What do you have here?"

Jeddok replied, "It's an unfinished tale which speaks of the Grhytans. My friend, Lohjji, found it under his grandpap's bed."

Hurshon sat up erect, "You say unfinished. What do you mean?"

Jeddok explained that the story had ended shortly after the Varrun sage's speech to the Council. He then exposed the bottom sheet containing the map.

"This is the last one in the bundle. The writing you see belongs to my pap." Jeddok continued, "Hurshon, my pap left mum and I three seasons back. He left only a strange note and a sword. When I saw this map with his scribes, it renewed hope in my heart that he may still live. That is why we come-to find my pap."

Hurshon stood up and began pacing the floor, swatting at the invisible insects once again. "I see you carry the awnaxe of a Lowland Yondut. I recognize the metal work. You are not the first Lowlander I have encountered since I moved to these regions."

Jeddok's interest grew. "Not the first? Who else has been here?"

Hurshon stepped over to the mantle and proceeded to fill his pipe. He withdrew a twig from a container and bent over to ignite it in the flames. The twig touched the pipe bowl, and he vigorously puffed until his head was encompassed with the aromatic smoke. He pointed up above the mantle at the hootchka head mounted in all its gruesome glory. He began to speak, "Another of your tribe and I slayed that monster together. I was using an awnaxe and he a sword. We met the hootchka head on as it charged toward us."

He paused to gather his thoughts, "This was not long after the Untras came to the Farlands. I had begun trading with them and I had learned some of their language. A group of the Untras had been over the mountain range beyond the Farlands. They brought back with them many trading goods. Among the goods were crude, brittle swords-if you could call them that. I inquired concerning their origin and the Untras would only tell me they came from over the mountains. I suspected that they came from the land of Grhytnod. I had heard the stories from my childhood, but that was the first time I pondered they might be true." Hurshon's face then grew tight with worry as he drew a deep breath. "However, I must share with you the most disturbing news I received from the traders. The Untras encountered a wicked clan of warriors on the other side of the mountains. The Untra word for them was 'yokpaza-niwaca', and the closest translation in Yondus is 'dark seafarer'."

Jeddok was growing impatient with the old Yondut's ramblings and interjected, "Please, what about the Lowlander? Who was he? Why was he here?"

Hurshon seemed annoyed that he had been interrupted. "I suppose you want his name? Well, that my friend, is an excellent question. I would be happy to oblige should it be dredged from my memory." He paused, looked up at the ceiling and swatted his hands at the invisible pests, "What I do recall is that he was somewhat somber and traveled with a metal crafter named Arunthal."

Jeddok said not a word, but stood up, approached the old Yondut and gave him a firm hug. He then walked around the table, patted his friends on the back, and seated himself again.

"Did I say something?" Hurshon asked.

Poodwah explained, "Arunthal is Jeddok's pap. He is the one we search for. What can you tell us about Arunthal? How did he come to be here in the Farlands?"

Hurshon began. "Let's see? A group of Yonduts arrived and told me they had come to survey the land. They searched for settlement acreage and ore deposits for smelting. I was growing weary of having only the Untras for company and looked forward to having fellow Yonduts for neighbors. They inquired of the lands beyond the mountains, but I could not tell them anything. I directed them to an Untra guide I had worked with before. Which brings me back to what I was beginning to tell you earlier." He took another puff on his pipe. "I interpreted for the wandering Yonduts and the guide agreed to take them into the mountains. They were gone around three or four phases and returned-well, some of them. The trip proved disastrous. The only members of the party to make it back were the Untra guide, Droegen, and the metal crafter-what's his name?"

Jeddok replied, "Arunthal."

Hurshon looked at him and said, "How did you know that?"

Before anything else could be said Lohjji spoke excitedly, "Did you say Droegen?"

Hurshon nodded. "Does that name mean something to you?"

Lohjji was barely able to contain himself. "Yes! That is my grandpap's name! He must be the somber one of which you spoke. Jeddok, don't you see? Your pap and my grandpap ventured here together." It was an unexpected revelation, but it explained a great many things.

# ⚜ CHAPTER 6 ⚜

## THE TALE BEGINS

### *The events to be described took place three seasons before the trio began their journey to The Farlands*

The sun began to change the dark to dawn and Arunthal and Droegen were already busy with the preparations. It had been many seasons since they had been on a survey. Droegen was aging; this was probably going to be his last venture beyond Yondusland. He had seen the Sea of Krell, the woodlands of the Untras, the desert of Erstra, and the steppes beyond it. He had never been in the direction of the setting sun. It was time.

His industrious friend, Arunthal, was eager to begin. He had only experienced the coast of Krell, and the Luurds-the less than pleasant inhabitants there. Now, Arunthal was ready to see more of what he did not know. Surely there were those out there who would engage in trading? Being a metal crafter, he was also always on the lookout for ore from which to smelt working ingots. Droegen was well-off enough and did not desire to increase his worth. He had acquired the sufficient means over the seasons to take care of himself and his grandson, who was the only family that Droegen had left. Arunthal's wife had agreed to take in Droegen's grandson while he and her husband were off on their trek.

Droegen and Arunthal were to meet the rest of the survey party just outside the village at daybreak. There was time remaining to spend with their families. They entered Arunthal's hutch; both the boys were still sleeping. Arunthal's wife, Ceshona, was already awake and preparing breakfast. She stepped into the sleeping quarters and roused the boys. Together they sat at the table and joined hands. Then Droegen, the eldest, asked for Theoas' blessings upon their meal, those on the survey, and those staying behind.

Just beyond the village edge, the survey party had finished gathering. The bonabeast and cart rigs were hitched and all was ready. Their travel pace went as quickly as the bonabeasts would allow. They followed a large river until it merged with another, creating a very wide confluence. Rafts were constructed and fiber ropes were weaved from the inner bark of a tree which grew in the area. The surveyors put their crude ferry to work and after many trips across the confluence, the entire caravan was moved to the opposite bank.

Along the route Droegen, a lifelong scholar, continued studying a language index he had acquired from the Luurds through trade a few seasons back. The index cross referenced Yondus, Luurin, and another language, thought to be that of beings called the Grhytans. The language was logically organized into phonetic combinations. As far as languages go, it was not complex. The Luurds were capable of sea travel and must have come upon the index during one of their excursions on the Sea of Krell.

The survey party reached an expansive hill region that preceded a mountain range far distant. After a few more days travel, they happened upon a Yondut settler in the area. He appeared to be comfortably prosperous with his little outpost at the end of a shallow valley. A large tribe of Untras had settled in the forested areas along the edge of the valley. With the help of the outpost owner, the group of surveyors was able to enlist the assistance of an Untra guide. Though Droegen was good with language, he had never dissected that of the Untras. However, the Yondut settler called Hurshon had developed a relationship with the tribe. His understanding of their language had developed enough to make basic communication possible.

The surveyors and their guide headed off through the hills toward the mountain range. They traded their bonabeasts for six-legged animals the Untras called "yatonkwa" in their language. The elevation of the land began rising and the air grew cooler. The first few days were spent making frequent stops at outcroppings to take ore samplings.

Traversing the rocky paths, they passed through a small ravine, and up on a slope they noticed an abandoned dwelling of unfamiliar construction. It was composed of well-placed stone work and heavy timbers. The Untra guide, whom they called Sunray because of his disposition, pointed at the dwelling and grunted out an unintelligible sentence. Sunray dismounted his animal and the rest of the party followed in kind. Upon examining the structure, they discovered it had been intentionally destroyed. The marks of awnaxes, or a similar type of tool, were seen on the timbers. A fire had been started, but apparently had not burned very far.

In a patch of weeds Sunray leaned down, picked up an object and held it high for everyone to see. It was a metallic helmet, well-constructed with bands and rivets. From the rim draped chain armor, also attached with rivets. The color of the metal was odd, unlike anything the metal crafters of the group had ever seen. The helmet was a deep black like charred wood. The color ran all the way through the metal. It was not apparent to the Yonduts what process, or metal, could produce such an item. The helmet was placed in a pack and the party went on their way.

A half days travel brought them down into a small valley. At the opposite end of the valley, they could plainly see a massive stone arch composed of colored stones. As they approached the arch, they could more easily see the exquisite stonework. Each joint of the stones fit perfectly with the next, with no space between them. There was no mortar; they were held together by their own weight. It was a truly unexpected and remarkable sight to behold.

Arunthal remarked, "This is an extraordinary work. What tribe of people created this wondrous gate?"

Droegen pointed towards the top of the arch, "Do you see those crude markings carved into the top stone? They closely resemble the markings on the language index I have been studying. If they were not so weathered I might be able to translate them."

It was at this point that Sunray made a loud proclamation in his own tongue, turned his animal around, and began to trot in the direction they had come from.

Droegen spoke with irritation, "I didn't understand anything he said. Where is he going?" He pursued the Untra, but before he could catch up, the guide stopped his animal. With a forceful tongue, the guide reiterated the phrase he had spoken just moments before. He pointed at the arch, pointed at Droegen, then nudged his animal in the haunches and quickly worked his way back into the woodlands. Droegen hurried back to his party and called them in close.

Arunthal was the first to speak, "By all appearances, the Untra fears the arch, or what lies past it. Do we take his actions as a warning or continue?"

Droegen looked down at the ground while his mind sorted out the options they had. He offered his thoughts. "What say we camp here this night and tomorrow we travel one full day's ride past the arch? If we find people to trade with, or ore for sampling, we will continue. If not, we turn around and head back to Yondusland."

Arunthal and the other surveyors agreed to the plan and made camp for the night. A meal was prepared and each member drew close to their sleeping pads.

In the dawn of the next morning, the survey party consumed a quick meal of dried foodstuffs and then mounted their animals for the day's travel. They uneasily plodded underneath the arch. Each one pondered what the day would bring. As they moved along the weedy trail, it gave way to a wide, open path. As the caravan approached a large creek, they saw a small dwelling on the opposite side. A ribbon of smoke rose from the flue of the dwelling. Though none spoke it, they all felt the urgency to turn tail and head back home.

The party crossed the creek; surely the splashing and clopping hooves of the animals would draw out those in the hut. Sure enough, the door swung open and crashed against the outside wall. Two large figures stepped out of the dwelling, both wielding stubby swords. In a deep voice, one of them hollered out a command that none of the party could understand. The party brought their animals to a standstill. Droegen and Arunthal were in the lead and were the first to dismount.

Droegen turned to his friend and whispered, "I believe we have just made contact with the Grhytans. If I am correct about that, I think I can put together a few simple words in their language." Nervously stammering, Droegen offered what he believed to be this phrase, "We are Yonduts who come exploring."

The two Grhytans looked at each other and lowered their weapons. The commanding one pointed at Droegen and waved him closer. Droegen cautiously approached. The Grhytans looked Droegen up and down, apparently deciding he and the survey party were no threat. He pointed at his own chest and spoke one word, "Kelta."

Arunthal was looking on and said, "That must be his name?"

Arunthal followed the Grhytan's example, pointed at his chest and spoke his name. Droegen followed in turn. Kelta pointed to the hut and said something to his companion. The second Grhytan stepped back inside and came out wearing a pack on his back. Kelta closed the door, waved in the survey party, turned around, and began walking down the path.

The Grhytans were imposing beings. They stood at least a head and a half above Droegen, who himself was tall for a Yondut. Their broad massive frames carried muscles like the stones and boulders that they worked with. Their faces bore wide chiseled jaws and deep crevices created by untold seasons of exposure to the elements. They wore upper garments of meshed tortoise shells bound together with wound fibers. The wide belts they wore toted the stubby swords pitted with rust. As they walked, their heavy boots made a solid thud on the soil.

The party followed Kelta and his companion down the path close to five lenads before they came to a clearing from which towered great stone walls. Kelta approached the timber framed entrance and pulled a thick rope which dangled out through a hole. The gates slowly opened, straining under their own weight. Within the walls was a large courtyard encircled by stone and timber dwellings. A Grhytan with snow white hair emerged from the largest of the dwellings and approached Kelta. The two had a short conversation, and then the White Hair turned and spoke to Droegen.

Unsure of how to respond, Droegen repeated the same phrase he had offered Kelta. "We are Yonduts who come exploring."

The eyes of the White Hair developed a curious glint and then he spoke. "We are Grhytans who fight Varruns."

This caught the survey party by surprise. How did this Grhytan know how to speak Yondus? The White Hair touched Droegen on the shoulder and drew him aside. He pointed the rest of the party to an open air oven across the courtyard and spoke something in his native tongue. The group of Yonduts didn't understand his words, but their stomachs made an accurate interpretation.

Droegen followed the White Hair into his dwelling and was offered a seat at the table. His limbs felt lost as they dangled over the edge of the enormous chair. The Grhytan stepped up to the pot suspended over the open fire pit in the center of the room. He ladled out a dip of the contents into a gourd bowl and presented it to his guest. Droegen thought to himself, "Grhytans like bonabeast!" He picked up the nearest utensil and speared a chunk of the meat, blew a few puffs to cool it off, and then stuffed the entire piece in his mouth. The Grhytan laughed as he went to the end of the table and opened a trunk that was by appearance as least as old as he was. Two tortoise shells bound together were tossed on the table and the fiber cord pulled loose. The Grhytan pulled out a sheet of parchment and laid it on the table.

Droegen almost spat his bonabeast out when he saw what it was. "This is remarkable." Droegen said. "It's an index identical to the one I acquired from the Luurds."

The Grhytan let out a bark and waved his hand in front of his nose. The meaning was obvious and both laughed like old friends. From that point on, Droegen and the White Hair spent many hours together and grew more skillful in their new languages. Droegen learned the White Hair's name was Tunska. He was an elder and chief of the fort. Droegen also learned of the threat that came inland from the Sea of Chime. Tunska and his soldiers were posted on this particular boundary of Grhytnod to engage the enemy as circumstances required. The Grhytan strategy was to build three circles of fully equipped forts along the perimeter of their borders. The three circles were separated by multiple lenads. The proximity of the forts allowed a substantial force to be quickly mustered anywhere within the bounds of Grhytnod. Any enemy breach could be contained in short order.

Droegen continued to learn more of the Grhytans, who proved to be gracious hosts. The party was thankful for the rest. One morning, as the sun's rays broke over the top of the fort walls and its inhabitants took to their morning tasks, Arunthal took interest in the fort's forge and attempted to converse with the resident metal crafter. Suddenly, there was a loud thud and sounds of scraping on the outer wall closest to the entrance. The huge gates buckled inward toward the courtyard and a deep growl could be heard increasing in volume. For a moment the noise subsided, but then the loud scraping began again on the outside stone. Suddenly, a shadow was cast on the courtyard, and as everyone's eyes turned upward, the Grhytans bellowed out, "Hootchka! Hootchka!"

Vibrations could be felt in the soil and a cloud of dust surrounded everyone in the courtyard. A Grhytan emerged from the cloud, traveling through the air and landing hard against the outside forge wall. By the time the dust had settled, everyone had armed themselves with whatever weapons they could find. Kelta stepped into the forge hut and came out wielding a long timber bearing an enormous metal ball mounted on one end. He belted out a growl that caught the attention of the hootchka. The monster pounded its clawed feet heavily on the ground and then charged directly at Kelta. The Grhytan reared back with his maul and timed his swing to meet the hootchka. The metal ball hit squarely between the monster's horns and it dropped like a rock. Kelta stepped forward and gave the monster a few kicks in the side. He turned toward Arunthal and smiled, exposing wide rows of teeth. Not waiting for any response, he pointed at the creature on the ground and proclaimed, "Good eat!"

Arunthal laughed and yelled at the top of his lungs, "Roasted hootchka all around!"

The excitement subsided and everyone settled back into their routine. Kelta dragged his prey behind one of the dwellings to clean the carcass. Droegen and Arunthal had joined Tunska at his dwelling. The three sat at the table with Droegen acting as an interpreter and a teacher for both his friends. Tunska had news from a messenger who had arrived at the fort a day prior.

He began, "For ages past, we have warred with the Varruns, but something has happened to them. An ordinary Varrun has skin with color much like your own. In recent phases, there have been attacks on our borders by a breed of which we have not seen before. They appear as Varruns, but with skin like wood ash. The armor they wear no longer gleams in the bright sun. It is dark like the night. We have taken to calling this breed the Darkrruns. The messenger who arrived at our gates brings news of a war party which comes close to our fort. They bivouac not many lenads from here. My Yondut friends, you should send your party back to your homeland. Staying here will only draw them into a battle which is not theirs-yet."

Arunthal spoke up, "What do you mean 'yet'? Your country is very far from Yondusland."

Tunska replied, "We have allies among the Frellsari Sages. They work as spies among the Varruns and their work has brought us details regarding plans to muster a great attack force. You see, Arunthal, the Darkrruns are not to be satisfied with the conquest of Grhytnod. They are looking beyond our borders. They know of the Untras, the Luurds-and the Yonduts."

Arunthal exclaimed, "Are you saying there could be plans to attack Yondusland?"

Tunska's demeanor grew serious. "There are such plans."

Droegen leaned in close to Tunska. "Have you any doubts concerning the information received from these spies of yours?"

Tunska shook his head. "No doubts."

Droegen turned to Arunthal and somberly replied, "Tomorrow we begin the trip back to Yondusland."

Tunska was not ready for their conversation to end. He endeared them to stay and hear a proposition. "Arunthal, you are a metal crafter, no doubt? The sword and awnaxe you carry-are they your work?"

Arunthal replied, "Yes. They are the work of my own hands."

Tunska continued. "Our skills with stone and timber excel above all others. Yet our metal work is a disgrace. You have seen our weapons-they do not hold an edge and they are brittle. You have seen the upper garments our soldiers wear. Shells-they are made of shells! Our metal does not bear up against the equipment the Darkrruns bring into battle. We need a teacher skilled in the metal arts. We need strong swords and strong armor. Arunthal, would you be that teacher?"

Arunthal was shocked by the question. "I have a family to care for. I must return home."

Tunska fixed his eyes on Arunthal. "Have you already forgotten what I have told you? Your fellow Yonduts will fight the dark warriors-it is only a matter of time. If we can crush them here in Grhytnod, they will never reach your borders. We need weapons and armor to match the strength of our soldiers. Do you understand what I am saying?"

Arunthal grew quiet and looked to his old friend. "Droegen, have you any wisdom for me?"

Droegen answered in an understanding tone. "Turn to Theoas and ask. Only his wisdom will make this clear for you."

Arunthal turned to Tunska. "I will give you an answer tomorrow, White Hair."

It was a fretful night for Arunthal and sleep was not to visit him. He struggled in conversation with Theoas for many hours, but by the awakening of the birds and beasts he had an answer for Tunska. He awoke Droegen and asked him to come with him to the home of the White Hair. The two crossed the courtyard to the dwelling, and Tunska was already up and about. He invited the two inside, and they sat down together at the table.

Arunthal began, "Your words last night gave my mind, and heart, much to consider. I have spoken to Theoas and he has answered. I am compelled to do what you have asked of me. You said the war force of the Darkrruns was not yet gathered. Do I have time to return to Yondusland and set my household in order?"

Tunska replied, "A second messenger arrived at our gates last night. We have news that the force will not mobilize until the ice of the far Chime has subsided next season. You have time, but you must first be educated on how Grhytans communicate over long distances. We have two methods, one being the position of the stars, and one using the pellsta."

Droegen asked, "Pellsta? What is a pellsta?"

Tunska continued, "It is a bird that remembers its master and its home. It is of adequate size to fly long distances and carry written messages. Each one of you must be introduced to a pellsta and you must spend your time with it. They will be your constant companions day and night. You must befriend your birds."

Arunthal and Droegen were filled with much curiosity about these pellstas.

Tunska arose from his seat and walked to the door. "We must visit the messengers this morn. Well, come on; you must meet your companions right away."

The three made their way through an opening in the inner fort wall and up a set of stairs. As they passed through the opening at the top of the wall, they saw a set of cages under a protective covering. The cages had no doors.

Tunska explained, "Pellstas are extremely loyal to their masters. There is no need to lock them in. Go to the cage on the far end." It was there they saw two of the brown mottled birds nestled together in the straw. "Arunthal, take this small tether and slip one end over your wrist, reach in the cage and gently pick one of them up." Tunska instructed. "Set the bird on your gloved hand and slowly slip the other end of the tether around one of its talons." Arunthal did as he was told and was surprised at the calm demeanor of the bird. Tunska then turned to Droegen, "Here is your tether. You are to do the same." Droegen followed the example of his friend and soon had a pellsta perched on his hand. Tunska continued, "Carry your birds with you at all times. We will provide you with seed pouches from which to feed them. You must talk to them so that they will come to know your voice. After one day, remove the tether and set the bird upon your shoulder. Stroll around the courtyard and see how the bird behaves for you. When it seems at ease and remains on your shoulder, then you have bonded well. From that point on let the bird fly freely, for it will always return to you, even following you in flight when you move about. Now, take your companions and go about your business. It would be wise to go encourage those of your survey party to begin their journey home."

Droegen and Arunthal returned to the courtyard and called their fellow Yonduts into a gathering. The party members expressed interest in the birds. They were told the birds were gifts from the Grhytans and they would be going back to Yondusland with them. The imminent threat of the Darkrrun war party was shared with them and it generated much discussion. Droegen also explained that he and Arunthal would stay behind for two days to finish some business dealings they had been working on with the White Hair. The Yonduts gathered their gear and loaded the oologs. By mid-morning they headed out of the fort gates.

The White Hair called his two friends back to his dwelling to finish their planning. "After the bonding of the pellstas, you two should journey home also. I will give you two Grhytan words the pellstas have been trained to obey: 'Hahkta' which means 'come' and 'Jahkta' which means 'go'. The birds remember the beginning and end of their journeys, and they will know what to do when they hear these commands. Once you reach your village, wave your arms at the pellstas and loudly yell, 'Jahkta'. They will return to the fort." Tunska then turned to Arunthal. "Now that you know of the pellstas, how do you plan to teach a hundred or more Grhytans how to master metal?"

Arunthal was stunned. "One hundred or more? That would require an enormous quantity of resources-dozens of forges and tons of rondra."

Tunska replied, "The inhabitants of Grhytnod will supply these needs. I once sat on the Council of Nernod and I still have great influence among its members. You give me the designs for forges, along with all else that is required, and we will build a metal crafters school while you are away in Yondusland."

Arunthal thought for a moment, "White Hair, give me parchment and ink, and I will draw out the design of a Yondut forge. To make the training time effective, we will need one forge for every two or three apprentices. The forges should be close to a rondra source. I will give you details on how to make sword and awnaxe blanks from ingots. Rough plates for armor must also be made. All these must be stockpiled in great abundance. Most importantly, you must know what to add to the metal to make it strong."

Tunska thought for a moment. "We shall build the school at Osrall and I will send the pellstas to summon you when we are ready. Keep yourself alive and remember your promise to return. The knowledge you share with us will protect your own homeland."

Arunthal replied with great earnestness, "Yes, I will return as I have said. My heart has peace in this matter."

Tunska smiled. "Very well; we will crush the enemy together."

"How shall the school and training be accomplished before the Darkrrun force comes to attack?" asked Arunthal.

Tunska replied, "We have thwarted our enemy before, and we will do it again. A Second Armada is almost complete and the warships are docked upon the coast of Rondur's Pier. It is our hope that the Armada can repel any coming attack and give us the time we need."

"I have not heard of this Second Armada or Rondur's Pier," replied Arunthal.

Tunska pointed to Droegen and said, "This Yondut has learned of our history. Ask him and he will tell you. You must only pay mind to the task ahead of you."

Arunthal agreed and then brought up an idea, "The helmet that we found on the way here-I must send it to the forge and see what it is made of. Maybe this will give us an advantage as we build the Grhytan arsenal."

Tunska replied, "Yes, Arunthal, do what you see fit."

Arunthal found the oolog packs and removed the helmet. He proceeded to the fort's forge and stoked it with rondra. The helmet was placed in the clamp tool and eased into the furnace. The metal began to glow, and suddenly an unearthly screech was heard in the fire. Arunthal, startled by what was happening, dropped the helmet into the pit of the forge. At first he thought the black smoke was coming from the rondra. Then the forge hut grew cold and the fire was extinguished. This was not smoke; it was something else. The dark cloud grew larger and began to take on a form.

"Droegen! Tunska!" Arunthal yelled as he ran out of the forge hut, "Come quickly!" The two ran across the courtyard and Arunthal pointed at the hut. "There is something in there!"

When he had spoken those words, a dark shadow in the form of a Varrun warrior emerged from the hut. The mass had no distinguishable features, only the shape of a Varrun in full armor, wielding a sword. Tunska yelled a command to his soldiers in the courtyard and they charged the entity. However, there was no fighting. The shadow quickly grew in size and lifted off the ground, then drifted up and above the fort walls. All those in the courtyard could only look on in bewilderment.

With the strange event over, Tunska spoke. "This is something beyond our experience. Have the Yonduts ever seen such a thing as this?" Droegen and Arunthal nodded with their mouths still open. Tunska continued, "I suggest we finish our day and calm our nerves. Please join me this eve for a meal at my home." The two Yonduts were quick to agree, and followed Tunska across the courtyard.

"Have you any idea what that entity was?" Tunska asked his guests.

Droegen responded, "I can only speculate. We can assuredly say it was a spirit and not a living being."

Tunska shook his head, "Grhytans do not deal with such things well. We know of things we can build and fight; things our eyes can see and things we can put our hands upon." He turned to Arunthal, who sat on the hearth by the fire pit. "I have heard you speak of Theoas. Who is this Theoas? I surmise this is part of the Yondut faith practices?"

Arunthal was quiet for a moment, "Theoas is the one from whom all things come. We do not see Theoas but we see what he has done."

It was evident Tunska's mind was busy. "Yes, I see. The Grhytans are not people of faith, but we do understand what you speak of. We have no cultural religion, but we do believe in a being we call The Maker."

Arunthal was curious, "How can you believe in The Maker when you cannot see this being?"

Tunska was quick to reply, "No doubt you passed under a grand arch when you crossed the border of Grhytnod? Is this correct?" Arunthal nodded and Tunska continued, "It was a wonderful work to behold, I'm sure you would agree? In your own mind, you had to have concluded that someone built the arch. It did not appear from nothing. It was the work of skilled hands."

Arunthal responded, "Of course."

Tunska went on, "Well, it is no different to gaze upon the sight of the sun setting behind a mountain, or to watch an oolog gracefully maneuver its six limbs in unison. To think these things came from nothing would be foolish. They must have a maker."

Arunthal smiled, "White Hair, we have more in common than you realize. Yet there is much more to the faith of our people. We also believe in The Rhyomas, who was sent by Theoas to all beings that have language. When you have time, maybe you would like to hear more?

Tunska nodded, "Yes, my friend, but this White Hair must rise early and the time for sleep has come. We will see one another tomorrow." Tunska walked to the opposite side of his dwelling and stepped behind a heavy curtain. The sound of his bed frame creaking and popping was heard as he settled down. Droegen and Arunthal quietly closed the door as they left.

The Yonduts woke early and untethered the pellstas, gently set them upon their shoulders, and walked out into the courtyard. They walked side-by-side along the path between the fort wall and the Grhytan dwellings. The pellstas hopped from one shoulder to the other, seeming a bit uneasy about their situation. On the third trip around the path, Droegen noticed the pellstas had settled comfortably and remained still while he and Arunthal continued their walk. Arunthal suggested they increase their pace to a trot and make another round. The pellstas, uncomfortable with being bounced about, took flight ahead of them. The birds made a wide arc above the fort wall and circled back. Droegen and Arunthal stopped and the pellstas landed upon the heavy leather pads the two had placed on their shoulders. It seemed the pellstas knew their masters now. Eager to tell Tunska the good news, they took off at a trot across the courtyard. The pellstas once again took flight in an arc around the courtyard and met the Yonduts as they approached the White Hair's door. Arunthal knocked and as Tunska opened the door he was pleased to see the birds perched in their proper places.

He greeted them. "Good morning, birdmasters! I see you have bonded well with your companions. Please come in and bring your friends."

Droegen and Arunthal stepped inside and the pellstas hopped to the nearest chair and made themselves comfortable.

Tunska spoke up. "It seems you are ready to begin your journey home. Let's have a final morning meal together before you get busy with your preparations." Tunska walked to a chest in the corner of the room and pulled out parchment and ink. "Please sit down. Arunthal, have you any last instructions for us?"

Arunthal pulled the parchment close to him and replied, "Yes. I have thought of a few more things which should be done. All the Grhytan forts should modify their forges in the Yondut manner. And they should also be supplied with the same materials that will be used in the apprentice training. Once the Grhytan metal crafters complete the school, they will be able to make a circuit among the forts and train others in the Yondut metal arts."

Tunska was encouraged, "Yes! A brigade of metal crafters to match the might of our armies. Please write all this down as best you can, and I will make translated copies to circulate among the fort chiefs."

The three finished their morning meal then Droegen and Arunthal headed to the stables to begin packing. Their pellsta companions perched themselves on the backs of the oologs.

The final pack was finished and Tunska met his friends at the gate. "Travel as quickly as you can. Remember to tend to the pellstas and send them back upon arrival at your village. Then watch the phases of the sky and be alert for the return of the pellstas. They will carry a message for you. Ride well, my friends."

The Yonduts bid the White Hair farewell blessings and headed out through the meadow toward the trail that would take them back to Yondusland.

# ⟫⟩⟨⟨ Chapter 7 ⟫⟩⟨⟨

## Arunthal Returns

The first full day of travel went well. The oologs, eager to be out of the confines of the fort, moved with great speed. The pellstas followed behind in leisurely flight, only occasionally landing on one of the oologs when the pace slowed down. Two more days of travel brought them to an area of dense vegetation on one side and a steep slope on the other. They slowed down, and far ahead they noticed unrecognizable heaps covering the path. As they came closer, it became evident what they were seeing. Strewn on the path before them lay the slain bodies of their fellow Yonduts and the oologs they had been riding. The sight was horrific. Droegen and Arunthal's hearts were filled with grief, fear and rage.

"This cannot be!" exclaimed Droegen as he dismounted his animal, "No! No! What has happened!? My companions are dead."

Arunthal dismounted also but could not speak. He moved to the edge of the trail, knelt down, and became ill. Finally able to form words, Arunthal wailed into the forest and cried out, "Who has done this evil!? Are you out there!? Come out and fight!"

He stood up and moved in among the bodies. The belongings of their companions were intact. Nothing had been taken.

Droegen stepped up to one of the dead oologs, grabbed a spear that protruded from its body and pulled it out. "Arunthal, look at the metal on this spear tip. It is like that of the Darkrrun helmet."

Arunthal nodded, "Now we know who the murderers are."

Suddenly, down the trail, they heard voices and the clopping of hooves.

Droegen grabbed Arunthal's arm, "We must hide in the forest. Lead the oologs into those thickets and I will disguise our tracks on the trail."

Arunthal did as his friend instructed. Behind the thickets he found a cavity under some large fallen timbers. The cavity was big enough to hide both of them and their animals. Secure in their hiding place, they waited as the sounds grew closer. From their vantage point, they could see dark figures mounted on four legged animals. The riders were covered in full armor as black as the night. Their faces were the color of gray ash, with beards the same color, beginning just under their black lifeless eyes, and flowing down to the middle of their chests. Each rider carried a spear and several other weapons. The riders halted their animals among the bodies and remained there in complete silence. They turned from side to side as they strained their ears, listening to the forest.

Droegen ever so quietly whispered to Arunthal, "Darkrruns. And they know we are here. Maybe we can wait them out?"

The oologs grew restless and one of them let out a low rumble. The lead Darkrrun turned his head in the direction of the thicket.

Arunthal whispered, "They know our location. What do we do now, Droegen?"

Droegen did not reply, but only lowered his head and quietly spoke, "Theoas make us a way."

In response Arunthal whispered, "Amoda."

Droegen turned to Arunthal. "The Darkrruns appear to be sensitive to sound. We must make a distraction, mount the oologs as quickly as possible, and then make a run for that gully which runs away from the trail. Maybe we can lose them there."

Arunthal removed the long leather strap he had draped over his belt, reached to the ground, and picked up a stone the size of his fist.

"Are you ready for this?" Arunthal asked.

Droegen nodded and carefully slid up on his oolog, lying close to the animal's back. Arunthal squeezed through an opening behind the fallen timbers. He stood and began whirling the sling above his head. He let the projectile fly in the direction they had traveled from. The stone cracked loudly against a tree on the slope and rolled down, splashing into a rivulet crossing the trail. The band of Darkrruns immediately turned toward the sound and kicked their animals hard. The riders sped down the trail, stirring up much dust behind them.

Without hesitation, Droegen emerged from the timbers, leading Arunthal's oolog behind him. "Arunthal, mount up now!"

Arunthal dashed from behind the hiding place and jumped onto the back of his animal. The two Yonduts pushed the oologs rigorously and were soon descending into the gully. The oologs navigated around the obstacles lying about and kept their pace easily. Riding up and out of the gully, the Yonduts could hear a great commotion; they had blundered into a skirmish between a Grhytan scout party and another group of Darkrrun riders. The two friends knowingly glanced at each other, drew their swords, and drove headlong into the chaos before them.

Arunthal swung wide around the Darkrruns. He charged from behind to the closest rider and his sword pierced the space between the helmet and torso plate. The dark warrior fell from his animal. At the same time, Droegen came around the other flank wielding his blade with a wide sweep, cutting the unprotected lower backs of two combatants.

The Grhytans bellowed a deep reverberating howl which made the hair on Arunthal's neck rise. The massive beings were reaching up and pulling the riders off their animals, slamming them to the soil. The Grhytans carried crude malls which proved to be deadly to the dismounted riders. The remaining Darkrruns knew that they would only meet with defeat and charged into the same gully the Yonduts had emerged from.

Droegen and Arunthal stopped the oologs; both animal and Yondut panted. They looked at each other not saying a word, each unsure of how to feel about what they had just experienced. Droegen pointed at Arunthal's shoulder. There was a bleeding gash possibly, from one of the Darkrrun spears.

The Grhytan leader approached the mounted Yonduts and smiled. "Good Fight!"

Droegen responded back to him in his native tongue saying, "Yes. Good Fight."

The battle over, Droegen said to Arunthal, "What say we find our way back to the trail and get out of Grhytnod as soon as possible?"

Arunthal nodded. "Let's avoid the gully. We might meet up with the dark riders again."

Making their way through the forest, they spotted the trail. As they turned their oologs onto the path, the pellstas swooped down and perched themselves on the oolog's backs close behind their masters.

Arunthal spoke. "I pray the remainder of our journey is quiet. What are we to tell the families of our fallen companions? For that matter, how do I tell Ceshona I will return here and put my life in danger once again? She will never agree to that, even if we explain the threat of war coming upon our people. Droegen, what a circumstance we are in."

Droegen took a deep breath. "My dear friend, my heart aches, as does yours. What if all this death comes to Yondusland? Have you any choice in the matter? You are not one to shirk such responsibility. I know you too well."

Arunthal remained silent for the remainder of the day's travel and into the evening.

Droegen found a likely spot for the night camp. "Give your soul a rest and see what the morning brings to you."

Arunthal halted his oolog and dismounted. He then busied himself with collecting wood and building a fire. The two had no appetite, but only sat together, staring into the flames.

Arunthal awoke to the sight of an oolog tongue in his face. The animal's breath quickly roused him to his feet. Arunthal blew life into the remainder of the glowing embers of the fire and then nudged his friend in the ribs with a stick while he lay on his sleeping pad. Droegen awoke in much pain, with a large bruise on one side of his head. He managed to stand up, but was barely able to walk without hobbling. He moved over to his oolog and pulled out the pouch of pellsta seed along with a bag of dried taeris fruit. He poured the seed out into his hand and then tossed it onto a large flat rock. The pellstas quickly found the seed and ate heartily.

Droegen handed the bag of fruit to Arunthal and took a seat next to the fire. "My seasons are speaking to me." He said in a gravelly voice, "Give me a bit more time to get around this morning-I am moving like a snail." It took a while, but Droegen eventually gathered his gear and got it packed on the oolog. "Shall we go home, my friend?" He said to Arunthal.

"Yes, Droegen, I am ready."

Once the oologs had warmed their muscles, the Yonduts increased the pace of their travel. Their minds were focused on home and nothing else seemed to matter. They descended in elevation and moved out of the mountains down into the hill region. The lenads passed quickly behind them, and they soon arrived at Hurshon's outpost. Hurshon was out near his forge hut with a group of Untras discussing a trade. The Yonduts stopped their animals just outside the hutch and dismounted. Hurshon could tell all was not well and left the Untra's standing by themselves as he hurriedly went to greet his visitors.

"Travelers, something is not right. Where is the rest of your survey party?" Hurshon asked.

Droegen replied as he dismounted, "A great tragedy has befallen us. Our companions have been killed. All of them."

Hurshon was shocked at the news. "Are you two alright? What happened?"

Droegen went on to explain the painful events which had transpired in Grhytnod. Hurshon called over the Untras to join them. He then relayed the

Yondut tale to the leader of the group. The lead Untra's face grew into a scowl and he replied in his native tongue.

Hurshon translated, "The chief knows of the dark riders that you speak of. Both he and the guide you called Sunray have encountered them on the opposite side of the mountains." Hurshon saw the gash on Arunthal's arm, "Please, let me treat that injury for you. My woodland friends have shared their healing plants with me."

He led Droegen and Arunthal into his hutch and they sat around the table. As Hurshon applied a salve to Arunthal's arm, he asked, "What will you do now?"

Droegen answered, "We go back to our village. Then we must share what has happened to our companions. I dread that task. It will be very difficult."

Hurshon offered to replenish their provisions and a place to stay in his hutch. Droegen thought for a moment. "Yes. We will accept your gracious offer of the provisions, but we must continue our journey." Arunthal nodded in agreement.

Hurshon answered, "Very well. Come to my storehouse and we will prepare you to continue."

With their travel pouches full, they thanked Hurshon, and turned back towards the trail. They traveled at a healthy pace, arriving at the confluence of the rivers in just a few days. The oologs easily carried them across the water.

Droegen spoke, "Let us stay the night here and renew our strength. If we keep this pace, we should arrive at the border of Yondusland within a phase."

Arunthal agreed. "Droegen, we should not speak a word of the evil we have encountered. We must offer our families and friends only the scarcest of details. There must be nothing in our words to bring alarm to our village or other any other Yonduts." He paused for a breath. "Theoas willing, I will return to Grhytnod as soon as the pellstas bring word. I believe the Grhytans can defeat the Varruns and Darkrruns and I am committed to help them do that. War must never reach our homeland, and we must not bring a cause for concern to any, unless it is absolutely necessary. What are your thoughts on this?"

Droegen replied, "I have already pondered on these things and I believe what you say is true. However, I must scribe our tale so it will not be lost. I will begin this eve to do so. We should also release the oologs some distance away from the village and walk the remaining lenads. These animals will only stir up more questions."

Arunthal agreed, though in his heart, he wondered if withholding information from his family and friends was the right thing to do. That night as Droegen sat by the fire, he began to write down their tale. Arunthal asked for a sheet of the parchment and began to draw a rough map of the areas they had traveled.

They arose early the next morning and began traveling, the intensity of their pace increasing as the day progressed. Even as the sun set, they did not slow down. Only when it grew too dark to travel did they stop for rest. Two more days and they entered the familiar territory of their homeland. They removed the travel pouches from the oologs and fashioned them into a form they could carry on their backs. They slapped the oologs firmly on the haunches and sent them back in the direction of the prairie. One more day of travel brought them within sight of their village. It was with elation and dread that they entered the Commons. They were overjoyed to be home, but the news they must share brought their hearts grief. As the two entered the Commons, a group of Yonduts gathered around them.

Droegen asked them, "Please, fetch the families of the survey party here to the Commons. We must speak to them urgently."

Droegen and Arunthal sat silently on the bench as the family members were gathered. Droegen then stood up on the bench so all could hear. "I bring painful news for you. A clan of warriors attacked our party and all were slain. Only we survived."

Some of the family members burst into wailing while some began yelling out questions. Droegen answered the questions as best he could, but the crowd grew louder as their hearts were filled with grief and anger.

Arunthal then stood up on the bench next to his friend and waved his hands. "Our hearts are grieved also and we cannot bring you comfort in these awful tidings. Let us reach out beyond ourselves for what our hearts need."

With that he lowered his head and began, "Theoas, our village grieves at these evil things we do not understand. We ask that you speak to us in only the way that you can. We ask that you come beside us and grant us what is needed in this time of grief. Amoda."

There were then many replies from the crowd, "Amoda."

Arunthal's simple prayer calmed the crowd. He and Droegen stepped down off the bench to embrace those who had come. Ceshona was quick to wrap her arms around Arunthal, and Jeddok held tightly onto both of his parents. Droegen sat quietly on the bench with Lohjji. The crowd dispersed, then Arunthal and Droegen made their way home.

This was the worst tragedy for the village in anyone's memory. It was going to take much time for their grief to travel its course. Slowly, the villagers settled back into their routines. Arunthal went back to his metal craft shop and began filling orders for farming tools and other utilitarian implements. He did not want to be reminded of the death he had seen and no weapons were to be created on his forge anytime soon. He began taking Jeddok to the

Commons and the village stockyards to teach him the business of trading. When school was not in session, he sent him to work at the outlying farms to learn the ways of agriculture. Arunthal had hopes his son would be more skilled in the ways of the land than he was. Arunthal's pap and mum had left him a substantial amount of acreage, but he had never pursued its cultivation, choosing rather to stay in the village and work with metal. He had only used the acreage as pasture to support the bonabeasts from his trading ventures.

Ceshona would often ask questions of Arunthal about the survey party. However, he was always reserved in the answers he gave. Jeddok asked about the birds that he and Lohjji's grandpap brought back with them. Arunthal would only say that the birds had returned home.

The phases passed and Arunthal was persistent in Jeddok's training. He was an excellent student and soon Arunthal allowed him to work some trades on his own. The lad did exceptionally well with livestock, but like his father, was proving to be only adequate with his knowledge of crops. Nonetheless, Arunthal was pleased at his progress.

Always in the back of Arunthal's mind was the nagging thought that he would be leaving his family again. Droegen, his dear old friend, could be depended on to watch over both Jeddok and Ceshona. This had already been discussed. Jeddok was maturing and would also be there for his mum. He had not thought of a way to bring this up with Ceshona without speaking of the encounter with the Darkrruns and the idea that foreign invaders could make their way to Yondusland. The thought of that disturbed him greatly. There was simply no way to explain his departure without bringing her alarm. Maybe it did not matter? The turmoil gnawed at his heart and mind continuously, though to keep his promise to return to Grhytnod was to keep his vows of protection to Ceshona.

Early one morning before the sun arose; Arunthal was working at the stables and noticed a bird swoop down and land on a railing close to him. He recognized the bird. He had long agonized that this moment would come. The bird hopped closer to him along the railing and Arunthal noticed a neatly wound fiber pouch tied to one of the pellsta's legs. He removed the pouch, untied the flap, and pulled out the small folded piece of parchment inside. He read, "The preparations have been made. The enemy has been turned back at the pier. Come teach us and fight with us. Tunska."

The time left to ponder on his departure was gone. It was time to make good on his promise. He would wait until Jeddok was away to morning classes and Ceshona had gone to the market. He knew his actions must not draw any attention. The stable work kept him busy outside until the hutch was empty. He scribed a short note, pulled his favorite sword from the storage trunk, and then laid both on the bed where Ceshona would see them when she returned. His heart ached as he stepped out of the hutch doorway and quickly made his way outside the village.

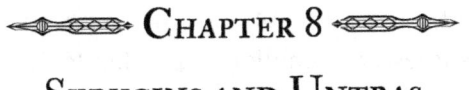

# Chapter 8

## Skrugins and Untras

### *Returning to the trio at Hurshon's Outpost*

Jeddok felt his strength renewed. "Just think. My pap and your grandpap were in this very room together only three seasons ago." Jeddok asked, "Hurshon, have any more Yonduts come this way since?"

Hurshon sat down and began working through his memory. "No, I do not recall. However, I expect a band of Untras here tomorrow morn. The Untras roam to and fro all over this land. It is possible they have seen something, or someone. We will inquire of them. Now enough of that. How about a meal and then a game of chunrots?"

Lohjji was pleased with the idea.

Poodwah chimed in, "My chums, let me cook for you. I have a tasty recipe for basted greetroot. We still have plenty in our pouch bags and it should be used before it spoils."

Jeddok's mind was busy with all that he had learned that day and his thoughts were taking him elsewhere. "Please proceed without me; I'm going out to the wood pile for a bit of awnaxe practice."

Hurshon glanced his way. "Watch out for the hootchkas; they get very frisky at dusk. Take some of my skrugins with you." Hurshon stepped over to a heavy timber box and pulled out some oblong metal objects somewhat smaller than Jeddok's fist. They were the color of rust and had a length of smelly fiber cord hanging from them. "You will also need some lighting twigs. Take two or three, lighting only one of them. They burn slowly and should last until the night comes. Wonderful little items they are-the skrugins I mean, not the twigs."

Jeddok took one of the objects in his hand and asked, "What am I supposed to do with this?"

Hurshon was eager to explain. "Do you not remember how we met? These objects are what gave the hootchka a permanent headache out on the hunting trail."

Jeddok smiled. "Ah yes, so I light the fiber cord with the twig to make it explode?"

Hurshon responded, "Yes, yes, that is all that is required. That, and running away, you can't forget that part. I'm missing a length of my finger because of that part. I must show you lads how to make these before you go."

Jeddok lit one of the twigs, picked up a second skrugin, and headed out the door. Poodwah was already busy at the grate over the fire pit. Lohjji had found the chunrot pieces and was setting them up on the table. Those in the hutch soon heard the unmistakable sound of metal hitting wood. Lohjji decided it was time to make his own sounds. He went out to his oolog, gathered his harp and went back inside.

The music was especially soothing to Hurshon, "I've not heard such a thing in, oh, so many seasons. You bring joy to an old Yondut."

Soon the greetroot was finished and Jeddok was called back inside. Poodwah set out the servings and all gathered around the table. Then he lowered his head, along with Jeddok and Lohjji. "Theoas, we thank you for our new friend, Hurshon, and his hospitality. We thank you for the meal you have given us. Let our lips and actions honor you as we go the way you lead. Amoda."

Hurshon seemed a bit surprised as everyone lifted their heads but said nothing.

As they finished the meal Hurshon spoke. "It's been so long since music, or blessings, were heard within these walls. My heart is touched." He continued, "Poodwah, no doubt you study the faith. I have not pursued such things since I was but a wee lad. My pap and mum were not prosperous and often it seemed their faith was all that sustained our family. Tell me little Yondut, what do you know of the faith of our Tribes?"

It had been sometime since Poodwah had been asked for any such teaching. "The basis of our faith is a belief in Theoas, The Rhyomas, and The Paracloas. The Creator, The Deliver and The Helper. They are distinct in being, but one in essence."

Hurshon commented, "I must admit I am only familiar with the words. I do not know what any of that means."

Poodwah continued. "To understand, we must first realize the nature of the beings which possess language. Our souls are born dark and will remain captive to the darkness until they are delivered."

Hurshon asked, "What do you mean we have dark souls?"

Poodwah shifted in his chair and leaned closer to Hurshon. "When we come from our mother's womb, the part of our being that we can see is part of the world we are born into. The part of our being we cannot see is what gives us life. The two parts make us a whole. However, the part we cannot see is separated from its Creator by its own darkness. We have no say in this; it is the nature of language beings. It comes through from the blood of those who came before us, going back to the first ones who chose to follow their own desires instead of the ways of Theoas."

Hurshon nodded, "So we are damned to darkness just by having been born? And just when I thought things were starting to brighten up."

Poodwah smiled, "I'm not done yet, my friend. Theoas desires that the created language beings desire him and love him. Because of the darkness of their souls, there can be no bond between Theoas and these beings. Because of His desire to love, and be loved by the souls who could choose otherwise, He sent forth The Rhyomas. This is the one sent to make a way for the language beings to be reconciled with Theoas. It was upon this world that we walk that he came. Taking upon himself the darkness of our souls and in self-sacrifice, wrought by the hands of others, he established a way back to Theoas-a bridge if you will. The language beings need only cross this bridge in faith and ask Theoas to release them from the darkness."

It was evident by Hurshon's demeanor that Poodwah's words touched something deep within him. He turned to Poodwah. "You have taken me back to the knees of my pap and mum. Thank you for these things you have said."

It was getting late and the time for sleep was near. The group knew they must wake early to meet the Untra traders and all went to their sleeping pads. The dawn had not yet broken when all arose, except Lohjji. He had to be vigorously shaken and awoke in a very unpleasant mood. Jeddok realized the urgent need to brew a pot of beanbud. Lohjji dragged himself to the table, sat down, and then plopped his head down on the hard surface. The beanbud began to bubble and its aroma filled the hutch.

Hurshon sat down next to Lohjji and patted him on the back. "Shake off the slumber, young one. We have skrugins to build before the Untra's arrive."

Poodwah exclaimed, "That sounds like fun! Can we pop off one of them?"

Hurshon smiled. "Of course! One cannot build skrugins and not pop one off!"

Jeddok served large steins of beanbud to everyone. Lohjji was finally able to get his shirt and britches on.

"Come on. Let's get to it," Hurshon said as he stepped through the doorway. The trio followed him out to the forge hut. "This is where we start. The first step is to make the metal containers. Jeddok, do you know enough of metal crafting to fire up the forge and heat ingots for forming?" Jeddok nodded and began shoveling rondra into the forge. Hurshon continued, "And you, little one, I will give you the formula for my mineral compound. I need you to mix the ingredients from the casks just outside the forge hut, next to the stable fence."

"At your service," replied Poodwah.

Hurshon turned to Lohjji. "Alright, my sluggish friend, I need you to pull the cover off that pile over there, take this mall and break the big pieces into little pieces."

Lohjji looked at Hurshon with a bit of disgust, turned and walked the short distance to the covered pile. He lifted the rocks holding down the top tarp and removed it, then a second. He noticed the small pile was glowing from underneath. As he pulled off three more tarps, the pile underneath grew progressively brighter. He yanked off the final tarp and was blasted by a very bright light. He threw his arms up over his eyes and yelled, "You old Yondut, what are you trying to do to me?" Jeddok and Poodwah moved in closer, shielding their eyes with their hands.

Hurshon spoke loudly, "Oh yes, I was going to tell you about that. You'll need this shield to protect your eyes." Hurshon handed him a small thin piece of wood with a slit carved down the center, on either end was a long fiber cord. "You'll need to strap this on your head," Hurshon calmly explained, "but do that before you pull off the tarps."

Lohjji turned away from the light and fumbled trying to get the shield tied to his head. Jeddok and Poodwah called Hurshon over to them.

Jeddok asked, "What are those objects?"

Hurshon replied, "Those are the rondracyte crystals I was telling you about."

Poodwah looked at Hurshon quizzically. "You never mentioned anything about rondracyte crystals."

Hurshon quietly looked down at the ground for a moment. "Hmm? I know I told someone. Well, anyway, the secret to the skrugins is crushed rondracyte crystals. They amplify heat and then release it with great force." Hurshon stopped, and his eyes grew wide. "Wait, Lohjji! Don't hit the crystals directly with the mall. Place them between two pieces of wood, and then hit the wood." He turned back to Jeddok and Poodwah. "That could have cost your friend a finger or two. All right you three, get to work. I'm going to wind and dip the fiber cords."

The group went to work at their assigned tasks, each being as thorough and accurate as they could be. Hurshon looked in on Jeddok just as the ingots began to reach the proper color for malleability. He took a clamp tool from the hut wall and pulled out a clump of the metal. With Jeddok closely watching, Hurshon formed the basic shape, and then pounded a wide spike into the still soft object. He took a smaller mall and finished off the edge and completed the form. "Do you think you can do that, young Yondut?" Hurshon asked.

Jeddok replied, "Of course I can. I am the son of a metal crafter, aren't I?" Jeddok took the clamp tool from Hurshon, pulled another blob of glowing metal from the forge, and laid it on the forming block. He followed Hurshon's example, and not missing a step, dipped the finished piece into the water cask and pulled it out. "How's that, old Yondut?"

Hurshon responded, "I don't know whether to give you praise or thump you for showing off." Jeddok took Hurshon's comments as praise.

Lohjji and Poodwah carried their work into the hut and laid it out on the work bench. Hurshon brought in his fiber fuses and Jeddok continued to form and cool the oblongs.

"We'll put these together when the oblongs have sufficiently cooled." Hurshon said.

"You say the rondracyte crystals are the secret to your skrugins. Where do these crystals come from?" asked Poodwah.

Hurshon paused for a moment. "I get the crystals by trade from the Untras. They gather them from the Canyon of the Nagaluu. I've never had the nerve to travel there myself."

Poodwah continued, "What do you mean by that? You do not seem to be one who is easily intimidated by anything. You seem to have no fear of hootchkas and they are the scariest things I've ever seen."

"You don't understand." Hurshon replied, "Beings which go into that canyon seldom return. I know more than a few Untras who have made the trip into The Canyon their last one. Of course, I believe there is a bit of a family skirmish involved there. It seems that ages back, the Untras and Nagaluus shared the same bloodline." Hurshon sat down on the stool next to the work bench. "I am also told by the roaming traders that The Canyon is a shortcut to the great city of the Grhytans. The only other passage is over the peaks-at least that is what I am told."

Outside the forge hut they heard the clamor of approaching hooves. On the far side of the pasture, a group of Untras emerged from the woodlands. Some were riding oologs and some were mounted on smaller four-legged animals.

Hurshon pointed to one of the animals and said, "The Untras call those creatures 'sukawa'. They bring them back from their forays into the mountains. Oologs have more stamina, but the sukawa are faster." As the band of Untra's drew closer, Hurshon commented, "I most assuredly did not expect so many of them. These are entire families, and I see the chief has brought his own children along."

The group was interesting to observe. The garb of the Untras was very colorful, being decorated with all manner of pigment. As they drew closer, Lohjji broke away from the group near the forge hut and walked out into the pasture. When the Untra's halted their animals it became evident what had drawn Lohjji away. Riding next to the Chief was one of the most beautiful girls the Yonduts had ever seen.

Hurshon joined Lohjji in the pasture and offered a greeting in the Untra tongue. He then leaned over to Lohjji. "I see you have noticed the Chief's niece. Quite stunning, isn't she?" Lohjji was transfixed by the young woman and gave Hurshon no reply. The Untras dismounted and the Chief offered Hurshon his own greeting.

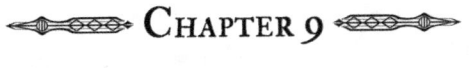

# CHAPTER 9

## LESHTI

Most of the band then wandered back to the edge of the woodlands, unpacking their provisions and preparing a campsite. Jeddok and Poodwah joined their friends in the pasture and Hurshon began his introductions, "My Yondut friends, I would like you to meet Chief Iyuski." He turned to the Chief and in the language of the Untras introduced each of the trio. Hurshon faced the girl and gracefully bowed, "I would also like you to meet Leshti." The girl offered Hurshon an awkward bow in return and spoke a short phrase. Hurshon turned towards his friends. "Leshti says she is honored." The greetings done, Hurshon waved the Chief and his companions to the benches at the front of his hutch. The Untras sat down and Hurshon went inside momentarily then emerged with his pipe and a sheet of parchment. He plopped down by the Chief, took a few puffs, and began to converse in the business of trading.

Jeddok and Poodwah were intrigued by the sukawa and walked out farther into the pasture to give the animals a closer look. Lohjji ran inside the hutch and returned with a leather water pouch. He walked over to Leshti and offered her a drink. Without changing the expression on her face, she took the cask from Lohjji and drank a hearty swig. She lowered the cask from her lips and leaned her head back releasing a tremendous eructation. Everyone in the vicinity peered curiously in her direction. Leshti handed the cask back to Lohjji. He looked at her, lifted the cask high and swallowed the remainder of the water. There was great suspense among the onlookers to hear what Lohjji was about to produce. He stood there a moment, gently patting on his stomach, and then his chest. He let loose and the sound seemed to echo all through the valley.

Not a soul could contain their laughter. Hurshon blew the herb and smoke clean out of his pipe, the Chief slapped his legs repeatedly, and Poodwah danced around in a small circle, clearly enjoying the moment. Recovering from his laughter, Jeddok gave Poodwah a gentle slap on the back. "If that isn't a perfectly matched pair, then I've never seen one!"

Lohjji ran back inside the hutch once more and this time he came back carrying his harp. He motioned at Leshti to join him under the shade of a tree a bit distant from everyone else. The harp music could be heard softly as it was carried across the valley on a gentle breeze.

Not knowing what to do with himself, Jeddok stepped into the forge hut and removed an awnaxe he had noticed hanging on the wall. He then walked behind the hutch to the woodpile and extracted his own awnaxe. Moving back a good distance he took aim, and began his practice. Poodwah went back inside, gathered one of his books then settled down on his sleeping pad. Hurshon continued his trading talks into the late afternoon. By then, Poodwah's snores could be heard behind the walls of the hutch. Hurshon decided it was time to finish up his business and took the Chief and his two companions to the storehouse where they completed their trades. They walked back towards the hutch and Hurshon called everyone inside. Except for Lohjji and Leshti who still lay slumbering in the grass under the padymir tree. After the group had gathered into the hutch, Hurshon pulled up trunks and stools around the table so everyone could have a seat.

Hurshon began, "Jeddok, I'm going to ask the Untras about any Yonduts they have seen during their forays." He then turned toward the Chief and spoke several phrases. Hurshon translated the Untra's response. "Chief Iyuski says he saw a lone Yondut near three seasons ago. They encountered him as they traveled over a mountain pass, returning to their tribe. The Yondut was going in the direction of the setting sun. He rode quickly on a lightly loaded oolog, not even stopping to acknowledge their presence."

Jeddok felt a slight pounding in his chest, "Is there anything else? Any more information?" Hurshon asked the Chief the same questions. The Chief nodded his head, and responded with a short phrase. Hurshon once again translated, "This is all I have to say."

Jeddok was encouraged by the news, but also disappointed he could find out no more. He thought of another question. "Hurshon, please ask him if the Yondut carried a sword like this."

As Hurshon asked the question, Jeddok pulled the sword from the scabbard strapped on his back and handed it to the Chief. The Chief looked the blade over carefully and spoke to Hurshon. "The Chief would like you to know he recognizes the handle, but leather covered the blade. He remembers the large symbol next to the hilt." Jeddok then knew the Chief had seen his pap. The metal crafter's symbols were unique to each family. The symbol of his family was a circle with three vertical parallel lines inside it.

Jeddok then asked Hurshon, "Will you please tell the Chief I am grateful for his words?" Hurshon conveyed Jeddok's thanks. The Chief smiled, nodded, and arose from his seat. The Untras left the hutch in the direction of their campsite.

The next morning, pots and utensils hit the floor with a terrible clatter, waking everyone in the hutch. "Oh my, did I wake you?" asked Hurshon. He leaned over to pick up the items and hit his head solidly against the basin table as he stood up. "Oolog Muffins!!" Hurshon exclaimed. "Our morning meal isn't starting out well at all. However, I am determined to prepare you boys some scrumptious eggins. Please, please, continue to rest. I have everything in order-I assuredly do."

Lohjji grunted something from under his cover. Poodwah arose from his sleeping pad. "My dear Hurshon, may I be of assistance?"

Jeddok interjected from under his blanket, "Yes, Hurshon, he can be of assistance!"

Hurshon accepted Poodwah's offer and the two arranged the griddle on the grate, stoked the fire pit, and began their work. Shortly, the smell of the cooking drew Lohjji and Jeddok to the table. Lohjji said something else unintelligible and laid his head down on the table. Jeddok looked at him, shook his head, and then got back up and went directly to the beanbud pot. He grabbed the largest stein he could find from the basin shelf and filled it to the brim with the hot brew. When the stein was set in front of Lohjji, his nose snorted against the table as he detected the drink in his vicinity. Without looking, he moved his hand over and grabbed the handle, lifted his head, and took a deep gulp. The heat never seemed to bother him. The meal completed, Hurshon and Poodwah put the servings on the table. As was their way, Poodwah offered the thanksgiving and then the hungry Yonduts grabbed their utensils and began to eat.

Poodwah spoke, "So, Hurshon, tell me of this girl Leshti that we met yesterday."

Hurshon grinned as he glanced over at Lohjji. "Well. I call Leshti the Chief's niece, but she isn't by bloodline anyway. The Dark Riders killed her father a few seasons back and then her mother passed away from a lengthy ailment. The poor girl was all alone and the kindhearted Chief took her in as one of his own. Let's just say the Chief took on more than he anticipated. The girl may be beautiful, but she has fire in her and is extremely mischievous. I know the Chief loves her, but I heard him threaten to throw her to the hootchkas on more than one occasion."

By this time Lohjji was wide awake. "How old is she?" Lohjji asked. Hurshon answered, "I wondered when you were going to join the living souls. Well, I reckon her to be in the proximity of nineteen seasons."

Lohjji just nodded and went back to his meal. Jeddok asked, "The Chief has other family, doesn't he?"

Hurshon replied, "Yes, two sons. Wanah and Wachin. They are twins. They were over in the campsite with the rest of the band yesterday and you did not get to meet them."

Poodwah joined in. "I am greatly interested in these rondracyte crystals. You say they come from a canyon. Where is this canyon?"

Hurshon scrunched his nose a bit. "If one were to follow the base of the mountain range towards the Sea of Krell, one would find it. I understand the Nagaluu are very aloof, though. If you ask an Untra about them, all they do is spit on the ground.

Anyway, the crystals grow in the caves and caverns throughout the canyon."

Poodwah continued, "Speaking of the crystals, are we going to complete the skrugins today?"

Hurshon's demeanor grew serious. "I am educating you young Yonduts about skrugins only, I repeat, *only* for the purpose of defending yourselves. I would be strongly offended if you took this knowledge and made ill use of it."

Poodwah leaned over to Hurshon. "Yes. I assure you we will only use them for their intended purpose. Although you did say we could pop one off."

Hurshon smiled. "Of course we can pop one off. We have to test them, don't we? Would you like to light it, Poodwah?"

Poodwah quickly replied, "And I can also assure you I will be the official tester."

Hurshon stood up and put on his hat, "Hop up, my friends! Let's finish our work out in the forge hut."

The trio got up from the table and followed Hurshon outside. He showed them the proper measurements and methods, for filling the oblongs, how to insert the fiber fuses and seal them in with wax. They carried the completed skrugins over to the pouch bags that were draped over the stable fence. Hurshon kept one out and handed it to Poodwah. He pointed towards a dead padymir stump which would make a good test subject. It was a safe distance from the hut and stables.

Hurshon spoke. "Poodwah, here is the lighting twig. Take the skrugin and place it in the knot hole over there. Light the fuse and run. This length of fiber fuse will give you plenty of time."

Poodwah walked over to the stump and followed Hurshon's instructions. He sped back to his friends, tripping over Lohjji's foot. He stood up and turned around just as the skrugin exploded. The chips of wood rained down on the Yonduts as they covered their eyes. After the smoke cleared, there was only a shallow hole in the ground where the stump was just moments before.

"Remarkable!" exclaimed Poodwah.

Jeddok piped up, "Now that is what I call a good method of self-defense!"

Lohjji nodded in agreement as he brushed the wood chips from his clothing.

Hurshon glanced toward the pasture. "I see the Chief is wandering this way. You three go clean yourselves up and I will see what he has to say."

The trio walked over to the water casks by the stable fence and washed themselves. They remained there until Hurshon returned from his brief meeting with Chief Iyuski. Hurshon looked at Jeddok. "Yesterday, the Chief noticed you practicing your awnaxe by the woodpile. He has offered you a challenge. Seasons ago, when I first moved here, I began crafting awnaxes for trade. The Untras found them very valuable and now most every male of their tribe carries one. They have also created a game to test the awnaxe skills of their warriors. The Chief has requested you join them out in the pasture."

Always ready to prove his mastery of the awnaxe, Jeddok replied, "Tell the Chief I will be there shortly."

Hurshon walked back the short distance to the Chief to convey Jeddok's reply. The Chief waved towards the campsite and several Untras walked towards him carrying poles and chunks of padymir wood. Jeddok went and gathered up the two awnaxes he had been using and met the rest of the group which had already gathered.

Hurshon grabbed Jeddok by the arm and took him to the targets which had been set up. "Let me explain the rules of the game. There are three targets, each one painted with geometric patterns. One of the Untra's will act as game master. This Untra has multiple pieces of bark, each with a specific sequence of patterns matching the ones on the targets. Each player is given three awnaxes. And as each player takes their turn, the game master will hold up a piece of bark. The player must throw his awnaxes, from left to right, hitting the patterns on the target matching the ones on the bark. It is a simple game of elimination. If a player once misses his mark on any target, he is out of the game. The last player is the winner." Hurshon continued, "The players are gathering in that group over there. Join them and wait for your turn."

Jeddok went to take his place with the other competitors. Hurshon and Poodwah sat down in the grass within easy viewing distance of the targets. Lohjji and Leshti had already found each other and had moved back away from the crowd with two sukawas. Leshti was apparently trying to give Lohjji riding lessons.

The game master approached his station by the targets and waved to the group of players. He spoke loudly instructions in his own tongue and the Untra warriors formed a line a few steps behind the pole marker which was placed a fair distance from the targets. Jeddok joined them in line, growing a bit anxious.

The game master issued a command and the first player stepped up to the pole marker. Having only one awnaxe, he was handed two more by the game master's assistant. The game master shuffled through the pieces of bark next to his feet and selected one. He issued a second command and flipped the bark over for the player to see. The pigments used for the paint were vivid and it was easy to distinguish the patterns on both the bark and targets. The player held two awnaxes in one hand, and took aim with the other. The awnaxe flew the distance and hit its mark squarely on the first target. The second and third throws also found their marks.

Jeddok thought to himself, "They can't all be that good, can they?" However, he was surprised at the skills the warriors possessed. Each player did very well and there were few eliminated. Finally it was Jeddok's turn. He was handed a third awnaxe and aimed. The first throw hit precisely where he predicted it would. His confidence strengthened, he continued to the second target and the third.

The final few players completed their throws and Jeddok was glad the first round was over. The line had dwindled but not by much. There was a short break to replace the targets and the game resumed. It went on through the afternoon and Jeddok held his own. The line was getting much shorter. The sun was nearing the mountain peaks when only three players remained.

Hurshon got up from his seat on the grass and approached Jeddok. "The taller of the two Untras is Wanah, one of the Chief's sons. I don't know the other one. You are making an impressive showing, my friend." He turned and went back to his place next to Poodwah.

The sun touched the tops of the far peaks and it was getting more difficult to see the targets. Wanah was the next in line and hit each of his targets. Jeddok went next and his aim was true. The third finalist missed his mark on the third throw. It was now down to Wanah and Jeddok. By this time, Lohjji and Leshti had moved in closer with the rest of the crowd. Hurshon and Poodwah hollered encouragements to Jeddok. The two players were given a short breather to loosen their muscles and then the game master issued the command to begin.

Jeddok went first. He raised the awnaxe and the head slipped down the handle, hitting his fist. He dropped the awnaxe on the ground, studied the small injury on his hand, and then motioned for another awnaxe to be brought to him. He readied himself, took aim and made his throw. All three were true.

Wanah glanced at Jeddok with a sneer and took his place at the marker pole. His first two throws hit their mark and he situated himself for the third. The awnaxe flew towards the target and hit the edge of the wood, bouncing away and landing in the grass. The crowd grew completely silent and then much murmuring was heard. The murmurs grew into a great uproar. Jeddok was enjoying the attention and strutted back and forth in front of the Untra's, waving his arms above his head.

Hurshon rushed towards him. "Please step this way. Come on, hurry!" Hurshon led Jeddok over to Poodwah and then called out to Lohjji. All of them being gathered together, Hurshon spoke. "I do believe I inadvertently failed to mention something very important."

Confusion evident in his face, Jeddok asked, "What are you talking about now, old Yondut?"

Hurshon continued. "The Untras-they are not cheering you. Let me express this in a different manner. Untras don't like to lose. I mean, they really, really, really don't like to lose."

The trio looked at one another as the meaning of Hurshon's words began to take hold.

Poodwah said, "I perceive we are in a somewhat perilous predicament."

Hurshon replied, "You have perceived correctly. You need to make your way back to the stables, pack your oologs, and flee from this place."

The group put on the most convincing smiles they could muster. Nonchalantly, they walked about the gaming area gathering up what few belongings they had brought along. Then one by one, going in different directions, they made their way back to the stables. Hurshon suggested they walk their animals back behind the hutch to draw less attention. The Untras had gathered around Wanah and Wachin and there appeared to me some kind of impromptu meeting. There was much shouting to be heard among some of the players. Shortly, the crowd dispersed and made their way back to the campsite. The Yonduts thought all was well and the Untra pride had acquiesced to defeat. However, their relief was short lived. Poodwah peered around the hutch wall and on the far side of the pasture saw a group of Untra warriors approaching, mounted on sukawas.

Poodwah exclaimed, "They are coming-a lot of them!"

Hurshon was very concerned. "You should get moving along. Not to worry, though; Untra's don't hold grudges for very long."

Jeddok turned to him. "I suppose that is an encouraging note. However, it seems they are holding on tightly to one at this moment."

The trio mounted their oologs and slowly moved out from behind the hutch, attempting to conceal themselves behind the storehouse. They heard a loud shout from the pasture and the Untra's increased the pace of their animals, heading directly towards the trio.

Lohjji spoke up, "I believe we might want to speed it up a bit. Or maybe a lot?"

The Yonduts gave their oologs a kick in the haunches and directed them to the edge of a nearby grove of padymir trees.

Jeddok turned around and could see the Untra's animals kicking up much dust as they charged towards them. "Follow me!" yelled Jeddok to his friends.

He turned his oolog into a small creek and raced up the hill. He had learned enough of the sukawa to understand that an oolog has the advantage on rough terrain. The creek branched off and Jeddok chose the direction which provided the most formidable obstacles. The trio could hear the shouting of the Untra's not far behind them. However, they were gaining the advantage and the shouts soon grew more distant. Jeddok continued to lead his friends up the hill. The oologs had no difficulty traversing the path. They continued their escape for a good span of time and when they could no longer hear the shouting, they slowed their pace. Moving into a dense thicket, they paused to listen. They waited; nothing of the Untras could be heard. It seemed that they had made good their escape. Emerging from the thicket, they were met with a great surprise.

There in front of them, mounted on a spirited-looking sukawa, was Leshti. They were all stunned, not knowing what to make of this development.

Lohjji nudged his oolog and approached her. "What are you doing here? Why have you followed us?"

Leshti was obviously not pleased with the tone of Lohjji's voice and offered her reply at a greatly amplified volume. Of course, none of the Yonduts could understand anything she was saying.

Poodwah spoke up. "I did understand one word-Luurd. Lohjji, I think she just called you a Luurd?"

Lohjji replied, "Poodwah, you are not helping matters. What am I to do now? We can't communicate with her."

Jeddok replied with a wry grin, "I find it impressive that she was able to keep pace with us. Lohjji, I don't think we are going to be able to stop her from following. I suggest you start working on the Untra language."

Lohjji exclaimed, "How am I going to learn Untra? I have trouble enough with Yondus!"

Jeddok turned to Poodwah, "Can you help our friend with his dilemma?"

Poodwah responded, "I would be delighted. After all, we have the best teacher we could ask for-an actual Untra. This is much better than any book."

Lohjji gave Jeddok a look of resignation. "Fine, where do we go from here?"

Jeddok thought for a moment. "Well, Hurshon did mention the Canyon of Nagaluu is the most expedient route to the great city of the Grhytans. I suggest that we find the canyon."

Poodwah nodded. "Yes, he said to follow the base of the mountains towards the Krell."

Jeddok replied, "I do remember that comment. All right then, we shall proceed towards the Krell. And Lohjji, please keep an eye on our new traveling companion."

Lohjji offered no reply and turned his animal in their chosen direction.

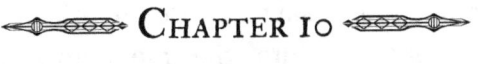

# Chapter 10

## Canyon of the Nagaluu

The group began their trek to find the canyon. They traveled the remainder of the day at a healthy pace, stopping only as the sun descended behind the mountains. A campsite was selected, a fire was made, and a small meal prepared. For the rest of the evening Poodwah sat with Lohjji and Leshti working on the exchange of languages. Poodwah had his pouch bag nearby and began removing objects, speaking out their names as he went. He would point to Leshti, and she would repeat the word with Poodwah assisting in her pronunciation. Then he would reverse, going from Untra to Yondus. Both he and Lohjji would repeat the name of each object in Untra as Leshti corrected them. This pattern continued for several evenings.

On one occasion when Lohjji had stepped away, Poodwah pointed towards Lohjji and said, "Smelly." Leshti looked at him with puzzlement, but followed his example, pointing at Lohjji as he walked away and repeated, "Smelly."

They traveled on for three more days, coming upon large rock formations that were much different from what they had seen before. Jeddok spoke, "Maybe we are drawing close to the canyon?"

As they continued, the landscape began to change drastically. As they rounded the point of an outcropping, they saw it. Before them was an expansive opening into the mountains, gradually descending off into the distance.

Jeddok looked up at the rock face closest to them. "Do you see that?" he asked while pointing up towards a group of painted figures. Leshti also pointed and said something in Untra.

Poodwah commented, "The pigment colors are familiar. They match those on Leshti's garment." The paintings randomly depicted a herd of oologs, an awnaxe, and what appeared to be a glowing rock.

Jeddok took notice, "That object could easily be a rondracyte crystal."

Poodwah nodded. "Yes. It could very well be. Shall we continue? Maybe there will be more paintings to see."

They resumed their trek, going down in elevation as they went. In the distance, they could see enormous natural arches extending off the canyon walls. Eager to get a closer view, they increased their pace and reached a large plateau. The opposite side of the plateau descended toward the canyon floor. They could see one end of an arch planted in the rock and the other end dropping down out of view. The oologs moved across the hot surface of the stone. They made their way across the plateau, going down through a rocky gully. More of the arch came into view. The gully made a sharp bend and opened into an area that gave them a full view of the arch.

Looking up, the group gasped. There, swinging from a fiber rope was the body of an Untra warrior. The body had obviously been hanging a great while, dried beyond recognition. Leshti spoke an anxious phrase in Untra and began an ominous sounding song. Lohjji drew near Leshti, and not knowing what to make of her behavior, quietly sat on his oolog next to her. Jeddok and Poodwah moved their animals closer to investigate the body.

Jeddok spoke first. "It would seem this Untra and his distant cousins were not getting along well at all."

Poodwah nodded. "That would be my observation also."

Leshti had quieted down and moved behind Jeddok and Poodwah. Lohjji followed closely, still not saying a word.

Jeddok spoke up, "We must continue and find an easily defensible position for a campsite." He proceeded under the arch and down the gully. Shortly, after another dip in elevation, they came upon a small waterfall pouring out from an otherwise dry cliff face. The water had created an inviting pool at its base and a grove of trees grew up around it. On one side of the waterfall was a large recessed area in the stone.

Jeddok led his party to the sheltered area and dismounted. "This will work well. We can make camp between the rock face and the boulders over there. We must take turns at watch this night. I do not believe this is a safe place that we travel in." The rest of them dismounted, unpacked, and built a fire. Jeddok commented to his friends, "We should rest here a day to refresh ourselves." Poodwah and Lohjji did not have to be persuaded.

The trio rotated watches but the night was uneventful. The next morning they awoke to find Leshti already working at a task. She had harvested the exposed, inner bark fibers from several dead padymir trees around the pool. Near one of the boulders, she had assembled a small frame of bound limbs weighted down on each side with rocks. On the horizontal part of the frame was a knot of fibers from which ran multiple strands going out for several paces. Leshti had the strands stretched taught, and with fibers in each hand, she twisted each pair together.

Poodwah was the first to figure out what she was doing. "Ingenious. She is making rope!"

Jeddok looked on. "If you ask me, she is planning to hang a Nagaluu. Nonetheless, rope could come in very useful. We should lend her assistance."

Everyone joined in the task and sturdy rope was speedily constructed. They continued working until the mid-day. Finally, Lohjji spoke, "My belly is complaining. When are we going to stop and eat?"

Poodwah was quick to respond. "Yes, my dear chum, we must tend to your noisy companion. I shall prepare a stew for us. Do continue your work and I will call everyone when it's ready."

Poodwah walked over to the pouch bags and gathered the dried bonabeast and grain seed. The metal pot took up much room in the bag, but under such circumstances, no one seemed to mind. He stoked the smoldering embers and went about his cooking. The group's hard work had produced many lengths of rope, coiled up neatly and laid aside.

Jeddok turned to Lohjji. "We should begin early tomorrow and not forget to fill our water pouches."

Lohjji replied, "Yes. There is also greetroot to be harvested on the marshy end of the pond. We should busy ourselves with that while Poodwah prepares the stew."

Jeddok agreed and they walked around the pool. Leshti dragged a sleeping pad underneath the shade of a large tree, close to Poodwah's cooking fire. She lay down and quickly fell into slumber. Poodwah said to himself, "She deserves the rest. I am glad she has joined us." He hollered loudly across the pool, "The stew is ready! Don't make me wait for you very long."

Lohjji dashed out of the water and started towards the campsite. Jeddok finished pulling a few more roots and followed behind. The remainder of the day was spent in leisure with Poodwah and Jeddok both reading and Lohjji strumming his harp. Leshti awoke a bit later, filled a small gourd bowl, and ate her fill of the remaining stew. As the evening grew near, the group gathered close to the fire and the language lessons commenced. This time Jeddok joined them. Poodwah had lately been working with Leshti on simple questions and phrases. Lohjji, Poodwah and Leshti were at a point where they could communicate at a very basic level. Jeddok felt a bit out of place as they practiced, but he did enjoy their companionship.

The cool dawn air was pleasant. The party did not speak much as they packed the oologs. With the water pouches full, they mounted and continued on their way. The canyon was opening wider and the riders were in quiet awe of the panoramic view before them. They followed the natural flow of the canyon floor, making their way alongside the cliff walls. Around mid-morning, just as the sun began to light up the rock faces, they observed what appeared to be brick dwellings nestled on the overhangs of the cliffs above them. They moved over to a small rise, just off the trail they were following and dismounted.

Jeddok strained his eyes as he tried to see more detail. "Those are, without doubt, brick-laid walls up there. It's not possible someone lives in such a place-is it?"

Poodwah commented, "It doesn't seem a hospitable place to call home."

At that moment a fair sized stone landed close beside them, causing the oologs a brief disturbance. That stone was followed by even more of ever increasing size.

Jeddok exclaimed to his friends, "This is not a rock slide. Someone is throwing those. Mount up and move!"

The party jumped on their oologs and sped down the trail for a short stretch and then stopped. Lohjji piped up, "There are no more stones. We are out of their reach now." Just as he uttered those words, crude wooden spears flew down at them, all of them falling short.

"Keep riding!" yelled Jeddok. With Jeddok leading, they rode inward towards the canyon, away from the cliff faces. Finding a safe gully, they stopped in the shade and dismounted.

Poodwah spoke first. "That must be the Nagaluu up there. We were apparently treading on their territory and they don't take kindly to it."

Jeddok replied, "Yes. And I caught a glimpse of one of them, dressed in a ragged animal skin. He threw down a stone and scurried away like a rodent."

The gully was home to a small spring. The riders drank their fill and continued. As the position of the sun moved in the sky, the side of the canyon they were on was cast in the shadow. Off some distance, a cave entrance could be seen not far up from the canyon floor. Poodwah pointed out the entrance. "We should explore a bit. Maybe we can find some rondracyte crystals."

Jeddok replied, "Why not? It would be an interesting side task. And I believe we could make use of the crystals in some fashion."

The group proceeded in the direction of the cave entrance and soon reached a point where they could climb up to the opening.

Jeddok dismounted first. "We should carry our side packs in case we find something. There will be little light in there. Gather up a few sturdy sticks. We can wind a length of fiber rope around the top and use them for torches."

Poodwah nodded. "Excellent idea. I shall start a tinder fire to light them."

He rolled the cord ladder down the side of his oolog, and then removed the striking stones from the pouch bag. Gathering a few dried twigs and pieces of a dead bush, he struck the small hard stones together creating a shower of sparks which landed on the tinder pile. Soon, a flame caught hold and ignited the pile. Jeddok and Lohjji had the torch limbs prepared and set the ends into the flames.

"These will not last very long. We will not have much time to explore. Hurry now!" Jeddok said as he moved up the slope towards the cave.

Lohjji handed Leshti his torch and pointed her towards the entrance. Poodwah followed Leshti. Jeddok entered the cave noticing a small fire pit on the floor, then continued down a short distance. He shouted, "I hope we will not meet the Nagaluu in here. Hello? Are you there?"

Poodwah replied, "I am right behind you, along with Leshti and Lohjji. Lohjji are you there? Lohjji!"

When Poodwah raised his voice, Leshti turned around. Lohjji was nowhere to be seen. She moved back to where they came in and saw Lohjji dawdling at the entrance.

She yelled, "Come, Smelly! Come!" It did not register with Lohjji that he was being called. Leshti repeated, "Come, Smelly! Come!"

From down a bit lower in the cave, Poodwah was laughing hysterically. Curious, Jeddok made his way back to Poodwah. "Did she just call him 'Smelly'?"

Poodwah, unable to catch his breath, nodded. He slapped the cave wall a few times and took a deep breath. "Yes, my dear chum, the girl is an excellent student."

Having just entered the cave, Lohjji exclaimed, "Why is she calling me 'Smelly'? Poodwah, what do you know of this?"

Poodwah answered, stifling more laughter, "Might it be a term of endearment in the Untra language?"

Lohjji scowled at Poodwah. "I do not think so. I must not leave you alone with her anymore."

Jeddok interjected, "We'll deal with this later. Let's keep moving." Continuing down into the cave, he rounded a turn and noticed a familiar glow coming from a side passageway and hollered, "My friends, we have found rondracyte crystals. Let's get close enough for the crystals to illuminate our way then set the torches aside. Remember what happens when rondracyte comes in contact with fire?"

Approaching the passageway, they propped the torches up in a nook on the cave wall. Shielding their eyes with their hands, they continued into the glowing room. Poodwah exclaimed, "These are beautiful! Let's collect some of the larger ones." It was clear the resident Nagaluu population had been harvesting the crystals. One side of the large room had already been picked clean.

Jeddok commented, "We should only pick a few that are fist sized. There is no need to add undo weight to our pouch bags." They scoured the walls, removing crystals of intermediate size. Having filled their side packs, they headed back out of the cave, each one holding a crystal in front of them to light the way.

Once outside, Jeddok said, "Let's get these in the pouch bags and find the night's campsite." They loaded the oologs and continued on their way. Finding a likely group of boulders, they settled in for the night. It had been an adventurous day and sleep was lying heavy on everyone's eyes.

Awakening early the next morning, Jeddok started a fire and went about rousing his friends. He came to Poodwah's sleeping pad but he was not to be found. He hollered out, "Poodwah! Poodwah! Are you out there!?" There was no response and he called out again. Jeddok's calls quickly brought Lohjji and Leshti to their feet. "What is wrong Jeddok?" asked Lohjji.

Pointing at Poodwah's sleeping pad, Jeddok replied, "I can't find Poodwah. He appears to have wandered away from the campsite. You and Leshti pick a direction and go search for him. I will do the same."

They all walked out among the boulders and through the sparse brush beyond. Shortly, Leshti was heard calling out, "Come! Look!" Jeddok and Poodwah ran her direction. She pointed at the ground, "Poodwah! This way!"

Approaching closer, multiple footprints could be seen in the sandy soil. Lohjji spoke, "These prints belong to more than one. See the smaller ones? Those surely belong to Poodwah. There are at least two other sets besides his."

Jeddok nodded. "Pack and mount quickly. Poodwah is in trouble and we must find him."

Wasting no time, they were soon following the trail of tracks. It led towards a cliff wall that veered back towards the left from their campsite. They continued to track while the sun rose but the trail stopped at a solid stone slope. The slope rose upward into a crevice in the canyon wall. They dismounted, and traversed up the slope. Moving deeper into the crevice they discovered a staircase carved into the stone, reaching to a ledge above on the crevice wall.

The ledge led into another crevice adjoining the larger one.

Jeddok stopped in his tracks, "There is a chance we will be entering another cave. We should take side packs with rondracyte crystals. We need to go back down to the oologs and fetch them. Strap on your sword and make certain your awnaxe is readily accessible."

They made their way back to the animals and gathered the gear. The extra weight made it more difficult to climb back up the slope. Jeddok turned to Lohjji. "We're ready now. Tell Leshti to stay between us." The staircase was steep, but the steps were well cut. They climbed to the first ledge and followed it to the next crevice. Carefully navigating the stones and boulders for a good distance, they came within viewing distance of a cavern entrance.

Lohjji spoke, "Jeddok you were right. We should each take hold of a crystal before we enter."

With the rondracyte in hand, they eased closer to the cavern. There was no sign of movement and nothing could be heard, so they slowly entered. The first area they entered was very large with extremely high ceilings. Water dripped through the cracks above them. Proceeding deeper, the passageway became smaller and more defined. None of them uttered a word, keeping their ears alert for anything which might bring alarm. Jeddok brought attention to paintings on the walls as the crystals illuminated them. Reaching a point where the passageway divided, the group stopped. Leshti knelt down and held her crystal close to the cavern floor. She pointed Jeddok and Lohjji to a set of footprints and what appeared to be drag marks.

Jeddok whispered, "Tuck your crystals away and I will mute mine with my jacket fabric. If our light is too bright, we will draw attention to ourselves."

Lohjji and Leshti put the crystals into their side packs and tied down the flaps. They proceeded with Jeddok holding his crystal underneath his jacket tail. They noticed the walls of the passageway had been chiseled and formed, creating small nooks on each side. Jeddok stopped, turned and pointed down the corridor, then slipped his crystal into his side pack. With Jeddok's crystal hidden, the glow of light farther down from them could be seen easily. They stayed there momentarily straining their eyes towards the direction of the light. Jeddok waved his companions on, and as the light grew brighter, they saw rondracyte crystals neatly tucked away in the nooks on both sides of the wall. Then they met another division in the passageway. Leshti once again directed them. The corridor grew wider and the light was growing brighter. Off to one side was an entrance. A makeshift door had been bound together and leaned against the entrance, with large stones holding it in place.

Jeddok looked through a crevice of the doorway but saw only darkness. He thought to himself, "There must be a reason this entrance is sealed." Turning to Lohjji, he pointed at the door, bent over, and began moving the stones. Leshti joined in the task, and soon enough stones were removed to pull the door aside. Jeddok removed the crystal from his side pack, held it up, and stepped inside. There, against the wall, was Poodwah. He was bound, gagged and unresponsive. Lohjji quickly ran to him, knelt down and began to remove the bindings. Poodwah was still unresponsive and there were several abrasions on his face. At that moment, a noise was heard some distance down the cavern. Leshti rushed into the room and took a position next to Lohjji. The noises grew louder.

Jeddok turned to Lohjji and spoke in a low tone. "Arm yourself, my friend."

With that, he shoved the crystal back into his pack and moved closer to the doorway. They heard voices but the language was intelligible. Jeddok peered around the edge of the doorway and saw silhouetted figures in ragged animal skin garments coming closer at a rapid pace. Jeddok thought, "This confrontation cannot be avoided." He stepped through the doorway directly into the path of the Nagaluu. Lohjji followed immediately behind him with sword drawn. Leshti had been able to rouse Poodwah from his incoherent state and helped him over to the doorway. Jeddok yelled, "Run!" Lohjji repeated the command with the same intensity in Untra. Leshti and Poodwah took off through the passageway back toward the entrance. Jeddok and Lohjji stood together in the corridor, facing three Nagaluu armed with metal pointed spears and small daggers. The fight commenced as one of the Nagaluu lunged at Jeddok with a spear and Lohjji deflected it with his sword. A large chunk flew off the spear handle, but the Nagaluu withdrew and came with great force at Lohjji, grazing his upper thigh. Jeddok engaged a second Nagaluu as he bowed low and came up under Jeddok's arms, cutting him on the side of the face with a dagger. Jeddok swung his sword, arching towards the attacker, but missed as the Nagaluu rolled backwards on the ground with great agility. The third attacker made his move, lunging toward Jeddok while he was still attempting to regain his balance. The spear grazed Jeddok's forearm and he dropped his sword. The Nagaluu swung the spear handle, coming from the opposite direction, hitting Jeddok behind his knees and knocking him to the ground. The attacker withdrew his dagger and jumped, driving his knee into Jeddok's chest. Jeddok was momentarily incapacitated as the wind was forced from his lungs. Seeing Jeddok was in trouble, Lohjji reared back with his sword and swung hard at the Nagaluu's back. Jeddok's attacker dropped to the ground. Jeddok looked up and saw one of their foes had readied his spear and was taking aim at Lohjji. In an instant, Jeddok pulled the awnaxe from his belt and threw hard, sinking the weapon into the Nagaluu's chest. The remaining Nagaluu ran back into the cavern, yelling as he went.

Lohjji moved over to Jeddok and hoisted him up from the ground. Jeddok spoke loudly, "My awnaxe! Fetch my awnaxe."

Lohjji propped Jeddok up against the wall and stepped over to the fallen Nagaluu, withdrawing the awnaxe. The two, moving as hastily as their injuries allowed, headed towards the cavern entrance. Just as they were in view of daylight, an echoing uproar was heard from where they had just emerged.

Jeddok exclaimed, "More fighters are coming! Waste no time getting to the oologs. I have an idea." They quickened their pace, ignoring the pain of their injuries. Traversing the ledges and then bounding down the staircase, they could see Leshti and Poodwah had already reached the bottom of the slope. Jeddok yelled, "Poodwah! Build a tinder fire! Hurry!"

They could see Poodwah scurry about digging in the pouch bags. By the time they reached the bottom edge of the slope, Poodwah had a fist-sized pile smoldering.

"Lohjji, break off small twigs from those bushes next to you and bring them to the tinder fire," instructed Jeddok. He then ran to his own oolog and extracted two skrugins from the pouch bag. Knowing what Jeddok had in mind, Lohjji knelt down and lit the twigs. Jeddok handed Lohjji a skrugin and retrieved a smoldering twig.

Jeddok spoke up, "We must climb back up the slope, getting as close as we can to the crevice." The two bounded up the stone, the sound of the angry roar was now moving closer down toward them. Jeddok turned to Lohjji. "Put that strong arm of yours to good use."

Lohjji lit the fiber fuse and heaved the skrugin up into the crevice. Seconds later the explosion was heard and large pieces of rock splintered from the side of the crevice wall covering the staircase.

Jeddok lit his own skrugin and handed it to Lohjji. "See if you can get this one in the same area."

Lohjji nodded and catapulted the object upwards. The second skrugin went farther than the first, landing behind the already shattered stone. The explosion jarred several great boulders down from the upper cliff. The echo of the Nagaluu yells could be heard faintly behind the rubble, but the Yondut's enemies were not going anywhere soon.

Jeddok and Lohjji made their way back down the slope. The group mounted their animals and sped away for a great distance. Slowing the pace, they continued to travel. The sun had begun its descent when Jeddok spoke. "Let us find a place to stop. I know we all need rest, but will have to maintain watches through the night."

His friends agreed. Moving into another gully, they happened on a likely camp area and halted their animals. The provisions were unpacked but no fire was started. They cleansed their injuries, determined the schedule of the watches, and the sleeping pads were laid out.

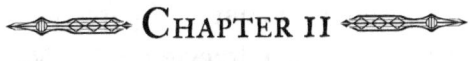

# CHAPTER II

## GRHYTNOD

The next morning was painful for the group. Each one felt the consequences of the previous day's events. Forcing their bodies to obey their minds, they rose to their feet and began the morning tasks. Leshti's concern for her companions could be seen on her face. Lohjji embraced her as if to say, "All is well," and continued packing the oologs. Poodwah's small fire brewed the remainder of their beanbud, while Jeddok hiked up the hill near their campsite to survey the landscape before them.

He moved back down the hill to the fire. "Thanks be to Theoas that we are able to be together this morn."

In unison Lohjji and Poodwah replied, "Amoda." Leshti looked at them curiously, not understanding their behavior.

Jeddok continued, "Poodwah, I have no notion of why the Nagaluu wanted to take you."

Poodwah replied, "Neither have I-though I do remember Hurshon saying this canyon made beings disappear."

Jeddok nodded. "Did they take any of your personal possessions?"

"My awnaxe was with the oologs, so all they were able to get was the side pack I had lying next to my sleeping pad. And there was nothing of value inside.

A few striking stones, a couple of parchments, a short length of rope, and a rondracyte crystal. Maybe a few more objects? I can't remember."

Lohjji joined in, "Were there metal objects of any kind?"

Poodwah thought for a moment. "Yes, two meal utensils, including my favorite bonabeast knife."

Lohjji continued, "I would guess they were after the metal and you were the easiest target. I do not think that they forge their own implements."

Jeddok turned to Lohjji, "That is an excellent observation. Yet I still don't understand why they would want to take our little Yondut."

Poodwah smiled. "I'm just happy to be back with my friends. What say we continue our day?"

"You are right," said Jeddok. "Let's be on our way."

The next several days of travel were pleasantly uneventful. They happened upon a spring and were able to replenish their water pouches, but the foodstuffs were running low. Continuing to follow the natural lay of the landscape, they began to see puffs of steam rising from fissures in the ground. An unpleasant smell filled the air, becoming stronger as they went. The rocks about them were of a composition unlike what they saw elsewhere in the canyon. It became increasingly difficult for the riders to discern a navigable path, so they moved closer along the canyon wall and there discovered a crudely hewn path. The trail was extremely narrow, seeming more suited for two-legged travel. The steam fissures were growing larger and more plentiful.

Jeddok, halting his oolog, turned back to his companions. "Our travel path appears to be turning for the worse. However, I did not see another route we could have taken. Stay close together and move your animals slower than the normal pace."

Lohjji replied, "I saw no other course either, my friend. We haven't any choice but to continue."

Poodwah agreed and they continued. The trail grew slightly wider as they traveled on and the landscape opened up. Some distance in front of them was a deep depression in the canyon floor, sloping steeply downward from all sides. Drawing closer to the formation, they could see the glow of a bubbling material at the bottom. The air around them became warmer and began to sting their eyes. The canyon wall was now pocketed with small caves, none of them appearing to be very deep.

Jeddok commented, "With all the steam spewing about us, I would say there must be a water source under our feet. We should look inside those caves for a pool of clean water and fill our pouches. Actually, if you don't mind, I would like to investigate that natural cauldron a bit."

Poodwah nodded. "You go right ahead, chum. I believe I will stick close to the caves."

Lohjji agreed. "I will remain with Poodwah and Leshti. Proceed without us, but watch carefully over yourself."

Jeddok responded with a nod, turned his oolog around, and moved towards the cauldron.

The remainder of the group turned towards the caves to begin their own investigation. Moving a short distance, Lohjji stopped his animal and dismounted. Leshti and Poodwah followed in kind. He leaned over, picking up a handful of small stones and spoke, "Move along the wall and toss the stones into the caves and listen for the splashing of water." Poodwah was impressed with the idea and followed his friend's example. Leshti remained by Lohjji's side.

Meanwhile, Jeddok moved close to the cauldron rim and could see the bubbling magma. The environment was extremely inhospitable. The oolog was nervous and skittish in the surroundings. The scene before him was something Jeddok had heard about during his school days; he was excited to see the source material for the study books. Curiosity overrode his better judgment and he moved even closer to the rim, but the oolog became more agitated and resisted Jeddok's guidance. Suddenly, the ground beneath them gave way. The oolog stumbled and Jeddok grabbed onto the mane loop tightly. The oolog went to its knees, two of its legs slipping over the edge of the rim. Jeddok's pouch bag slid off the animal's back towards the cauldron; he grabbed one end of the bag before it dropped. The flap on the opposite end came open and the skrugins tumbled out, along with all his rondracyte crystals. The objects rolled down the slope, heading into the deep pit towards the molten rock below. The oolog righted itself as Jeddok watched the items from the pouch bag continue to slide down the slope. Knowing something awful was going to happen when they reached the bottom, he kicked the animal in the haunches and charged back to his friends. The oolog was having difficulty traversing the rough surface at such a pace and stumbled several times.

When Jeddok came within shouting distance of his friends, he yelled, "The caves! Move into the caves!"

The other three glanced toward Jeddok, not knowing what to make of the situation, but Jeddok yelled again, "Get into the caves!"

They quickly led their animals into the larger of the two caves that were closest to them. There was a low rumble now coming from the cauldron and the ground began to vibrate. As Jeddok drew nearer to the cave, a plume of dense smoke rose from the cauldron and the ground beneath him shook with great violence. There came a deafening roar and the air filled with a mixture of smoke and dust, while large chunks of stone slammed against the canyon wall. A heavy crash was heard in the back of the cave.

The roar subsided and soon only a low rumble could be heard. They coughed as the smoke dissipated. They frantically looked about in the cave trying to find one another. Then, towards the back of the cave, they saw a large boulder had fallen on Leshti's sukawa. The animal was not moving and Leshti could not be seen. Running behind the boulder, they found Leshti lying on the ground with one of her arms pinned under a large stone. She was unconscious and had a large gash on the side of her head.

Lohjji cried out her name, "Leshti!" as the trio knelt beside her. She was still breathing. Lohjji grabbed the boulder lying on her arm and tossed it aside as if it had no weight at all.

Poodwah exclaimed, "We must get her out of here!"

Jeddok and Lohjji gently lifted her and carefully carried her outside. As they laid her down in a flat area, she began to cough as she came to consciousness. Jeddok stood up and walked away. He began to pound his fists hard against the rock face. "You fool! You idiot! You stupid, stupid fool! Why did I bring us to this place?"

Poodwah went over to his friend and gently patted him on the back. Lohjji's attention was intently focused on Leshti and said nothing. Jeddok turned and looked at Lohjji. "I am so sorry. This is all my doing, and I am sorry. We must get her far away from here."

Lohjji, still silent, took one of Leshti's shoulders in each hand. Jeddok took hold of her legs and together they lifted her up. Jeddok followed Lohjji's lead as they moved towards his oolog standing just outside the cave entrance. They carefully placed her on the animal's back and supporting Leshti with his hand, Lohjji mounted the oolog. Jeddok and Poodwah gathered up the pouch bags and other items strewn about in the chaos. Shortly, they began down the path once more, veering around boulders as they went.

Leshti was incoherent, waking only for short periods. Lohjji held her tightly as they went. The group remained quiet as they pushed the oologs as quickly as they dared. By late afternoon, they emerged from the cauldron area and the canyon grew wider and flatter. The path they were traveling became more easily navigable. Eying a dry grassy area, Jeddok halted his oolog, "This is the best site we've come across to stop for the night."

Jeddok and Poodwah dismounted, assisting with getting Leshti down from the animal. They both offered their own sleeping pads, and along with Lohjji's, laid them out on the densest part of the grass. Leshti was more awake now and was able to stumble along with Lohjji holding her up. She groaned as they moved, clutching her injured arm. She was gently settled on the sleeping pads, and then Lohjji fetched a water pouch and a rag of fabric from his oolog. He knelt down beside her and began to cleanse the injury on her head.

Jeddok pulled a coil of the thinnest rope from his pouch bag and cut off a length. He went around the edge of the campsite picking up some of the larger pieces of brush stems, cleaning off any protrusions with his awnaxe. Moving over to Leshti's sleeping pad and kneeling, he spoke to Lohjji. "We must fashion a splint and sling for her arm."

Lohjji just nodded, stood up, and moved aside. Jeddok, ever so carefully, assembled the branches as best he could. Finishing, he spoke, "It's not the work of a healer, but it will give her arm some support. Lohjji, I am deeply sorry."

Lohjji responded, "You speak as if you have done this to her?"

Jeddok told his friends of his mishap on the cauldron rim. Speaking to Lohjji once again, "My friend, I regret bringing all of you here. I am a fool for doing so."

Lohjji looked at Jeddok in the eyes. "Jeddok, we were not forced to join you. Poodwah and I chose to come on this journey of our own free will. You could not have known what would happen at the cauldron. And I am as responsible for Leshti's injuries as you are, for I should have drawn her close to me while we were in the cave. I did not protect her as I should have." Lohjji's forgiving heart was a testimony to his grandpap's teaching.

Jeddok looked down at Leshti. "Please, Lohjji, tell her I am sorry."

Lohjji knelt down beside her and spoke two short phrases. She simply nodded and lay on the sleeping pads. Night was upon them and the trio had settled down into the dry grass, trying to make themselves as comfortable as possible. The exhausted riders were soon deep in slumber.

The next morning Leshti's condition had improved. The riders now had one objective: to get out of the canyon. The trail now afforded a healthy travel pace and the group traveled continuously, only stopping for water. Leshti was alert but very weak and unable to maintain a firm grip on the mane loop, relying on Lohjji's support to stay on the oolog. For four days, they moved at an exhausting pace. By mid-morning of the fifth day, the canyon exit was in view, opening up to a large forest. They completed the remaining lenads out of the canyon and began towards the forest. Reaching the top of a ridge, they saw an enormous stone arch towering over an opening into the trees. The riders slowed down as they approached.

Poodwah spoke up, "What is this? What place have we come to?"

Jeddok halted his animal, his friends doing the same, then reached into his jacket and pulled out a rolled leather case. Unfurling the case, he removed the map, glanced at the parchment, and again at the arch. His voice seeming stronger, he spoke, "I believe we have just entered Grhytnod."

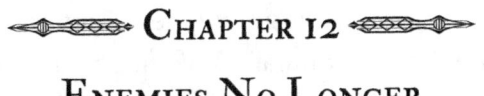

# CHAPTER 12

## ENEMIES NO LONGER

**_A vast distance away
across the Sea of Chime,
the Varrun homeland experiences
a great internal struggle between
the two factions of power_**

The growth of the Ehkkahn ceased when there were no more Varruns willing to merge with it. Varrunas tumbled into chaos. Dissension increased and several minor battles were waged between the Varruns and Darkrruns. With the threat of a civil war, the Varrun king, Ulfur, initiated an alliance with the Chief General of the Darkrruns. It was agreed to focus their energies on expanding the dominion of Varrunas and invasion plans were drawn, but details of the strategy became a point of contention. Political and power struggles ensued, with the plans becoming mired down in the process. Tensions rising, King Ulfur became distressed at the possibility of losing his position. Choosing a diplomatic approach to the crisis, he summoned his generals and the most powerful Darkrrun leaders to an assembly in the Varrun capital.

King Ulfur pounded his staff upon the floor. The sound echoed throughout the cavernous meeting hall. He shouted at the crowd before him, "Restrain your comments! The Chief General will continue to speak!"

His voice lowered as it grew quiet. "The arrangement is by my edict. Our domain must not be divided, and I have proclaimed this resolution. The Chief General is now co-regent along with me, and the lands of Varrunas will remain as one kingdom."

Chief General Graeog approached the gray stone podium. "As you well know, the forces of our two armies are evenly matched. We agree that there is nothing to be gained by warring among ourselves, and the truce has been somewhat successful for a full season. Yet, you still continue to call us swine and vermin. Even the Grhytans show more respect and use the name 'Darkrruns'. Nevertheless, we share the same blood and mutual lust to expand the dominion of Varrunas. The forces of your King Ulfur and the forces of the Darkrruns will subjugate all lands and cultures that we desire. The time is now to execute the attack plans which have been established. The continued postponements only exhibit the weaknesses of those who will not join us."

The crowd was in uproar. King Ulfur began violently beating his staff on the floor. He lifted his hands high, in an attempt to quiet the crowd once again. "Chief General, I called you here to speak to my generals, not insult them!"

Ulfur faced the crowd and shouted, "You are dismissed until further notice." Turning towards Graeog, he angrily spoke, "As for you, Darkrrun swine, we will continue this discussion in my chamber."

Graeog replied, "Very well, dotard."

The two entered King Ulfur's chamber and seated themselves at the heavy timber table. Ulfur spoke first. "You will not inspire unity with my generals by using such words as that. What are you thinking?"

Graeog, pouring himself a drink from a pitcher on the table, responded, "I grow weary of waiting for your generals to take action. Their failure to join our ranks makes them weak."

Ulfur stood. "And by 'weak', you mean they choose not to submit themselves to that rogue sage whom you follow?"

Graeog jumped up, throwing his drink to the floor, "We do not follow a sage. We follow ourselves. The sage has only shown us the way to the freedom that is already within us."

Ulfur began to pace the floor. "Relinquishing one's mind, spirit and body to the dark entity will not bring freedom. You are a fool. I am my own master. I will not relinquish my will to anything or anyone."

Graeog seated himself again. "You have no understanding of what can be achieved through the freedom that my brothers and I have been given. You and your kind are restrained by foolish notions of honor and rules of war. You do not decimate your enemies; you leave the females and offspring to propagate even more enemies. You do not slay the officers-only hide them away in that antiquated prison of yours. You let such ideals make you and your armies weak." Graeog paused. "Do not be deceived; even your own sages teach that all beings belong to the darkness of their souls. No being is its own master."

Ulfur seated himself on the opposite side of the table, "I am a Varrun warrior. During my seasons I have slain more beings than I can remember. I have casks of blood upon my hands. However, there are things I simply will not do and killing young offspring is one of them. My conscience will not allow such a thing."

Graeog slammed his fist on the table, "This is what I speak of! The dark entity can release any being from such restraint. You are already mastered by the darkness of your own soul-why do you resist the opportunity to embrace that darkness? That is the power and the freedom the Darkrruns have been given. There is no shame, guilt or regret in any action that we take. No female, offspring, or animal is shown mercy when we march. We lust for power, wealth, and all those other things that your sages declaim against. Without the petty restraints of our hearts, we are free to pursue all these by any means at our disposal. This is freedom. This is power!"

Ulfur barked, "Do not slam your fist at me. Show respect. It was my decision to give you co-regent status in order to hold this kingdom together.

Remember that." Ulfur paused, scratching his beard. "The freedom that you speak of is not the freedom that the Frellsari Sages proclaim. Their words say a soul can be released from the darkness that holds it. I am not a follower of that faith, but as my seasons advance, I oft wonder if I have missed something."

Graeog rose from his seat and sneered. "You will not hold a kingdom together with such notions." He stormed out of the chamber, slamming the door behind him.

King Ulfur again paced the floor, murmuring to himself. "What has become of Varrunas? What has become of me? I am a pathetic king. I believe my soul would have been more content had I remained with my father to harvest the sea."

Glancing towards the widest wall of his chamber, he pondered all the spoils that he had mounted there. "Have my conquests achieved anything of consequence? My heart questions if the Frellsari Sages speak words of truth." He stepped closer to the wall, drawing a finger across the blade of a Yondut sword. "The people called Yonduts hold to a faith much like that of the sages. Have they a knowledge that has escaped me for all these seasons?"

He turned away from the wall, pacing again. He swung open the door to his chamber and hollered out, "Sentinel! Fetch me the Yondut prisoner and bring him to my chamber. He must be questioned." Being a king, Ulfur was schooled in many languages and could converse in the tongues of several cultures. Shortly thereafter, the sentinel pounded on the door, Ulfur opened it and there stood the Yondut, squinting and dirty. "Bring him in and shackle him to the table," commanded Ulfur. Seating himself on the opposite side of the table, Ulfur was silent, seemingly at a loss for words.

Not looking up from the table, the Yondut spoke. "Why do you bring me here, Varrun?"

Ulfur responded, "Are you not the one responsible for the weaponry and armor the Grhytans now carry?"

With head hung low, the prisoner replied, "Yes. I am the one."

Ulfur continued. "You are not of the Grhytans, but you hold rank in their army. A reward for the metal work, I presume? Do you understand your rank is the only reason you still live?"

Lifting his head, the prisoner replied, "Yes. That is what I have heard. Varruns do not slay ranking prisoners."

Ulfur stood. "That is correct. It is fortunate you were not captured by the Darkrrun faction; they do not abide by such engagement rules." Ulfur walked over to the wall, removed the sword, and brought it to the table, laying it in front of the Yondut. "I have always admired the metal work of your people. This particular blade-I understand it is the work of your own hands. Is this correct?" The prisoner nodded and

Ulfur continued. "Tell me Yondut, the symbol on the hilt is unique. What significance does it have?"

The Yondut replied, "It is the metal crafter's mark of my family. It has been handed down for generations. I now carry it on. All those who see it know that this work was crafted by Arunthal."

Ulfur asked, "But what does it mean? It must represent something."

The prisoner shifted slightly on his seat. "Yes. It symbolizes the faith of my people."

Ulfur was curious. "Explain. I find great interest in this."

Arunthal sat erect and replied, "The lines symbolize Theoas, The Rhyomas, and The Paracloas. The circle symbolizes that they are three, but one. This is our belief."

Ulfur leaned closer, "Tell me more. What of the lines? What do you speak of?"

Arunthal sensed the sincerity of Ulfur's questions and his mind grew more at ease. "I speak of The Creator, The Deliverer, and The Helper."

Ulfur nodded. "Tell me, what do these scribes on the blade mean?"

Arunthal pointed at the words on the sword. "In our 'oldsay', the words are pronounced, 'Diodef Gwirion', and they mean, 'Truth Endures'."

Ulfur sighed. "I am weary and my seasons have made my heart yearn for things that my youth did not consider. The wall you see behind me has not brought peace to my soul. Rather, it seems to have brought only strife. My heart now grieves for peace and truth."

Arunthal felt compassion for the old Varrun warrior who sat across from him. He thought to himself, "Ulfur seems not an enemy to me at this moment." In response, Arunthal offered these words, "Theoas can grant you peace. In ages past he sent The Rhyomas, the Deliverer, to the world upon which we walk. He was despised and rejected by those whom he walked among. He knew sorrow and grief as we do and was subjected to oppression and affliction at the hands of those he came to deliver. In the greatest act of self-sacrifice ever conceived, he took the darkness of the souls of every being upon himself. In death, wrought at the hand of others, he gave the offering Theoas required. Yet his tomb would only hold his body for three days, for on the third day, he rose again. Even this day he is reunited with Theoas."

Arunthal paused. Ulfur remained silent, but his eyes spoke clearly. "Ulfur, if you truly desire what you speak of, it is within your reach. Confess the darkness within you, accept the sacrifice of The Deliverer, and make Him your master. Then you will have what your heart yearns for." Arunthal could see a small tear forming at the corner of Ulfur's eye.

Still silent, the King looked out the window of his chamber for a few moments, turned back to Arunthal, and spoke, "This, I do. Yondut, your words have wrought a change within me. My heart is not as it was. I must ponder on these things." He turned towards Arunthal. "I do not know what to do now; you seem not my enemy any longer. Nevertheless, I must send you back to your cell. However, do not be concerned with this. We will speak again very soon."

Arunthal smiled. "Yes. King Ulfur, I would like that very much." Ulfur opened his chamber door and called for the sentinel, "Take this prisoner back, and give him a basin of water for washing and some decent food. Do you understand?" The sentinel looked at his King quizzically, but acknowledged his orders and led Arunthal down the hall.

Arunthal was escorted down the isolated passageway to the stone room where he had spent the past season. The sentinel locked the door but shortly returned with the items the King had requested for the prisoner. He waited for several moments as the sentinel walked way, and then hollered to the cell adjoining his, "Therak! Are you there?"

A gravelly voice responded, "Yes Arunthal. I have just returned from my garden walk and I'm settling down for a fine meal."

Arunthal laughed, "Then that would make me your servant, because I have some delectable portions to share with you."

His neighbor replied from the other side of the wall, "And how, might I ask, would you come to be in possession of said delectable portions?"

Arunthal pressed his face closer to the bars and turned his head towards his prison mate, "I have had an audience with King Ulfur. Look what I have for you!" He wrapped the food in a cloth and slid his arm through the bars towards the adjoining door.

Therak took the bundle, unwrapped it, and exclaimed, "You speak the truth! How did this come about?"

Arunthal withdrew his arm and replied, "I haven't a notion? Earlier you heard the sentinel come to fetch me?"

Therak answered, "Yes. I feared the worst."

Arunthal continued, "I was escorted through the meeting hall to the King's chamber, then shackled to his table."

Therak asked, "For his amusement?"

Arunthal replied, "I was greatly puzzled, as the King spoke not a word when I first entered. He just sat at the table with me. He then began asking questions about my sword-it was hanging on his chamber wall."

Therak asked, "Why would Ulfur be so inquisitive about your sword?"

"I am still bewildered," Arunthal answered, "yet the discussion turned towards the faith of my people. Therak, I gave the words of Theoas to Ulfur."

There was complete silence, then Therak asked, "And how did he respond?"

Arunthal shifted his position on the bars. "I believe his heart has now turned."

Therak pressed closer against the bars. "This seems impossible. Are you certain of this?"

Excitedly, Arunthal answered, "I saw his demeanor change towards me and he ordered a wash basin and a meal be brought to me."

Therak commented, "That does not sound like the Ulfur that I know. However, if a heart such as mine can be turned, then why not Ulfur's? For we are much the same, more than I would care to confess."

"I am weary my friend," said Arunthal, "What say we finish our meals and rest? We can talk about these things tomorrow." Therak agreed, and soon both were settled on their sleeping pads.

# CHAPTER 13

## ESCAPE

Therak, last King of The Grhytans, had been discovered, with a handful of his soldiers, on one of the outlying Varrun islands. His soldiers were slain and he was taken captive. Two Varrun kings had passed during his incarceration, with Ulfur being the third to watch over him. He had languished in his dank prison cell for all those seasons, growing in bitterness and anger all the while.

Change came for Therak in a way he could not have anticipated. A new prisoner was placed in the cell next to his, a devout Yondut who had been fighting with the armies Therak once commanded. The two became friends as the season passed, sharing stories of family, friends, and country. Therak conveyed the story of the First Armada and its demise. With great detail, he described the dark tempest that came upon them in the Sea of Chime, like tentacles emerging from the Varrun homeland. He went on to tell how he and a few of his boatmates had survived the disaster, drifting to the bank of an island and living in concealed dwellings until their discovery and subsequent capture by the Varruns.

Arunthal explained how he had been recruited by the Fort Chief, Tunska, and how he had left his family in Yondusland to oversee the metal crafter's apprentice school constructed in Osrall. He went on to tell how he had been called to enlist as a soldier in the Grhytan army as a Weaponry Chief, and then by circumstance, became part of the Battle of The Plain. He told of his capture by the Varruns, and how he missed his wife, Ceshona, and his son, Jeddok. Arunthal also told Therak of his faith, and the displaced Grhytan King would eventually grow to understand and accept it as his own. Together, they waited, but for what they did not know.

A clamor was heard at the end of the dimly lit passageway; it echoed past the cells of the prisoners. There was the clanking of metal upon metal and then silence. Footsteps could be heard as they shuffled towards the prisoners. Therak and Arunthal strained against the bars in an attempt to see who approached. A figure emerged from the shadows, draped in the animal skin robe of a sage. However, instead of parchments, the figure held a blood stained sword. The two prisoners quickly stepped back far into their cells, not knowing what might befall them. The figure approached Arunthal's door and its free hand reached up and removed the hood of the robe.

"Ulfur?" exclaimed Arunthal. "What are you doing here? What have you done?"

He responded, "What I have done is come to make right what is wrong. My soul has been restless within me since we spoke in my chamber. Sleep would not visit and my conscience demanded I come to you. In doing so I have relinquished what little remaining power I had among the Varruns. Therefore we must make our escape together."

Therak hollered from his cell, "Have your senses left you? Only a fool would take such actions as this!"

Ulfur stepped in front of Therak's bars. "You are right Grhytan: I am a fool. However, the plan has been put into motion and it cannot be halted."

Therak responded, "Is this what Theoas has asked of you?"

Ulfur's eyes grew wide and he glanced towards Arunthal, who was still pressed against his bars. "How does he know of this?"

Arunthal replied, "Therak has known Theoas for many phases now, and he knows of the words we spoke in your chamber."

Ulfur turned back to Therak. "Can a Varrun and a Grhytan mingle without the shedding of blood?"

Therak was quiet for a moment, "This I know-my heart is not as it was. And because of this I say 'yes' to you."

Ulfur looked intently at Therak. "Then we shall test this faith. You will join our escape."

Therak replied, "Yes, we shall test it."

Ulfur reached under the robe to retrieve a set of keys. He unlocked the cell doors and explained his plan for escape. "We must make our way to the stables. The steeds will give us transport to the coast. There I have a fleet of fishing vessels; we will take possession of one and make our way to the island of the Frellsari Sages. They will grant us sanctuary and give us time to define our next actions. We must move without delay."

With Ulfur in the lead, they made their way down the dank passageway. Ulfur knew the tunnels of his prison well. Navigating the maze, he led them to a metal grate in the floor. Ulfur reached down and attempted to lift it up, "Therak, will you help?" he asked.

Together they were able to remove the grate from its setting in the stone. Ulfur pointed down into the hole. "This will be extremely unpleasant, but the sewer under our feet is the most expedient way to escape."

Ulfur slid himself inside, followed by Arunthal and then Therak. It was unpleasant indeed, but their efforts were undeterred. It was exceptionally difficult for Therak because of his large, burly frame. It seemed to them a dreadfully long time before they came upon the barred exit. The passage had widened enough for Therak to squeeze by his companions and he knocked out the barrier with a forceful kick.

They emerged a good distance down from the outer prison wall. They continued down the slope towards a creek at the bottom of the ravine. Ulfur lost his footing half way down and tumbled the rest of the way. Therak dashed down quickly and lifted him up out of the water. Ulfur had received no life-threatening injuries. Thanking Therak, he continued following the creek downstream, and then climbed up on the bank after a short distance.

"We are near the outer stables. Stay close behind me," instructed Ulfur.

Passing through the trees, they could see lanterns glowing about the stable building. Some were stationary, but others were being carried by the stable sentinels. Ulfur had an impressive herd of steeds he had bred over the years and many in Varrunas had tried to acquire them without the King's permission. Ulfur spoke, "Stay here and I will send the sentinels off on some erroneous errand."

He moved out of the trees and up to a path along the stable fence. Arunthal and Therak could see Ulfur conversing with the sentinels. They appeared confused with the situation, but soon started trotting down the path away from the stables. Waiting until the sentinels were out of sight, Ulfur waved in his companions. Once inside, Ulfur quickly opened three of the stalls. "These are the best of my stock. Therak, the large stallion is yours. Take these bridles and prepare your steeds. We must move without hesitation. The sentinels will be back shortly."

In short order they mounted their animals and sped into the forest. Ulfur increased their pace and seemingly navigated from memory through the forest. The trees opened up to farm land and they began a gallop. They traveled at a full pace for many lenads before the moonlit ripples of the sea came into view.

Ulfur continued to the coast, veering down towards the piers. There were several fishing vessels tied up there but not a soul could be seen. They led their animals underneath the pier closest to them and made their way to the wooden walkway.

Ulfur turned to Therak, "Mind your steps here. We do not want to rouse anyone awake." Stepping across the planks as quietly as possible, they came to a likely looking vessel and boarded. Ulfur untied the rope then turned to the Grhytan. "Therak, give us a hearty shove off, will you?"

Therak leaned over the edge of the vessel, laying his hand on one the posts, and with a tremendous push they glided out into the water. Ulfur instructed, "Take hold of an oar and gently stroke the water. No splashing." The three made their way out of the small harbor and headed across the channel. Ulfur pointed upwards to a prominent constellation, "That ascending trail of stars will guide us to the cloister landing. The sages will be beyond themselves when they see me show up on their doorstep."

The sun was just peaking over the edge of the sea when they grounded upon the beach.

# Chapter 14

# A King Returns Home

A lone sage on his morning walk beheld an odd sight. There on the beach ahead of him, three figures stepped out of a small fishing vessel. Moving closer, he determined they were not harvesters of the sea. He recognized a Varrun, a Grhytan, and what appeared to be a Yondut. He stopped his pace, staring at the ragged looking group. Fearful to approach, but extremely curious, he yelled out, "Visitors! Who might you be?"

Ulfur hollered a response, "It is your King and his companions!"

The sage's eyes grew wide, for he did not believe what he heard. He asked, "And why would my King come to this island? There is nothing here for royalty."

Ulfur approached and the sage scurried away from him. "Stop!" yelled Ulfur, "There is nothing to bring you concern."

The sage stopped and faced Ulfur. "Why are you here? Are you really King Ulfur?"

Ulfur replied, "Look at me. Do you not recognize the King of the Varruns?"

The sage studiously looked him up and down, then glanced towards Therak and Arunthal, "Yes, I recognize you. Yet why do you come with these strange companions?"

Ulfur took a few more steps closer. "Your King is no longer King. I now hold no more power in the land than do you. The two who are with me and I have escaped from the prison on the homeland and we seek sanctuary among your brotherhood."

The sage, still incredulous at what was happening, replied, "What are these things you speak of? You are no longer King? Why were you in prison?"

Ulfur waved his hands at the sage, "Please, we will answer all the questions that you have. Will you grant us what we ask?"

The sage nodded. "Yes, follow me."

He began walking the direction he had come from then turned back inland. The boatmates followed closely. Not far from the beach, the sage led them to a complex of nondescript buildings. They approached the doors of the gate and the sage gently knocked. As the gate opened, they could see a beautiful courtyard with many trees. A few curious sages milled about, but it was very quiet.

The sage brought them to a small room on the far side of the courtyard. "Wait here. You must meet with the brothers who lead."

The sage exited. Ulfur and Arunthal sat on the edge of the bed but Therak sat on the floor, leaning against the wall. Ulfur commented, "I have much to explain to the brothers."

Arunthal nodded in agreement. Therak piped up, "And I have even more. They now have a Grhytan among them. I would say that constitutes a historical event for the sages."

Ulfur chuckled and footsteps were heard approaching. The sage entered followed by four of his brothers. "We must know your purpose here before we grant the sanctuary that you ask. My name is Tethio and I will be your liaison." The brothers pushed aside the table and sat on the floor as a group. Tethio continued, "We are ready."

Ulfur spoke, "Be comfortable, for we have much to say."

Ulfur began his story, starting with the alliance he had made with the Darkrruns, pausing occasionally to answer the brother's questions. Arunthal and Therak also shared their stories and the meeting extended well past mid-day. The sages were exhausted, for this was much to absorb in one sitting.

Tethio stood. "I believe I speak for us all when I say you are welcome here." His fellow sages heartily agreed. He continued, "Brothers, we must tend to our guests. Let us fetch them a meal, and point them to the water basins. I do believe they are in dire need of a good washing." Pointing at Therak, he commented, "We must also put them in the bunk room; that is the only space large enough to hold this Grhytan."

The three were led to their reassigned quarters where they washed themselves and their garments and a meal was brought to them. With their bellies satisfied and the trials of the previous day upon them, each one drew close to his sleeping pad.

The next morning they arose and joined the brothers in the gathering hall. After the morning meal, Tethio called a meeting to order. He stood up on a bench and announced, "My brothers, as you have already seen, we have guests among us. One you may recognize, for he was formerly known to you as King Ulfur. However, he has requested that we do not address him as King. I have asked Ulfur to speak to us in regard to what has transpired on the homeland. Ulfur, their attention is now yours."

Ulfur stepped up on the bench and relayed the events of recent phases which led to him being on the island. He finished, seated himself at the table, and then the questions began. There was much discussion among all in attendance.

Tethio then spoke. "Ulfur, what do you know of Stolt and the dark entity? The arms of Ehkkahn continue to move about the surface, but most recently they have been seen stretching toward the direction of the rising sun-towards Grhytnod."

Ulfur responded, "The Ehkkahn no longer increases in strength as it did prior. The Darkrrun transformations have all but ceased. Those Varruns willing to submit have already done so, and there are no more fields for its harvest."

Therak interjected, "There is no need to fear for Grhytnod; the entity's power cannot reach across the Sea of Chime."

Tethio looked at Therak with puzzlement. "And have you not heard of the Pier?"

Therak responded, "What is this 'pier' you speak of?"

Tethio explained the construction which had taken place while Therak was in prison. "You have been trapped on the Varrun homeland for the rule of three kings. It brings no surprise you have not heard of these things."

Therak turned to Arunthal, "Why did you not tell me of this?"

Arunthal responded, "Forgive me, but I have never set a foot upon the pier that they speak of. While working at the school in Osrall, I knew of it, but there were many other tasks that were required of me and I gave it no thought. My mind did not turn to it in our conversations."

Therak asked Tethio, "And you say my people took this upon themselves to search for their King?"

Tethio replied, "Yes, as we have come to understand, the inhabitants of Grhytnod faced a dilemma. It was your last order that directed the citizenry not to venture beyond sight of the Grhytnod coast. They desired to honor their King's command; yet there were some who desired to search for possible Armada survivors among the outer islands. In the Grhytan's reckoning, The Pier offered opportunity to afford both. It could well be said that your final edict was the impetus for The Pier. There were other survivors, were there not? Was not the final edict transported to your land with a handful of Grhytans in a small dory vessel?"

Therak's mind went back to that time. "Yes. It was the only remaining vessel left of the Armada, just large enough to carry four. We had been on the island for a phase when we discovered the dory grounded on the beach. It had drifted in with the wreckage, as did we." Therak continued, "The Pier-such an immense undertaking. And it was all done for me?" He grew quiet, searching his thoughts.

Arunthal spoke up, "What does the Pier have to do with the Ehkkahn?"

Tethio explained, "The Pier has grown close to the outer islands. The Grhytan's have built a Second Armada and its ships are docked along the length of the pier. It appears they are preparing for an assault on the homeland. I surmise both the Varruns and Darkrruns see this as an opportunity to engage the enemies within their own dominion."

Ulfur commented, "You have surmised correctly. The Pier was to be the primary target of the first assault. However, it was the Darkrruns who proposed the elimination of all life on the Pier. The inhabitants of the Pier were to be brought to extinction. This did not abide with our engagement rules and I fervently resisted the idea."

Arunthal asked, "How does any of this relate to the Ehkkahn? I don't understand."

Tethio replied, "The Grhytans continue to build; their pace has increased. Some of our brothers have traveled across the waters and have seen this with their own eyes. Do you not understand? The Pier will soon be within the grasp of the Ehkkahn. And no doubt it will find submissive souls among the Grhytans. Its power will increase and there will be nothing to stop it from moving to the interior of the continent. Again I say: the strength of the dark entity is sure to increase, and who will be able to defeat it? Can anyone here offer an answer? Can the Ehkkahn be defeated? Ulfur, you have experienced what the Ehkkahn has done to our homeland. The same fate will befall all other countries the entity comes upon."

Therak had remained silent during most of the morning's discussion. Suddenly he slammed his fist on the table with great force, jarring its timbers and knocking utensils to the floor. He stood. "The inhabitants of my land have shown their loyalty and I will not allow such a thing to befall them. I will return to my home, muster the armies, and lead them against the enemies who threaten my people. This WILL be done. I must leave your island."

All in the room were stunned to silence. It was not wise to speak against an angry Grhytan.

Finally, Ulfur spoke. "If you allow, I will join your fight, for your enemies have now become mine."

Arunthal quickly followed, "I, too, will fight, as I was doing before my capture."

Therak bellowed out, "It is done!"

The three visitors gathered their belongings and loaded them into their fishing vessel. They boarded and slipped the vessel into the water. That very moment, far distant across the Sea of Chime, at the outer boundary of Grhytnod, Jeddok prepared to lead his party through the arch.

# CHAPTER 15

## TO OSRALL

Jeddok rolled up the map and placed it back inside his jacket. They nudged their animals forward, passing under the arch.

Poodwah asked, "What do we do when we see a Grhytan?"

Jeddok answered, "We show no sign of fear."

Poodwah nodded, "Yes, that is a simple statement for you to make. I believe I will move to the back." Poodwah turned around his oolog and moved behind Lohjji.

"What if they come from behind?" asked Lohjji.

Poodwah, obviously irritated, replied, "You would have to open your mouth, wouldn't you?" However, he kept his position and they continued down the path.

About mid-day, they heard a pounding on the soil. It was coming from up ahead. They slowed their pace but kept moving. Soon they saw a troop of Grhytans marching towards them. Poodwah yelled from behind, "What do we do?"

Jeddok hollered back, "Keep moving, and remain silent."

As the distance between the two groups narrowed, a Grhytan stepped out into the middle of the wide trail and held up his hand. He bellowed out a command and the troops behind him ceased their marching. However, he continued forward. Jeddok halted his animal and held his position. Those behind followed his example.

The Grhytan continued toward Jeddok, stepping right up to his oolog, and paced around it. He said not a word and seemed to be analyzing every hair and fiber of both Jeddok and the oolog. He looked up, pointed at the sword in Jeddok's back scabbard, and said, "Yondut!" The party was startled and anxiety was building. The Grhytan stepped in front of Jeddok's oolog, reached behind his back, and quickly withdrew his sword. Jeddok reached back and withdrew his, Lohjji did the same. Poodwah and Leshti were frozen with fear. The Grhytan held up his hand and in a commanding tone, said, "Cease!" Jeddok and Lohjji paused as the Grhytan moved the sword into a vertical position in front of his chest. He lifted his free hand, pointed at the hilt, and repeated, "Yondut!" It took Jeddok a moment for the reality of what he saw to take hold. However, there it was, as clear as the mid-day sun: the metal crafter's mark of his pap.

Jeddok yelled back to his friends, "It's my pap's marking. He is here!"

Lohjji and Poodwah cheered as they shared their friend's good fortune. Jeddok held up his sword in the same manner as the Grhytan and clearly spoke the word, "Arunthal!"

The Grhytan grinned widely, "Yes! Arunthal!"

Jeddok once again yelled to his friends, "They know who he is!" Speaking to the Grhytan, he asked, "Where is Arunthal? How do I find him?"

The Grhytan, obviously not understanding Jeddok's words, pointed at his chest and said, "Scout Chief Kelta."

The Grhytan's command of the Yondus language was crude, but Jeddok knew what was being communicated. He pointed at himself and said, "Jeddok." Turning around, he pointed at each of his companions, speaking out their names. Before anything else could be said, a white haired Grhytan approached in a noisy cart pulled by a single oolog.

Coming closer, the White Hair announced, "Welcome to Grhytnod. I am Makkros, healer among the forts, and interpreter on occasion. What venture brings you so far from Yondusland?"

Jeddok replied, "My companions and I have come seeking my pap, Arunthal."

Makkros replied with surprise, "Do you tell me that Arunthal, the metal crafter, is your father?"

Jeddok answered, "Yes. That is so."

Makkros turned to Kelta, explaining this discovery. Kelta looked at Jeddok, stood erect, and spoke, "Good weapons! Good fighter!"

Makkros explained to Jeddok that his father was held in high regard by the Grhytan armies. He gave detail of the metal crafter's apprentice school in

Osrall, Arunthal's service with the army, and his capture by the Varruns at the Battle of The Plain.

Jeddok felt his heart drop into his bowels. "My pap is dead?"

Makkros shook his head. "No. No. Listen to me. The Varruns are vicious in battle, but hold to their own code of war; they do not slay those who hold position. Your father held the rank of Weaponry Chief, and he was taken to the prison on Varrunas."

Jeddok felt some relief and asked, "These Varruns- are they the ones called the 'dark riders'?"

Makkros responded, "Yes and no. It would take much time to explain. Let me just say they are of the same blood, but a different breed." Makkros glanced back towards Leshti, sitting with Lohjji on top of his oolog. She was holding her splinted arm tightly next to her chest. "What ails the girl's arm?" He asked.

Jeddok replied, "It was crushed under a stone in the Canyon of the Nagaluu."

Makkros nodded and approached Lohjji's oolog. Leshti pulled back, leaning in closer to Lohjji. Makkros looked at her and said, "I am a healer." Leshti did not respond, leaning farther away from him. Makkros looked up at Lohjji, "Does she not hear?"

Lohjji replied, "She knows only a few words of the language."

"Tell her I am a healer. Will you?" asked Makkros. Lohjji spoke softly into Leshti's ear and she grew more at ease. Makkros pointed to her arm and Leshti moved it out slightly towards him. Makkros instructed, "Get her off that animal and bring her over to my cart. I can help with her arm."

Lohjji assisted Leshti off the oolog and followed Makkros to his cart. He pulled back the cover to expose multiple compartments, each one containing either a cask or leather pouch. The outside of the cart was covered with gourds, dangling from fiber cords. Makkros reached in and pulled out one of the pouches, untied a gourd, and pulled the plug. He handed Lohjji the items. "Here, have her chew some of these herbs and then drink the contents of the gourd to wash it down. All of it."

Lohjji explained the instructions to Leshti and she proceeded to chew the herbs. It was evident by the pucker of her cheeks that the taste was very unpleasant. She lifted the gourd, and drained its contents, expressing herself with a heartfelt, 'Yuck!'

Makkros spoke, "Take the cart cover and spread it out on the ground, then ask her to lay down on it." Lohjji did as he was asked and helped Leshti to the ground. Makkros shouted and waved to Kelta and pointed at Leshti's feet. Kelta knelt down and tightly grabbed her ankles. Makkros instructed Lohjji to hold down each of her shoulders firmly, and then removed the splint from her arm. It was evident that he was accustomed to working on soldiers, as he was not the least bit gentle with her. With the splint off, he encircled her arm with his large hands, both above and below the break. Without warning, he gave her lower arm a sharp yank, and she cried out in pain.

Lohjji yelled, "Stop! What are you doing?"

Makkros looked up, "Nothing now; it is finished. Her arm will heal as it should. Put the splint back on and I will give you two or three more gourds to take with you. Tears flowed from Leshti's eyes as Lohjji helped her up. He said nothing, giving Makkros a look of contempt. The old healer simply said, "Your gratefulness is not necessary, Yondut."

Jeddok approached Makkros, "That's it? Her arm will be whole again?" Makkros nodded as he picked up the cart cover and began strapping it back on. Jeddok continued. "I must seek help to rescue Pap from the Varruns. To whom do I turn? Who would be willing to take on such a task?"

Makkros replied, "You father has many friends in Osrall-especially among the fighting forces stationed there."

Jeddok asked, "Very well. How do I find this city?"

Makkros looked at him. "I would be willing to lead you. I have been out among these soldiers for much too long and I yearn to visit the city, any city."

Jeddok responded excitedly, "I can't thank you enough! May Theoas bring you blessing."

Makkros smiled. "You Yonduts are always throwing that name around. Your gratefulness is appreciated. And I do hope this Theoas of yours does bring me blessing."

Makkros and Kelta drew away from the rest of the group and had a short council together. Returning, Makkros grabbed the bridle of his oolog, turning away from the Grhytan troops. He started down the path and hollered back, "Yonduts! If you are going to Osrall, you must follow me."

Jeddok and his friends scurried to mount their oologs and caught up with Makkros. The White Hair moved at a hearty pace and seemed never to tire as he moved along the trail for the remainder of the day. The landscape changed from mountains to hills but they remained in a forest of cone trees. When the sun began to descend, Makkros finally stopped, pointing at a small spring against the hillside. "We will spend the night here."

Lohjji and his friends dismounted. Poodwah began to go through the pouch bags, only to realize all that was left was a few strips of dried bonabeast and a handful of grain kernels. He called to Jeddok, "Come over here. We have a bit of an emergency."

Jeddok stepped closer. "What is it? What is the problem?"

Poodwah replied, "We haven't anything left to eat."

Jeddok was quiet for a moment. "Yes, that is an emergency, especially for Lohjji."

Jeddok walked over to Makkros and drew him aside. Then Makkros could be heard laughing and exclaimed, "I travel with an army. Of course I carry portions for your bellies." He grabbed the cart cover and pulled it back, dug through the compartments and began pulling out an assortment of grains, roots and dried meats. He loudly spoke, "Eat well, Yonduts! And do not forget to prepare me a bowl."

Poodwah ran toward the pouches, snatching them up off the ground. "I am at your service! Lohjji, do help with the gathering of wood."

Poodwah and Lohjji went about their business. Leshti took a swig from one of the gourds and then reclined on her sleeping pad. Jeddok sat down with Makkros on a fallen timber and began to ask questions. Much was discussed and Jeddok learned of the people called Grhytans. He was astonished to discover how old Makkros was and was even more so when he learned that was not out of the ordinary for a Grhytan.

Poodwah finished preparing the meal. He had done well with what he had been given and all in the group were satisfied. Makkros yawned, "This White Hair must visit his sleeping pad. We will arise early in the morning. You would do well do pull your pads close also." All slept deeply as the fire burned down to embers.

In the dark of the next morn, the party wasted no time continuing their trek. The days of travel had stretched into a full phase and half again when they began to move along the edge of a high bluff overlooking an undulating plain. Makkros commented, "One more day and we should be able to see Nernod. We will not venture there, but our capital is a sight to behold." Around mid-morning of the next day Makkros halted his cart, pointing towards the edge of the bluff at an opening through the trees. He spoke, "Jeddok, take your friends through there and follow the edge of the bluff."

Jeddok nodded and did as Makkros directed. Jeddok and his companions had journeyed over many lenads to see the city of Nernod. Here upon a massive outcropping of stone they gazed at the grand view before them. Makkros came up the path to join them. "Impressive, isn't it?"

Lohjji commented, "Never have I seen such a sight as this."

After a few moments Jeddok spoke, "I do not desire to spoil our moments here, but we must continue. Osrall awaits."

Makkros nodded, "Yes. We still have many lenads to travel. As many as we have already come."

The group made their way back to the path and settled into the pace with which they had grown accustomed.

In just under two phases they came to the outskirts of Osrall. Makkros led his Yondut companions to view the expansive apprentice school where Jeddok's father had instructed. Continuing, they found a stable keeper with empty stalls and left the animals with him. Walking through the streets for half a lenad, they entered the city proper. Makkros veered down a side path and stopped in front of a comfortable looking dwelling nestled against a slope. Makkros spoke, "Did I ever mention that Osrall is my ancestral city?"

Jeddok replied, "No, not once."

Makkros pointed at the dwelling. "This is my home and it has been many phases since I have been here."

Hardly had the words left his mouth when a figure burst through the door of his dwelling. It was a female Grhytan. Other than bosoms and long hair, they did not appear any different from the males. They were just as large, and carried the same muscle mass on their frame. The lady Grhytan approached Makkros, speaking loudly and shaking her fist. It was quickly determined by the onlookers that she was not happy with the healer. An argument commenced in their native tongue, with the female ending it when she forcefully stomped down on Makkros foot. He yelled out in pain, turned to face his travel companions, and hobbled towards them. He spoke, "I would like to introduce you to my dear wife, Ershrun. However, it seems she has already gone back inside. I will get you three settled into the outbuilding. That will allow her time to quench the fire."

Poodwah asked, "What was all that about?"

Makkros responded, "She does not like it if I do not write while I am away."

Jeddok and his friends made themselves comfortable in Makkros' outbuilding. It afforded a place to sleep and wash. There was a fire pit with implements for cooking just outside the door. Poodwah was delighted. Makkros eventually went back inside and all was quiet the rest of the night. The foursome was happy this part of the journey had ended, yet all wondered what was yet to come.

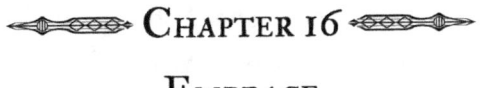

# CHAPTER 16

## EMBRACE

The sounds of banging metal were heard approaching the outbuilding. The noise quickly roused all those inside. Jeddok hopped from his sleeping pad and ran to the door. He swung it open and there stood Ershrun, holding two cooking pans. "My dears! Why do you still slumber?" She exclaimed with volume which proved very disturbing so early in the morning. She continued, "My husband has yet again brought home strays for me to tend. Come my little strays, the morning meal is ready!"

Poodwah had already gathered himself and was heading towards the door. Leshti, with her one good arm, was attempting to help an incoherent Lohjji rise from his sleeping pad. Jeddok just shook his head and walked about searching for his boots. With Lohjji finally on his feet and somewhat stable, they walked toward the back door of Makkros' dwelling. Ershrun had it standing open and waved them inside. "Please sit down anywhere. Make yourselves comfortable."

Poodwah had already staked out one end of the table for himself. He stood on top of the chair, leaning across the table attempting to retrieve a morsel from the serving dish. Ershrun spied his action from the corner of her eye and gave him a quick slap on the back of his hand. She commented, "You will wait until your friends are settled."

Poodwah gave her a sheepish grin and slid back down on the chair. Makkros was at the other end of the table, intently reading a long parchment, oblivious to everything going on around him. With everyone finally seated, Ershrun spoke up. "You may now proceed." There were none bashful and they filled their bellies with much abandon.

Everyone satisfied; Makkros pushed his bowl and utensils to the side and laid out the parchment he had been reading. "I have been away so long-there is much news to become acquainted with."

Ershrun glanced his way. "The most interesting news is not in that parchment of yours."

Makkros asked, "What do you mean by that? I don't want to hear any of your gossip."

Ershrun gave him a look of annoyance and continued, "I am not speaking of that. If you want to hear what I have to say, you will treat me kindly."

Makkros nodded. "Yes, my love. Please forgive my rudeness. You were saying?"

Ershrun seated herself close to her husband. "This sounds beyond belief, but just yesterday, it was heard that King Therak has returned and he is in Osrall!"

Makkros jaw dropped open. "Incredible! Are you certain? It would be remarkable if it were true."

Jeddok interjected, "Are you speaking of the King who led the Armada?"

Makkros and Ershrun looked at Jeddok and Makkros exclaimed, "How would a young Yondut know of that?"

Jeddok replied, "Lohjji's grandpap wrote down the story. Part of it anyway. I have it tucked away in my jacket if you would like to see it. Assuming you can read Yondus?"

Makkros responded, "Yes. I am an educated Grhytan and I can read both Yondus and Luurin. Please bring it in."

Jeddok trotted to the outbuilding and brought back the parchment. Makkros unfurled the roll and began to read, while Jeddok and his friends assisted Ershrun in cleaning up the meal. Makkros finished. "The map is different. Not made by the same hand?"

Jeddok replied, "Yes, that was drawn by my pap. The story and the map were unknown to any citizen of the village until Lohjji discovered it."

Makkros commented, "It seems they were hidden away purposely? Well, if we are to find adventurers to help you search for your father, we should make our way to the square. That is the best place to recruit."

Ershrun spoke up, "As I understand it, the square will be filled by mid-day. It has been said our returning King has called an assembly, including the provincial councilors."

Makkros replied, "That assembly is something we must be part of. Jeddok, I do hope you and your friends will come along."

Jeddok replied, "If I may find assistance for my quest, we will most assuredly accompany you."

Makkros nodded, "Very well, let us finish what tasks we have to get ready."

Jeddok groomed and watered the oologs, Poodwah cleaned out the pouch bags, and Lohjji helped Makkros mend a damaged axle on his cart. Leshti went with Ershrun to the market. They were an oddly matched pair but seemed to enjoy each other's company.

As mid-day approached, the trio and Makkros had finished their tasks and prepared to leave for the square. Ershrun and Leshti had not returned so they proceeded without them. They approached the city center, but even before reaching the square, the streets grew crowded. Much murmuring was heard among those who gathered. Makkros leaned towards Jeddok, "The inhabitants believe this assembly is just some gossip gone awry. I agree, but still, we must see if King Therak appears."

The four squeezed their way through the bodies, attempting to get close to the elevated speaker platform at the center of the square. Then the crowd grew quiet; something was happening but they were still too far away from the platform to see anything. They pushed through even harder with Makkros making a path for the Yonduts. Most Grhytan's would step aside for a White Hair. Suddenly, Makkros stopped in his tracks. His eyes grew wide, and he pointed towards the platform, "It is true! Unbelievable!" He pushed through a few more paces to the edge of the platform and yelled, "King Therak! King Therak! It is I, Makkros!"

The distinguished looking Grhytan on the platform moved closer. He smiled at Makkros. "You crusty dotard-join me. Come up."

Makkros turned and motioned for the Yonduts to remain in their places. King Therak took position front and center with Makkros standing some paces behind with a small group of dignitaries.

Therak raised high both of his arms, commanding the full attention of the crowd. He spoke in a resounding tone. "My heart is elevated beyond words to be back among my people. For too many seasons I have been away. It has become evident to me that the Council of Nernod has shown great wisdom and care in leading Grhytnod during my imprisonment on Varrunas. There are many of you, especially the White Hairs, who know the tragedy of the Armada so many seasons ago. By circumstance, I have survived and now I have assembled you here to issue my final orders as King of Grhytnod."

There were many gasps and other comments from the crowd as they shifted restlessly. Therak continued. "Hear me out, fellow Grhytans! There is a threat just beyond our borders like none we have ever faced. You know of the Varruns with whom we have warred for ages. You know of the Darkrruns, the evil dark riders, who have made many incursions inland. However, there are only a handful of Grhytans who know the origin of the Darkrruns. I am one of them. The force responsible for the Darkrruns and the destruction of the Armada is a dark entity from the bowels of Varrunas. It moves its limbs about the surface world as if it is alive, but it is not. It is composed of the spirits of the dead. I have heard tales in our land about a dark being many have called The Not. However, I assure you, this is no tale. It is real and it seeks out Grhytnod!"

The crowd grew rowdy and many yelled out in Grhytan fashion, "Destroy the beast! Crush the monster! Attack and conquer!"

Therak once again motioned for the crowd's silence and continued. "Yes, my kindred warriors, this is what we will do. As my last act of King, I appoint myself Chief General of the Armies and I will lead Grhytnod against The Not."

The crowd grew exuberant, shouting praises of Therak. He responded with a booming voice, "Do not give me praise. I have not told you how I came to be here. I have not told you of my escape from the prison. You must trust my words now. Yes, the Varruns are our enemies from ages past. Yet my freedom was gained through the sacrifice of a Varrun who came to me within the walls of the prison. The King called Ulfur is the one who made my escape possible. In doing so, he has relinquished the throne of Varrunas."

There were shouts from the crowd mocking the Varruns, but Therak put a quick end to them. "My words are true and I owe my freedom to Ulfur. He has requested to join our armies and fight the dark forces which come against us. There is much turmoil on Varrunas and now is the opportune time for attack. Ulfur knows the land and the people and I have made him my second in command."

There was great agitation and yelling from the crowd. Therak, in a booming voice which shook the stones of the square, commanded, "You will show my companion in arms respect. Do you understand? All those who oppose will step forward!" The crowd grew silent and Therak motioned back to the small group behind him. A figure draped in an animal skin robe stepped forward and Therak removed the hood. There were a few hostile looks, but most were shocked. Therak continued, "Grhytans, this is Ulfur. He will be respected and obeyed as you would obey me. I give you my words of truth; Ulfur and I are not as we were. Our hearts no longer war with each other and we will fight as brothers. This is all I have to say to you now. I must meet with the provincial councilors."

The crowd dispersed and the small band of dignitaries followed Therak off the platform. Jeddok motioned for his friends to follow but was caught off guard as he turned back around. His mind could not fully comprehend what his eyes beheld. He yelled, "Pap! Pap!"

Arunthal's eyes were directed towards the voice. He pushed aside one of the Grhytan councilors standing next to him and ran across the platform. Jeddok darted up the steps, tripping as he went, and landed on the stone. Arunthal knelt, scooped up his son, and wrapped him in a full embrace. Tears flowed freely as they held tightly to each other. Arunthal gathered himself. "Jeddok! My eyes do not deceive me. It is you!"

Jeddok replied with much emotion in his voice, "Yes, my Pap, it is I."

Arunthal leaned back a bit and focused his eyes on Jeddok, "How have you come to be here? I do not understand? And your mum? Is she with you?"

Jeddok up righted himself on the stone. "No, she is still in Yondusland with Seeanna. And they are well." He continued, "Pap, we were told you were a prisoner on Varrunas. How are you here?"

Arunthal assisted Jeddok to his feet. "I escaped with Therak. We were imprisoned together. However, you still haven't told me what you are doing so far from home."

Jeddok wiped his nose. "We have come in search of you, all the way from Yondusland."

Arunthal looked at Jeddok with puzzlement. "Who is 'we'?"

Jeddok pointed down the steps towards Lohjji and Poodwah, who were grinning ear to ear. Arunthal laughed, holding his arms open wide, "Come to me, boys! Theoas be praised!"

Therak and the dignitaries took notice of the commotion on the platform. Makkros made his way back up the steps and asked, "Jeddok, who is this Yondut?"

Jeddok reached an arm around his pap and proudly announced, "Makkros, I would like you to meet Arunthal."

Makkros eyes gleamed as he held out his hand, "It is with great honor, sir."

Jeddok continued, "Pap, meet Makkros, our friend who led us all the way from the outer boundary to Osrall."

Arunthal looked Makkros in the eyes. "The honor is mine, White Hair. Thank you for what you have done for my son and his friends."

By this time, Therak had approached the group. Introductions were made all around, and he invited the Yonduts to join him as he met with the councilors. The group walked down one of the side streets to a civic building. There were several long tables inside and everyone found a seat. Therak stepped to the front of the room and began: "Councilors and friends, our armies must be mustered to Osrall and new recruits enlisted. I charge all the provincial leaders here to prepare your pellstas for flight to your regional forts bearing this message. In two phases, we begin boarding the ships of the Second Armada. Ulfur will guide our forces to the shores of Varrunas. The forces under my command will make landfall on a strategically remote beach located near the entrance of a narrow watershed canyon. Ulfur's forces will come by way of Reitrius and the Balchdur Gorge. Both armies will then make intrusion inland to the fortress complex of Ilkraador. The strategy comprises a simultaneous attack from the two gorges, which lay opposite one another across the valley. The movements of our two armies must be in precise unity for the plan to work. Now, unless there are questions, go about your tasks immediately."

The councilors nodded in agreement or from fear of debate with Therak. As the room emptied, Therak sat down at the table with the Yonduts and Makkros. "Arunthal, you have already fought with us, and I expect you are willing this time. I would not ask this of the young Yonduts."

Jeddok replied, "With respect, I say to you we have fought our way here over many phases and many lenads. It is my wish to fight by my pap's side. My friends must make the decision of their own will."

Poodwah spoke. "If I have understood everything I have heard thus far, it is reasonable to surmise that in due time, the enemies of Grhytnod will become the enemies of Yondusland. I do not wish war to come upon our families and loved ones. It seems the honorable action is to fight with the Grhytans."

Therak turned to Poodwah. "You are a perceptive one. Small of stature, strong of heart."

Lohjji commented, "I don't think Poodwah should join us. Look at him."

Poodwah, in an unusually stern tone, replied, "I can use an awnaxe. And have you forgotten I know how to use a skrugin? We still have several between your pouch bag and mine."

Jeddok interjected, "He does have a good point about the skrugins."

Arunthal asked, "What is this 'skrugin' you speak of?"

Jeddok answered, "Pap, it is something we will just have to show you when the time comes. Please trust me on this."

Arunthal replied, "Very well. Lohjji, do you have a decision for us?"

Lohjji looked around the table. "You know me better than that. I will fight to protect all Yondusland, and Leshti."

Arunthal looked at Lohjji. "Who is Leshti?"

Jeddok put his hand on Arunthal's shoulder. "She is Lohjji's Untra maiden. They are quite the pair. You will get a chance to see them together this eve."

Arunthal grinned. "Where is she now?"

Makkros spoke, "She is with my wife, still at the market, I presume. However, you are welcome to join your son and his friends at my home. I would be delighted and Ershrun won't mind another belly to tend. At least I don't think so."

Therak stood. "My friends, I must dismiss myself. I have much planning to do. We will speak again soon." The rest of the group agreed it was time to leave and walked back to Makkros' dwelling.

## ◆══ CHAPTER 17 ══◆

# THE ELDER AND THE GENERAL

Graeog descended the stone staircase leading underneath the Altar of Ehkkahn. He pulled open the heavy timber door and felt the damp meet his face. Proceeding down the narrow corridor, his armament rattled with each stride.

Farther down the passageway, off to the side of the octagonal vestry, the lantern light flickered on the walls of the sobo. Stolt lifted his eyes from a worn parchment and glanced through the doorway. "General, I see you have finally returned from that assembly of fools. Have you anything of consequence to share with me?"

Graeog sneered. "Elder Stolt! I see you remain firmly planted on your haunches. Has Your Excellency achieved anything of consequence since my departure?"

Stolt slammed his fist on the small desk as he rose to his feet. "Your insolence will not be tolerated, you boorish ingrate! What I have done is not of your concern. Now, have you anything to report?"

"Did I not insist the assembly would provide nothing of strategic value?" Graeog barked back. "All I have gleaned is confirmation that Ulfur has lost his grasp on reality. He is no longer of any use to us. I now hold position as Co-Regent of Varrunas-that is the only thing of consequence."

Stolt smirked. "Ah yes, that does hold great significance for the dark children-and for you, General. Surely you have come to realize that loyal service to the Ehkkahn is generously rewarded? No doubt your newly acquired power will be exercised to expand your dominion to the lands beyond the Chime?"

Graeog paced the floor of the vestry. "Why have you called me here? What do we have to discuss? Or do you wish merely to engage in mindless chatter for your own entertainment?"

"You have no patience, General," Stolt replied, "We have a very important matter to discuss. I have eyes and ears among those of my old brotherhood, and I have recently received information that substantiates your estimation of Ulfur's mental condition."

Graeog stopped. "What information? What do you speak of?"

"Do not let your jaw come unhinged!" Stolt snapped. "Listen! It has been no less than two phases since the assembly was dismissed. No doubt you dawdled your time away. Even after the messenger delivered my directive to return to the Altar, were you engaged in the pursuit of females? Perhaps wagering on chunrots? You mindless dolt!"

Graeog's face contorted in anger. He drew his sword and assumed a fight stance. At the same time, the serpentine spawn of the Ehkkahn stealthily emerged from a recessed well port just beyond the

General's field of vision. Slithering arms wrapped around his ankles and lifted him to the vestry ceiling. With blood running to his head, Graeog's body began to slowly spiral. The speed of the twirling increased and brought the General near the point of unconsciousness. Abruptly, he was released at the dizzying speed and slammed against the stone wall with crushing force.

Stolt strolled over to the dazed General and looked down. "The Ehkkahn and I are of one mind and one purpose. It will let no harm come to me. Do you not remember that you are powerless to destroy me? Nor do you and your Ehkkhan brothers have the power to destroy one another? Only I have that power!"

Graeog looked up at Stolt with disgust, but said nothing.

Stolt continued his ranting. "Your body and mind exist in the temporal, yet your spirit resides in the bowels of the Ehkkhan. It is I who allow you to walk about in this realm as if you still had life. Remember this."

Graeog braced against the wall and pushed himself upright. "Elder Stolt, you are most persuasive. Please continue-you were speaking of the report you received from the Frellsari emissary."

Stolt stepped back away from the wall. "Your old enemy, Ulfur, has indeed gone off the pier. He has left Varrunas-and he has taken Therak with him."

General Graeog's eyes grew wide as he stared in disbelief, "How did...that can't...what do you mean? Can this be true?"

Stolt nodded, "I have confirmed the message. Ulfur also has a Yondut prisoner in his company. The three escaped from the old prison and made their way to the coast where they absconded with a dory vessel. They took refuge with the Frellsari sages; shortly thereafter my emissary made haste and came directly to me."

"What significance does that have for us?" Graeog asked.

"That is precisely the point I wish to make Graeog!" Stolt exclaimed, "We do not know what significance it has for us. You will gather a force of warriors and go directly to the Island of the Frellsari. You will extract all information from the sages regarding Therak's plans. You will then destroy the Frellsari complex and all its inhabitants. Do you understand?"

Graeog grinned widely, "Why yes, Elder Stolt, I do understand. And I am indebted to you for entrusting me with such a delightfully invigorating task. May I leave your presence now that I might begin the preparations immediately?"

Stolt nodded and waved Graeog back up the corridor. "General, do not tarry on your mission. You have exactly three nights to complete your task. When that time is finished, I will summon the Ehkkhan to the island. You would do well not to be there when it arrives. Now go."

The General offered no reply except to hoist his belt into place and proceed to the surface.

With Graeog gone, Stolt prepared for his nightly invocation. He entered his sobo, moving to the rear wall and pushing a heavy curtain aside to ascend the lengthy staircase to a precipice alcove overlooking the chasm. He knelt down, extended his hands toward the abyss below, and cried out, "Master of the Blessed Darkness, your servant calls to you. Arise and receive your adoration!"

The walls of the chasm shook. The mournful wail of a multitude of spirits grew louder as the entity ascended. The dim starlight was blotted from the sky as the Ehkkhan enveloped the altar-and then there was silence.

An oddly soothing voice emanated from the dark mass. "Servant, do you bear an offering of more language beings that I might consume their essence? My time of solace has long ceased. My forbearance is no more and I desire to journey beyond this isle."

Stolt bowed. "Master of the Blessed Darkness, each day the pier of the Grhytans grows closer to Varrunas. In a short while we will find more beings willing to join with you. The Grhytans know only the realm of the temporal and they hold to no faith of their own. They understand and respect the ideals of authority and jurisprudence. Above all else, they understand prudent actions that will allow them to achieve their objectives. And that is the crux at which we must meet them."

"A very wise assessment, loyal servant." answered the Ehkkhan, "As was your reckoning of the Varrun warriors. Their own code of honor needlessly restrained them- rigid rules of war ingrained on their hearts and minds for centuries. Their foolish sentiments enabled the bloodlines of their enemies to linger. Searing their consciences has proven most effective. Tell me, loyal servant, what do the Grhytans desire? And, what restrains them?"

Stolt replied, "Master of the Blessed Darkness, the Grhytans are prosperous, yet they desire more. They yearn for their wealth and culture to grow beyond their primitive walls of stone. They yearn for the admiration and respect of kings from other lands, yet they lack the knowledge to fulfill such desires. They lack the resolve to move beyond their own borders, remaining indifferent to what they do not understand."

"Yes, this is where we will meet them." replied the Ehkkhan, "The Grhytans will be offered the gift of temporal knowledge. It will be through this gift that they achieve all which brings them pleasure. A few willing disciples will be all that is needed. Once the Grhytans observe what the converts can achieve, they will understand how immeasurably prudent it is to join with me. Go now; continue to learn more of the

Grhytan's will and ways. Learn more of the pier and its inhabitants. Send a group of faithful proselytizers to them that the path for the joinings might be prepared."

Stolt rose and bowed. "Master, your loyal servant will do all that you ask of him."

General Graeog made a hasty ride to the coast, gathering a force of warriors as he went. Reaching the waterfront, he brought the column to a halt in front of a long timber lodge. The entrance faced the sea; all manner of steed, stock, and cart were tethered to the posts along the outer walls. The bellowing of the rabble inside was of such volume, it nearly overpowered the crashing of the nearby waves.

Graeog turned to his lieutenant. "The proprietor of this latrine has a keen ear for the local hearsay. With the Island of the Frellsari just across the channel, he may have culled useful information from the resident vermin. Hold the column here; I shall return in a trice."

Dismounting, the General worked his way through the menagerie of creatures to a wooden walkway. Each step he took made the aged planks groan. He gave the weathered door a hearty shove and moved through the dense smoke that filled the dimly lit interior. Approaching the bar slab, his foot came down heavily on something composed of flesh and bone; a cry of pain came from the floor. Graeog smiled, lifted his foot, and forcefully rammed it downwards. Nothing more was heard.

A haggard Varrun on the opposite side of the bar slab peered up at Graeog, "You appear to be a warrior I once knew. Yet your visage is that of a corpse and your fragrance is reminiscent of the same. General, what circumstances bring you to my regal establishment? Or, do I address you as King?"

Graeog quickly reached across the bar slab, grabbed the proprietor by the collar, and pulled him up close. "Hold your tongue, Tarkus. No doubt I have enemies about and you are well aware of that."

Tarkus smirks, "Of course, General, please excuse my careless behavior. May I interest you in the basted krellfish? It is our specialty."

Graeog released his grip and moved back, "Is this what becomes of aged warriors? Shall we see if you can still be of some use? Tell me what you know of Ulfur and do not claim ignorance. Otherwise, you are certain to discover how creative I have become in the art of extraction."

"Calm your senses. You are as irascible as I remember. I would have thought these many seasons would have dampened your fire somewhat." Tarkus paused, tapping his fingers on the bar slab. "So, the subject at hand is Ulfur-expatriated King of our beloved homeland? Hmm? I only know that he has left Varrunas and nothing more."

Graeog fixed his eyes on Tarkus. "This I do not believe. Your patrons share much as they partake of the drink. Do not stir my anger-tell me what you have heard!"

Tarkus raised an eyebrow and rested his elbow on the bar slab. "I have only this-near two phases back, a crew of crab riggers came in. They had been out on the flats and went ashore upon the island of the sages to trade for foodstuffs and sterk ale. Several of the crabbers cursed the sages, saying they were told by one of the leaders that there was no sterk ale to be traded and none of boatmates were allowed inside the cloister to select bonabeast cuts from the smokehouse. They were simply told to leave the island."

"What importance does this trivial piece of information have?" Graeog gruffly replied.

"You don't understand." Tarkus leaned across the bar slab, "In all the decrons I have presided over this establishment, not once, under *any* circumstance, has *any* crew been turned away by the sages. There is something askew on that patch of soil."

Graeog scowled. "All you have really told me is that I still must travel to that cursed little isle of dullness for the information I seek."

From the far end of the lodge came a booming voice. "Darkrrun! Have you come to fill this place with your stench, or do you seek to wager with warriors on the chunrots?"

Unable to see clearly who challenged him, Graeog stomped in the direction of the voice, knocking over chairs and patrons along the way. There, sitting around a large oblong table, a group of Varrun warriors were engaged in several very well provisioned rounds of chunrots.

A Varrun, bearing a sergeant's insignia, held out his hand with an offering of game pieces. "Darkrrun, have you the fortitude to engage in battle upon this table? Or have your knees become weak?"

"Who are you?" shouted Graeog.

The sergeant calmly replied, "My name means nothing to you. Nor do I have an interest in yours. I merely wish to separate you from your most recent allotment."

Graeog pointed at the game pieces in the sergeant's hand. "I do not have occasion for such things I have been charged with a task and I must complete it without delay."

The sergeant rose to his feet, "You are rejecting my challenge? I should have expected as much from one who has the odor and strength of a Luurd. Why do you disgrace the company of these valiant warriors with your continued presence? Be gone!"

Anger welled up within Graeog. He shouted back, "Verkgilma!"

The boisterous crowd grew silent. Then there was an explosion of voices shouting, "Verkgilma! Verkgilma!" Graeog and the sergeant exited the lodge, discarding their armament, outer garments, and boots as they moved toward an open patch of soil. The crowd followed the warriors outside, forming a wide circle around them.

The lieutenant grew curious about the events transpiring. He dismounted and moved to the front of the crowd. Upon seeing his general and the sergeant milling around the inside of the circle with bare feet, he realized what was occurring. Working his way back to the column, he hollered out, "Verkgilma! Dismount!" The Darkrrun warriors promptly joined the crowd for the festivities.

It was unknown how or when 'verkgilma' came to be on Varrunas, but the rules were simple. The challenge was a match of strength and a wager. No weapons of any sort could be used, only bare fists and body parts. Any violation of the weapons rule was deemed forfeiture. The match continued until one of the participants was rendered unconscious. The losing party was roused awake and given the choice of sacrificing a digit from a hand or foot, with the selection of the digit to be determined by the winner, or relinquishing his personal possessions to the victor. For a Varrun to decline a verkgilma challenge was anathema. It was considered one of the most deplorable expressions of weakness that could ever be committed.

The crowd surmised this would be an entertaining match, as each participant retained all their appendages. Either they had never engaged in any verkgilma matches, however unlikely, or, they had never been defeated. Many side wagers were made among the observers, including the Darkrrun warriors who mingled with the crowd.

"Varrun, take your stance!" growled Graeog as he shifted his feet into the starting position.

The sergeant prepared himself and nodded at the onlooker who had taken it upon himself to officiate the match. The judge glanced at Graeog, who also nodded. Turning around to face the crowd, the judge raised his hands and then dropped them. In unison, the crowd shouted, "Wealth or Maim!" The match began.

Graeog and the sergeant charged each other. Both combatants brought a shoulder downward to ram the other's chest area. Instead of crushing blows to the lungs, they rammed shoulders, knocking each other backwards to the soil. Both fighters were instantaneously back on their feet, and shuffling along the curve of the circle around them. The sergeant dashed towards the center, calculated his angle of attack, and then dove in the opposite direction at the last moment. Spinning his body around, he kicked Graeog behind the knee, causing him to collapse. Graeog quickly rolled off to the side but the sergeant came down fast, driving his knee into Graeog's rib cage. Still on the ground, Graeog rolled, wrapped his legs around the sergeant's neck and began squeezing tightly. The veins in the Varrun's forehead protruded and grew discolored. In a burst of strength, the sergeant forced himself to his feet, taking Graeog with him. Graeog lost his leg hold, but righted himself in a fashion that allowed him to take a wide sweeping punch to his opponent's temple. Graeog was surprised his strike did not have the anticipated effect. With both participants on their feet, they began to move about the circle once again.

The crowd was ecstatic and cheered loudly. Some of the onlookers commented that neither fighter was even drawing a heavy breath. Their cheers increased in volume as the fighters executed the most skillful verkgilma movements they had ever witnessed. Graeog and the sergeant continued their assaults, with neither opponent gaining the upper hand. As the sun began to set behind the nearby peaks, they both collapsed to their knees within arm's reach of each other. From their kneeling positions, they began striking one other. The sun continued to descend and the blows became fewer and further apart. Just as the sun disappeared behind the mountains, the sergeant fell over. With a final effort, Graeog stood, raised his hands above his head, and then collapsed next to the sergeant.

The crowd drew a collective sigh of disappointment. All knew that according to the traditional rules of verkgilma, this match was a draw. There would be no decisions of wealth or maim this evening. Nor would any side wagers would be settled. The judge addressed the crowd. "Leave them be until the morrow. These fighters have earned their rest." All in attendance agreed. Leaving the unconscious contestants lying on the ground, the mob retreated into the lodge to engage in further drunken behavior. The Darkrrun lieutenant reckoned his warriors could use a bit of merriment and encouraged them to join the patrons inside.

Tarkus began his morn with the usual drudgery. On a back wall, he propped up the guests who had consumed more drink than their constitutions would allow. The floors were swabbed with a concoction of lye and sea water. The chairs and stools were set in place. An inventory of steins was completed, as they tended to break upon impact with skulls. He completed his chores and the first few patrons began to arrive. Soon, the lodge was filled with the usual dregs demanding their drink and sustenance. A bit past mid-day, the judge from the previous night's verkgilma match approached Tarkus, "Where be our mighty fighters this fine day?"

Tarkus called toward the crowd, "Has anyone caught sight of the sergeant and the Darkrrun?"

A slurred voice shouted, "They still slumber where they fell!"

"It seems I have failed to finish cleaning up all the debris," Tarkus mumbled to himself. He grabbed a pail and rope from under the bar slab and stepped out onto the elevated walkway just beyond the lodge entrance. He lowered the pail into the water below, filled it to the rim, and then moved to the area where the fighters still lay in the soil. He doused both with the cold water.

After a few groans, Graeog sat upright and shook his head. The sergeant soon did the same. They said nothing as they shared glassy-eyed, blank stares. Still not clear of mind, Graeog turned to the sergeant, "I must cross the channel; there are sages to slay." Then, with greater clarity, he recalled Stolt's directive. "Curse you Varrun! You have delayed my assignment! Where is the lieutenant?!" He jumped to his feet and gathered his garments and armament from the ground. Continuing to the opposite side of the lodge, he yelled out, "Lieutenant! Lieutenant! Sounder! Where is my sounder?!" He rounded the end of the lodge and glanced up at the crest of the gentle slope before him. There, on the dense grass, his entire force lay in sound slumber. Charging up the hill, he spied his sounder and gave him a kick in the torso. "To your feet! Sound the ready call-now!"

The blasts of the horn quickly roused the warriors. The General commanded, "Untether your steeds and make ready your feet!" Stumbling about, they managed to gather themselves into a ragged formation. General Graeog led the column to the waterfront and onto the longest of the piers. The waterfront did not provide suitable docking for large war vessels so the General was prepared to improvise. Toward the end of pier, Graeog spied a craft of adequate size to carry the company of warriors. Barging onto the deck, he promptly grabbed the captain by the scruff of his neck and heaved him overboard. After adequate threats were offered to the crew, he focused his attention on the pilot. "Take us to the Island of the Frellsari! Now shove off!"

The crew of the vessel commenced launching in a flurry of activity. In short order the sail was filled, and the Darkrruns were on their way across the channel.

Elder Stolt sat quietly listening to his Frellsari emissary. The messenger had just made a second, and unscheduled, trip to the Altar of Ehkkhan. The wily sage had attended the meeting in the gathering hall when Ulfur and Therak addressed the brothers. He revealed to Stolt that Therak was returning to Grhytnod with Ulfur and the Yondut metal crafter, Arunthal. Upon arrival in Grhytnod, Therak would take command of a fleet of vessels to lead an invasion force against Varrunas.

"Excellent, my old friend. I now have a strategic advantage against Therak," smiled Stolt. "I have charged General Graeog with the task of retrieving the information you have just conveyed. He is already en route; no doubt there will be some frivolous affair which will distract him. I believe the General has become a troublesome liability. It now seems judicious to modify the schedule of his assignment. If the Ehkkhan consents, its fury will be upon the sages this eve."

The emissary nodded, "Have you any further tasks for me, Elder Stolt?"

Stolt pulled a sheet of parchment from the drawer and began writing on it. "Take these orders and ensure they are communicated to my captains and marine officers stationed along the seaboard. They will know what to do. Then proceed to Tarkus' lodge; disguising yourself in the manner of the local rabble. Be discreet and unobtrusive; keep alert for such hearsay which might reveal more detail of the Grhytan's plans."

The emissary tucked the parchment beneath his robe, pulled up his hood, and quickly made his way to the surface.

Elder Stolt situated a small stool in front of the archive rack. Stepping up, he reached to the topmost shelf. He grabbed the exposed end of an antiquated scroll, sliding it out of the nook. The scroll was his favorite; it contained the 'Invocation of Wrath'. His predecessor, Elder Balchdur, had successfully used it to destroy the First Armada of the Grhytans, and was rewarded with uncommon longevity. Stolt had studied every word of the journal left by the previous Elder. The last entry described the events; it also spoke of Balchdur's imminent full joining with the

Ehkkhan and its descent into the depths for the time of solace.

Stolt had discovered the chasm of the Ehkkhan a decron after Balchdur's last journal entry was scribed. It would be many phases later, during construction of the Altar, that he would unearth the passageway to the sanctuary complex beneath the unfinished Altar. He had already summoned the Ehkkhan through sheer persistence and happenstance. The discovery of the sanctuary and the archives brought his bond with the Ehkkhan to fruition.

Shortly thereafter, Stolt executed the 'Invocation of Wrath', making a heavily populated costal city the target of the Ehkkahn's savagery. Stolt had sent a legion of proselytizers to the city, but to no avail. The citizens arose in mass and drove them out. Not content to yield, the proselytizers erected a camp outside the city walls. News of the event reached the Elder and he seethed with anger at the city's arrogant resistance. The Ehkkhan was summoned, consent was granted, and the city became engulfed in a shroud of death. The serpentine arms of the entity emerged from the mass in all directions. Becoming as cyclones, each arm produced gales of wind with sufficient strength to dismember flesh and bone. The roar of the wind was deafening, interspersed with the horrendous wailing of the dead and those who soon would be. A barrage of black lightning, oft called the 'dokkbolts', exploded downwards from the upper formation of the entity, annihilating buildings, beasts, and beings while leaving smoke-filled furrows carved across the landscape.

Upon witnessing the carnage, Stolt came to fully realize the entity's power. When summoned in this manner, the Ehkkhan made no distinction between ally and enemy. The entire camp of proselytizers was decimated-none survived. Stolt wondered if he had somehow overlooked a notation in the scroll, or if he had simply not grasped the implications of what he had studied. Of one thing he was certain: that particular invocation should only be used ever so rarely.

Stolt made his way to the precipice alcove once again. Carefully opening the scroll, he began, "Master of the Blessed Darkness, arise in fury, arise in wrath, arise for your pleasure, arise for your servant." As he continued to read from the scroll, the chasm filled with a mist that stung the eyes and nose. Tremors shook the mountain. Stolt could see his Master ascending.

"Elder, whom do you desire that I meet? Have you chosen well?" the Ehkkhan asked. Stolt responded, "Master, I have called you to visit the sages who reside on the Island of the Frellsari. For ages, they have served our greatest enemy. Now they offer aid to the temporal enemies of Varrunas-those who would come against us upon our own shores. The existence of the Frellsari vermin is a great offense to your children."

After a brief moment of silence, the mass began to rise even higher above the chasm rim. "Yes, loyal servant. This would bring Ehkkhan great pleasure. Your request has been granted, and your wise choice will be rewarded."

The Ehkkhan grew in mass and density as it ascended. The darkness began a slow rotation as it extended itself farther past the chasm rim. A rumbling like distant thunder echoed through the nearby peaks. A haunting chorus of mournful spirits emanated from within the entity. The sages would know the tranquility of their island no longer.

The pilot leaned heavily on the steering beam; the starboard side of the vessel tipped down. General Graeog yelled, "Back off! Keep us level!"

Offering no response, the pilot kept his grip on the beam and held the angle. A moment later, he glanced at the cronubus mounted next to his station. The needles now fell where the seasoned boatmate knew they should. He turned to Graeog, "Blow it out your moke, you big, ugly carcass! Or did you really want to go visit the Luurds? I'll steer, though under protest, and I will get this vessel to the island. However, hear me now-a gafspear will find its way into your gullet if my darling doesn't make it back home in good order."

Graeog could only grin with admiration at the small, stout Varrun. Rarely did he encounter a noncombatant with such fortitude. He nodded, "Well spoken. Continue with your task."

The shore came into view as the evening came upon them. The crew busied itself bringing the vessel to a halt and the anchors were dropped. General Graeog sternly directed the landing. He and the other ranking warriors boarded the few dory vessels; the underlings removed their armament and packed it into the remaining empty spaces. The sea waters surrounding the vessel were churned to froth as the Darkrruns dove in and swam to shore.

The dories reached the beach first; the boatmates disembarked and dragged the vessels onto the sand. The swimmers followed close behind, retrieved their armament, and awaited orders. General Graeog dispatched a group of warriors to block any attempts at escape through the rear walls of the cloister complex. He and the remaining force trudged through the sand towards the main entrance. After leading them only a few steps, Graeog stopped in his tracks and turned around to face the sea. "Do you hear that?" he asked.

Curious, the group of warriors also turned to face the sea. One of them answered, "Yes. It is but the clamor of a storm. The meeting of water and sky is clear; it must be far distant."

Graeog intently surveyed the horizon. "That is not the rumble of a sea squall. I have heard that roar only one other time in all my seasons." He pointed back in the direction they had traveled from. "There, do you now see the darkness that comes towards us?"

A mass was moving across the open sea at astonishing speed. The veteran warriors knowingly looked back at Graeog. The rest of the group merely stared in disbelief. General Graeog yelled, "Stolt has betrayed us! Back to the dories; back to the ship-now!"

No time remained to flee; the Ehkkhan was upon them. The sky became as the bowels of a bog. The foul odor of sulfur permeated the atmosphere. Beach gravel was hurled with such momentum, it peeled the ashen skin away from the Darkrrun's bones. Chaos ensued and the warriors lost their bearings in the haze. The entity discharged a series of dokkbolts which blasted deep craters into the sand. The once proud warriors stumbled into the pits and were quickly buried by the twisting gale. The cries of the doomed war party were eternally muted.

The maelstrom plowed through the cloister complex, wrenching stone from stone and timber from timber. Debris was caught up into the cyclonic arms of the Ehkkhan as it sifted for a morsel of sustenance. None were found; the entity roared with anger. A multitude of limbs were birthed from the expanding mass, extending over the entire island. A cacophony of earsplitting howls resounded for lenads in all directions. A battery of dokkbolts pulverized the cloister's remaining foundations. After one final surge of destruction, the gales diminished and the Ehkkhan withdrew into itself, slithering limbs receding back into the body that bore them. The darkness rose skyward, retreating across the sea waters as rapidly as it appeared.

Rays of light shot over the hills by the setting sun. Seabirds could be heard as they resumed their incessant screeching. One of the larger birds set down upon a floating timber. The creature made several hops and peered curiously at the other occupants. It was greeted with the swipe of a hand across its feathers. The remaining passengers on the timber looked back towards the island. Not a building, a tree, or greenery of any sort could be seen. No living creatures were moving about; even the seabirds avoided the shores. All that remained was a landscape of soot and rubble. Gripping the pitch-covered wood tightly, the survivors tried to shake the trauma from their minds. The bird hater turned his eyes towards Varrunas, shook his fist in the air, and bellowed, "Graeog will not be betrayed!"

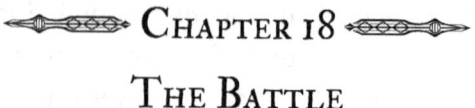

# CHAPTER 18

## THE BATTLE

The two phases passed quickly for the trio. The events to come weighed heavily on their hearts but they chose to dwell on the simple pleasure of enjoying their friends and family. Arunthal had spent many hours at a local forge building Poodwah his own special armor. Unlike the Grhytan soldiers, he would have shields covering his lower body as well. He also gathered armor of appropriate size for Jeddok, Lohjji, and himself.

The splint on Leshti's arm was reworked with a lighter dressing. This freed her hand to more easily perform light tasks. She would remain with Ershrun while the Yonduts went off to battle.

The day had come to board the ships. The Yonduts donned their battle attire, except for Poodwah, who had convinced Lohjji to push his armor and the remaining skrugins in a small handle cart. After a tearful goodbye, Arunthal and the trio began the short trek to the pier and the Armada.

As they drew near, they were awed at the sight before them. All the armies had gathered in large bivouacs at the landing area near the pier. Jeddok admired the well-formed armor covering the heads and torsos of the Grhytans. He especially took notice of the swords they carried in their back scabbards. Each one bore the mark of his pap. The gathered force appeared immense but it was well known that the Varrun armies were much larger. It was said there were six Varrun warriors for every Grhytan soldier.

The blast of horns was heard over the noise of the crowd and the Grhytans quickly gathered themselves into formation facing the arch at the entrance to the pier. A second blast of the horns was heard and the ranks began moving under the arch to their appointed vessels. Arunthal motioned for the trio to follow him and they headed towards a small tent near the arch. Stepping inside, they found Therak, Ulfur, and a group of officers and deputies. Therak greeted them and turned to one of his officers, "The Yonduts will join me on the first flagship. And you, Colonel Jakkur, will join Ulfur on the second."

The Colonel promptly responded. "Understood, Chief General." Ulfur responded in a like manner and quickly stepped out of the tent with Colonel Jakkur close behind. Therak looked at his friends and fellow soldiers. "It is time."

Therak led Arunthal and the trio outside the tent where a makeshift stable had been constructed. It held six adorned oologs. Therak pointed at the animals and said, "This is to honor those who fight as Grhytans but do not come from our land."

Arunthal was stunned, "Therak, this is not necessary. Let us walk as do the other soldiers."

Therak responded, "You do not know Grhytan ways. We would so honor Luurds, should they choose to fight with us."

Jeddok piped up, "They are so large. Won't they sink the ship?"

Therak winked at him. "You have not yet seen our flagships."

With their departure at hand, Lohjji helped pack the skrugins into a pouch bag draped over one of the animals. Poodwah was lifted to the top of the oolog; the others mounted their animals, leading the remaining one on board on Ulfur's ship. Therak led the group at a healthy trot down the center of the pier's well-worn path. The ships were docked closely together on either side of the pier. Each one was filled to capacity, with rows of Grhytans gripping large oars which partially hung out of the side portals. Therak continued down the path and over a stone bridge of great height and width. A Grhytan vessel could easily traverse from one side of the pier to the other underneath the enormous structure. On the opposite side of the bridge, the flagships displayed their proud beauty. They were of the same design as the other Grhytan vessels but on grander scale.

The flagships had three levels with rows of oars extending from ports on the lower level. The deck was wide and open, having a large single mast from which hung an unfurled sail. The riders guided their animals up the ramp, boarded, and dismounted. The oologs were led down inside to stables in the stern. Pieces of taeris fruit were placed in the troughs. The animals consumed their treats and nestled down in the thick layer of hay. On the top deck, Therak took his post and motioned towards the sounder. The Grhytan lifted his horn high and let loose with a series of blasts which carried all the way up the pier.

Jeddok watched as the boatmates removed the tether ropes and pushed away from the pier with long poles. Looking down towards the lower level, he saw movement among the oars, as they settled into position and began short sweeps in the water. The other vessels were following in kind, easing away from the pier. Having moved clear of any obstacles, the boatmates extended their oars to full length and took longer sweeps. Jeddok looked back at the other vessels as they formed up behind the flagship. He could see the ships on the other side of the pier as they passed by another of the enormous bridges. The fleet on the opposite side matched their speed.

Their journey went swiftly and after four days of travel they reached the end of the pier. It was at that point, upon his return home, Therak called for its construction to stop. One more day brought them within sight of the outer islands. Ulfur's fleet had altered course the night prior. It would take an additional day's journey for his fleet to arrive at its appointed landing site at the ruins of Reitrius.

At mid-afternoon, Therak called the Yonduts together. "By the dark of tomorrow morn we will be upon the shores of Varrunas. We will go ashore in full battle gear and march towards the fortress at Ilkraador. The day thereafter, Ulfur's forces will reach their point of landing and commence to march through the Balchdur Gorge towards the opposite side of the valley. May Theoas rule our strides that our arrivals may be in unity."

The Yonduts smiled and responded in agreement, "Amoda."

The group noticed the wind became stronger, and then forceful gusts blew down on the fleet. Poodwah hollered, pointing towards the horizon. "Over there? Is that a storm approaching?"

Therak shouted, "The Not is upon us! Get below!" His mind went back to his previous encounter with the entity and great dread came over him. As Arunthal stepped down to the lower deck, Therak said, "Call upon Theoas."

Arunthal nodded and continued down the steps. Therak issued commands to the topside boatmates to rope everything securely. He offered a silent petition to Theoas for protection as the waves grew higher and crashed against the side of the vessel. The sky became dark and the wind grew even stronger as the entity came upon them. Black lightning flashed in the sky, filling the air with the smell of sulfur. A bolt of the malevolent force struck the base of the mast, snapping it clean away from the deck. Another charge blasted a ragged hole near the stern, splintering a large portion of the half deck. The vessel was jarred violently; listing heavily to the starboard side, the cap rail licked the waves. It seemed inevitable to the horror-struck passengers that the ship would soon capsize.

The deafening roar was more than wind. The eerie voices of a thousand angry spirits could be heard. The fingers of the mass reached through the ports and faces could be seen forming in the darkness. The Yonduts and the boatmates huddled together in fear; the oologs roared as never before. The dark mass swept over every being inside the ship, then retracted back through the ports. The atmosphere of the deck became oddly serene. Each being sat in stunned silence with a mix of terror, relief and confusion reeling through their minds.

Poodwah was first to break the stillness, "What have we just experienced? I look about and see that all remain; the ship is broken, but we are not." The group nodded in agreement with Poodwah's comments, but remained as they were-waiting for someone to offer direction.

Shaking the fog from his head, Therak stood up and motioned for everyone else to do the same. "I fear for the smaller vessels." Pushing debris aside, he made his way back to the top deck. The Yonduts followed, surveying the devastation the ship had sustained. Therak spied a lone pellsta perched on the side plank. He turned to the Yonduts. "Loudly yell out 'Hahkta' in all directions."

By this time, many of the other boatmates had come topside and joined them as they called out to any surviving pellstas. Three more of the loyal birds landed on the deck, and then another two. Therak asked the Yonduts, "Have you pen and parchment?"

Poodwah reached into his new side pack and pulled out the items. Therak tore the parchment into smaller pieces and quickly scribed a short note on each one. He instructed the Yonduts, "Bind these to the birds and send them off."

Therak stepped to the bow and released the final pellsta. He shouted at the sea in his native tongue and turned to face the Yonduts on the deck. With anger in his eyes, he said, "We will destroy this enemy!"

Poodwah responded with an authoritative tone, "Chief General, the Grhytans are mighty, yet all their strength is not enough. Only Theoas has the strength to defeat this enemy."

Angry, but keeping his composure, Therak replied, "There was a time when I would have slain you where you stand. However, I now know words of truth when they are spoken. And you are correct, little Yondut."

As the sun began to set, pellstas began returning, Therak read the parchment fragments they brought with them. More pellstas had returned than had been sent out. After a time, no more arrived; Therak called the Yonduts together. With his head hung low, he spoke, "My friends, it appears I have lost at least a third of my fleet. I pray Ulfur's vessels were spared. I am determined to continue. We will press on."

Arunthal responded, "We are with you, without reservation."

Therak offered a quiet "Thank you" and moved to the bow of the ship in silence.

The vessel bounced with the roll of the waves just as it had done for the last four nights. The wait had become tiring, but the single passenger remained inexhaustibly patient. Living with the others for so long, he had become accustomed to the trials that came with lengthy journeys aboard a sage wherry. He said to himself, "It will be worth the grief. The Grhytans will be most grateful for the gifts I bear."

Hurdroy reached into the bag of smoked krellfish and removed the remaining scraps. Moving to the compartment at the stern, he was pleased to see there were still several firkins of water and sterk ale. "If necessary, I could remain a while longer, though I soon hope to observe some sign of their arrival." Still pondering, he mumbled to himself, "Am I in the correct location? I have gone to and fro only in this one area. Of course, I am where I need to be-this is the most logical entry point. Then again, maybe my time would have been better spent exploiting drunkards with my 'special' chunrot pieces? Possibly, I should consider opportunities beyond these islands? The Luurds have a taste for the ale. Perhaps, my own brewstill on the far shores of the Krell? Enough of that-set your mind on the task at hand." Shifting around to face the open sea, he found a comfortable position against the mast pole. Humming a lodge ditty, he concentrated his gaze where the water met the stars.

How long the slumber had lasted he did not know. Now fully awake, he was certain of the sounds that had roused him. The distinct clunking of wood against wood, interspersed with a splashing of water that seemed out of place. Surveying the sea waters surrounding the wherry, he caught sight of an obscure silhouette against the glow of the moon. Once again, he heard the rhythmic clunk-splash-clunk-splash. It was louder and more defined than it had been earlier. Waiting a few moments longer, he could clearly see an enormous vessel moving in his direction. "Dirgenhoots!" he exclaimed. "Hurdroy, you are too clever! My estimation was accurate—now I must attempt to befriend these bulky boatmates. I must first draw their attention."

The flagship had just entered the outer boundary of the Varrun waters. On a course separated from Therak's fleet by several degrees, Ulfur heard the night sentry cry aloud, "Lantern-port side!"

Ulfur hollered down the entryway to the lower deck, "Colonel Jakkur! Come topside quickly!"

Jakkur bounded up the stairs. "Chief General, what brings you alarm?"

"The sentry has spied lantern light off the port side," said Ulfur, "Though I do not yet know with what we have to contend. Drop a neshorn dory off the side and accompany a group of soldiers to investigate. Take a sounder with you also; he might be required."

Jakkur nodded, "As you command, Chief General."

No time was wasted and within moments the Grhytans were plowing through the water towards the light. Nearing the vessel, the soldiers discarded their armor, bulky garments, and boots and then securely strapped snub spears to their backs. Though not the fastest of swimmers; the Grhytans compensated with their enormous lung capacity and sheer endurance. Engaging the oars once again, they quickly moved towards their target.

Wafting through the night air, a rollicking lodge ditty issued from the tiny deck of the mystery vessel. Colonel Jakkur commented, "What breed of sea creature have we found?"

Once close enough to see the passenger, the befuddled Grhytans attempted to decipher the situation. In the glow of the lantern they could see him clearly. Hurdroy was leaning against the mast pole with his feet comfortably propped up on the edge of the boat, singing and swigging from a firkin of ale.

Hurdroy stood on the platform with outstretched arms. "Greetings, mighty warriors of large proportions! Your arrival is both timely and welcome. May you accept my solicitations with great inadvertence. I bring gifts of great significance to the leadership of this impressive flotilla. Let there be no more delay-I must have an audience with the superior in charge. Off we go now-bustle and dash! No haste makes waste!"

Colonel Jakkur tilted his head. "Huh?"

Offering a graceful bow, Hurdroy continued. "And I am tremendously pleased to make your acquaintance also, Lieutenant." He looked at the other crew members of the neshorn. "My felicitations to you, able boatmates. Your weapons will not be required; there will be no acts of aggression on my part. As you will soon note, I come only with expressions of good will and proposals to benefit my own monetary welfare. Yes, yes-I can tell by the glint in your eyes that you show interest in what I offer. Let me begin with a thorough introduction-starting with a brief outline of my pedigree, and—"

Jakkur bellowed, "Silence! No more words! They do not understand your speech, Varrun! We will tow your craft to the flagship. You will explain yourself onboard."

Hurdroy replied, "You are most gracious, Lieutenant. I am honored, and let me just say—"

"Nothing!" Colonel Jakkur fired back forcefully.

A rope was cinched to Hurdroy's craft and towed the short distance. Arriving at the ship, the Grhytan's tied up, put on their garments, and gathered up their armament. Colonel Jakkur was the first to ascend the rope ladder.

Hearing the clamor, Ulfur leaned over the edge just as Jakkur reached the deck. "What have you found, Colonel?"

Jakkur hesitated. "I do not know."

"You do not know? That is an unacceptable report, Colonel. What do you mean you do not know?"

Looking back over the edge, the Colonel shouted at one of the underlings still on the neshorn, "Get that Varrun aboard!" He turned to face Ulfur, "You will understand shortly, Chief General."

After a few moments, Hurdroy pulled himself over the railing. He set foot on the deck and without so much a pause to catch his breath he immediately initiated a conversation. "King Ulfur!? . . . Captain Ulfur? . . . Sir . . . how awkwardly unexpected. How do you come to be on this vessel? Of course, you must be asking the same thing of me. Well, such surprises offer generous seasoning to our lives. Don't you agree? To answer your question: a series of interesting circumstances have brought me here. Where to begin? As a young Varrun, I was very unsure of myself, lacking direction and purpose. You see, I lost my dear father at an early age. Though I am not certain of the details, I understand he met his demise on a battlefield in Erstra, or some such place. My mother, a being of strong will and determination was not one to yield to self-pity. She uprooted the family from our home in the mountains and moved us to the coast. Finding employment at one of the waterfront lodges, she was able to provide meager sustenance and living accommodations for my siblings and me. Speaking of my siblings, there are my two sisters who . . ."

Ulfur cupped his hands over his ears, "Silence! Silence!" He looked over to Jakkur, "As you have said Colonel-I now understand." Ulfur directed his eyes toward Hurdroy. "Understand this: I will ask direct, concise questions and you will only give me answers that are of a pertinent nature. Are you clear on this point?"

Hurdroy offered a timid nod.

Ulfur continued, "Excellent. I am neither King, nor Captain, and you will address me as Chief General. Now, who are you? And why are you here?"

"Chief General, my name is Hurdroy, formerly of the Frellsari Brotherhood. I have come to barter information that could be crucial to your immediate plans."

"And how would you know of my immediate plans?"

"Well, Chief General, I was in attendance at the Gathering Hall when Therak announced his agenda upon returning to Grhytnod. It brings no surprise that you do not remember me, as I tend to keep a low profile-well, when it benefits my commercial concerns."

"Commercial concerns?" responded Ulfur.

"Yes, Chief General, I spent well over a decron with the sages, it was a secure and pleasant life. However, the life of a sage did not lend itself to opportunities outside the cloister walls. I volunteered early on as a courier; taking messages and supplies to and from the main island. Let's just say I expanded from there. I continued to pursue more lucrative endeavors while still residing at the cloister."

"Hurdroy, why are you here? How does floating upon the sea in the dark fill your coffers? What does all this have to do with my 'immediate plans'?"

"Yes, Chief General, that does require some explanation. Is there a more private place where we could discuss these matters?"

Ulfur grabbed Hurdroy by the arm, "Colonel Jakkur, please accompany our 'guest' and me to my cabin."

Descending below the deck, they entered the Chief General's quarters, lit a lantern, and set their visitor down at the small table.

Ulfur continued his questioning. "Get to the point Hurdroy. Why are you here?

"Chief General, you are most impatient. Nevertheless, I will put this as succinctly as I can. As I did not want to limit my marketplace, I contacted The Elder. You know him simply as Stolt. We were acquainted from our time together with the sages and I offered him my services as a courier. He offered the 'honor' of joining with the Ehkkahn, but I chose to accept more material compensation which he has provided in satisfactory measure."

Ulfur sneered with disgust. "Stolt is responsible for the civil chaos and division that now reigns on Varrunas. He and the dark entity have brought only grief and destruction upon our land and populace. Why should I trust one who has engaged in ventures with our enemy?

"May I just say, Chief General, that I do understand your concerns. However, my relationship with Stolt was strictly for monetary gain. I hold no loyalty, or regard, for him. His obsession with dark, other worldly matters and his unbearably grim demeanor had become communicable and burdensome. Our assemblages brought me a great compulsion to dive from the nearest cliff and greet the stones below. By coming to you, I have willfully severed my ties with The Elder."

Ulfur thumped his fist down on the table. "Your arrival on this ship means nothing!"

"Hear me out-please," pleaded Hurdroy. "Before leaving the Altar of Ehkkahn, I was entrusted with a message to be delivered to Stolt's military puppets along the seaboard. The orders directed the forces to congregate about the ruins of Reitrius along the coast. As you know, Chief General, that area is the gateway to the Balchdur Gorge, and the most expedient route to the fortress valley from any side of Varrunas."

Taking great interest in these comments, Ulfur and Colonel Jakkur seated themselves at the table with their guest.

Hurdroy grinned. "Yes, noble officers, it seems that I now have you attention."

"Do you have these orders? Show them!" Jakkur insisted.

"Patience, Grhytan; I have not yet finished. You see, one of my remarkable skills is the ability to duplicate the writing of any hand. So much so, that my copy is indistinguishable from the original. This brings us to the first contribution that I have made to our forthcoming partnership. It seems the orders that Stolt intended for his officers to receive were not the orders that were delivered to them. At this very moment, his scouts and ships are traversing aimlessly along the far shores; beyond the web of gorges and far distant from the ruins of Reitrius, and your landing site. This service has been rendered to you without compensation as an offering of goodwill."

Colonel Jakkur and Ulfur looked at each other across the table, sharing expressions of suspicion.

Ulfur leaned close to Hurdroy. "And how might you be privy to the whereabouts of our landing?"

Hurdroy displayed an arrogant smirk. "Chief General, thank you for asking. It was a well-studied reckoning on my part-a very clever one at that. The Balchdur Gorge is the most expedient route to the valley of the fortress on Varrunas. There could be no better point from which to deploy an invasion force."

Ulfur grinned at Jakkur. "Colonel, would you say that our guest has an uncanny skill for divulging the obvious?"

Laughing heartily, Jakkur stood up from his seat and slapped Hurdroy on the back. "Varrun, your knowledge of military strategy is beyond compare. It bids well for our forces that you have chosen to ally yourself with this humble fleet."

Hurdroy squirmed in his seat. Waves of confusion coursed through his mind. "I don't understand. Are you not pleased that I have misdirected the Darkrruns? Your invasion force will not be met with resistance. Why do you laugh?"

Ulfur's expression grew more solemn. "We do have strategic reasons for choosing the ruins of Reitrius as a landing point; though, not as you have stated. And yes, your act of deception is worthy of acknowledgment. Unfortunately, it is improbable that Stolt relied solely on your services to communicate his orders. No doubt there are other couriers; and no doubt your deception has already been exposed.

Hurdroy's countenance projected defeat, but only for a brief moment. "There remains another item of information-one of which I'm certain you do not have. For this, I would require a diminutive consideration of only one thousand Varrun peindols, or the equivalent value in Grhytan grollets."

"That is absurd!" roared Jakkur. "Have you a notion of what you ask? What could you offer that would have that kind of worth?"

Hurdroy calmly replied, "What I offer is a weapon not yet experienced by the Darkrruns." He turned towards Ulfur, "Have we an agreement Chief General?"

Rising from his seat, Ulfur glared down at Hurdroy. "If what you say is true, then yes. If you have wasted our time, be aware that Colonel Jakkur has orders to toss you into the sea."

Hurdroy's mouth grew dry as beads of sweat formed on his brow. "Being of the military occupations, you both would be aware that Darkrruns have an aversion to fire. The knowledge you do not possess is that wood alone does not create a flame of enough intensity to disperse a Darkrrun."

Jakkur asked "What do you speak of-'disperse'?

"A flame of sufficient intensity will turn a Darkrrun into vapor. On several occasions, while Stolt was consumed with his nightly invocations, I was left to my leisure at the Altar of Ehkkahn. This allowed me occasion to pilfer his archives. I learned many things.

It was near that same time, through exchange with a fleet of Luurin traders, that I acquired a mineral compound capable of fortifying a flame to the degree of intensity required. If you had not noticed, my vessel which you commandeered has an unusual draft for a craft of its size. It bears the weight of this substance under its deck planks. A carefully measured quantity of this substance, mixed with pitch, and slathered on the metal point of a spear, would provide an effective weapon for your forces. If you wish, let us arrange a presentation. However, we must be cautious not to repeat the mistakes of others. The Luurd who demonstrated the mineral's properties for me apparently did not carefully think the task through. It did not turn out well for the hapless chum. I would have never imagined that a Luurd could combust in such expeditious fashion-quite disturbing, really."

"Enough talk! We shall see this weapon now!" Colonel Jakkur insisted.

Hurdroy scowled. "Are all Grhytan's so indignant?"

Ulfur briskly arose from his seat, "The Colonel is justified in his indignation. We have no more time to squander. Colonel, accompany Hurdroy topside and assist in the arrangements for this demonstration. It must be executed as quickly as possible. Hurdroy, you would do well to obey his instructions promptly and without debate."

A pail of pitch, a small bag of the mineral compound, and a broadboar spear were collected and brought to the half deck. A substantial audience including officers, underlings, and couriers gathered in a semicircle. Hurdroy's previous experiments had prepared him for just such a moment. He dipped a cup into the bag of granules, filling it to a third. He began at one end of the line of observers and passed the cup under their noses. "Take careful note of what you see; scribe it on parchment, and scribe it on your mind's eye. Use no more, no less; otherwise your flame will soften the spear point or the flame will not be of sufficient intensity to disperse your enemy."

Hurdroy continued, "Also take careful note of the other preparations that must be completed. Remove the spearhead, shave the shaft down slightly and wrap it tightly with a layer of oolog fleece, then securely reattach the spearhead. The oolog fleece resists the heat, and inhibits charring of the shaft. Bending over the pail, he poured in the contents of the cup, and stirred the concoction using the end of the spear. Satisfied with the mixture, he extracted the spear and motioned for the boatmate with a lighting torch to approach. Holding the tip of the spear just over the edge of the cap rail, he gave the boatmate a nod. "Wait! Not just yet." He turned towards his audience, "It would be beneficial to tighten your eyes to a squint." He gave another nod, and the torch was lowered to the spearhead. Crackle! Whoosh! Hiss! A white ball of flame engulfed the spearhead, emanating a large sphere of very intense light of the same hue. The observers jumped backwards, shielding their eyes with their hands. Shouts and expletives were profusely expressed all around. The spear illuminated the deck of the flagship from stern to bow.

"Very impressive!" exclaimed Ulfur. "Are you certain this flame will dispatch a Darkrrun?"

"Without a doubt, Chief General." replied Hurdroy. "Let's just say I've had the opportunity to execute a field test with a weapon very similar to this. The Luurd's instructed me fairly well, and I spent much time investigating variations of the flame spear. All I lacked was a definitive test to prove the design of my prototype. As timeliness would have it, I was offloading some mineral bags at an undisclosed location, when I saw a Darkrrun's head bobbing up and down just on the other side of a rise. Ducking behind the low outcropping where I had moored the wherry, I readied my instrument and engaged my spark stones to create a small tinder fire. Then he appeared, charging over the rise on the most beautiful of stallions. I extended the head of the spear over the fire, and—"

"Enough! Enough! I do not need to hear your story!" shouted Ulfur. "I will take you at your word." He paused for a moment to gather his thoughts and then faced the observers. "You have heard and seen what is required to create these weapons. Colonel Jakkur, search out the Quartermaster and order him to gather all the pitch pails we have on board. Send a detail to the stable deck; order them to shave the oolog's manes and gather them in bundles. Officers, soldiers, and couriers, you will scribe briefing instructions to send with the pellsta's back down the fleet line. The other vessels will need to gather their inventories of pitch as well. Then, load the neshorns with as many mineral bags as feasible, along with sufficient oolog fleece. Your most critical task is to train the Chief Adjutants on each of the smaller vessels, directing them to train their troops in the same manner. However, do not leave this ship until I issue the battle briefing. Fall out!"

As his orders were being executed, Chief General Ulfur scribed out the final details of the landing. He had sufficient opportunity to survey the Grhytan fleet before leaving Rondur's Pier. The Second Armada, as it was known, consisted of vessels with significant features unknown to the prior fleet. Each Grhytan warship, called a "drocmog," and its supplement of specially designed dories, called "neshorns," were equipped with double-layered hulls and heavy ramming beams fully clad with metal shielding. The beams were extensions of the keel and protruded from the bow. The ramming beams were specifically designed to puncture the hull of a Varrun drakkar at water level. His plans would fully utilize the new designs and the Grhytan muscle that propelled them.

Alone in his cabin, Ulfur sat staring at the words he had just penned. His fingers nervously tapped the table, his breathing felt labored, and fretfulness gripped his heart. He questioned whether his tactics would be successful. His counterpart on the other side of Varrunas was depending on him to reach the valley according to schedule. The combined attack against the fortress was dependent upon it.

Pondering, he considered the circumstances surrounding the moment, "How strange this is. I have allied with a Grhytan, once my enemy, now my friend. I lead Grhytan forces to attack my own nation- to battle warriors that I once commanded. I am no longer King, I am certainly not a Captain, and I surmise my commission as Chief General will expire once this operation has concluded. I have no home, and I have no family among the living. I have no understanding of my purpose beyond this day. Never has this Varrun been found in such a way." He lifted his eyes, catching a glimpse of the stars through the small portal. "The Yondut would tell me to speak with Theoas. How simplistic and childlike that sounds. In my former life I would have laughed at the suggestion and engaged in yet another frivolous pursuit. Yet now it seems that is all that remains." Speaking softly he began. "Theoas, in my understanding, you hold authority over all that has been, is, and will be. You are the one I now serve and my petition is simple. Issue my orders and I will obey. This I also understand and this I will do. So be it."

Strength and determination took hold where anxiety once resided. Ulfur bounded up to the deck. Jakkur and the Quartermaster stood near a lantern at the starboard capstan. Ulfur called out, "Colonel! Come quickly-the final orders are ready."

Ulfur briefed Jakkur on the execution of his orders. "Now, gather the mission leaders back together and get these instructions distributed. They are to be replicated precisely; I want no misinterpretations. Do you understand?"

"Yes, Chief General. Any, further orders, Sir?"

"Come to my cabin when you are satisfied that my directives are clearly understood by all. I will then give the order to disembark. Also, escort Hurdroy to the brig. He is to remain there until this engagement is over."

Colonel Jakkur gave an affirming nod, "As you command, Chief General."

After a brief span, the battle orders had been issued and the mission leaders had disembarked. All that remained was to wait on the stars to reach the position that had been designated as the advancement signal. The eyes of the fleet watched the sky with anticipation as the preparations were finalized. The hastened training on the flame spears appeared to be successful. The pitch mixture had been prepared and distributed among the vessels. The fleet was poised to engage the Darkrruns.

Chief General Ulfur stood on the deck next to the pilot. From both sides of the flagship he could hear the sounds of the fleet coming into position. From the farthest ends of the line of battle he could see the faint glow of the signal lanterns appearing sequentially. The lights continued toward the flagship until the final two were ignited; one on the port, and one on the starboard. He moved to the forecastle, took a breath, and then cast his eyes upward to observe the constellations. The stars dictated that the time had arrived. Ulfur picked up the lantern at his feet, turned up the wick, and with a swinging motion presented the advance signal. The signal passed back out toward the ends of the battle line. Ulfur moved aft, swung his leg over the railing, and boarded a waiting neshorn. A chorus of reverberating Grhytan battle howls was the final signal. Across the battle line rowers dug deep into the water. The Grhytan's propelled the drocmogs and neshorns towards Varrunas with vengeance. Ulfur was astonished at the swiftness of the vessels. He felt an inner confidence. "Theoas has directed me here. So be it."

The faintest hint of morning glow could now be seen behind the outline of craggy peaks. All across the line of battle, Grhytan oarswains called out the thunderous, methodical commands, "Tog! Tog! Tog!" The rowers responded with powerful strokes that moved the vessels along at an ever increasing speed. Chief General Ulfur sat in quiet amazement; he had not thought such a pace could be achieved in a water craft. Ulfur gave his oarswain a nod, the cadence increased, and their neshorn raced ahead of the others. The Chief General's incursion plan placed the neshorns in the forward line of battle, with the drocmogs trailing slightly behind. A Darkrrun ship would be targeted by five to six neshorns in attack formation moving at full speed. The intent was to inflict as may hull punctures as possible in a single assault. The neshorns would immediately pull back, and then divert their course to engage other drakkars in the same proximity. If the tactic was successful, the sea would consume the Darkrruns and their vessels, leaving the Grhytan's free to run the drocmogs aground. This would be completely unexpected by the enemy, as no naval force had ever done such a thing. The soldiers would then promptly disembark and move inland with flame spears poised to dispatch whatever Darkrrun resistance they might encounter.

The coast of Varrunas had become dimly visible to the neshorn crews. Also coming into view were the distinct outlines of Varrun drakkars. An extensive line of ships was guarding the beach at Reitrius. Leaning forward, Ulfur tapped on the sounder's back; the blast of the horn was loud and clear. The other vessels in the fleet responded accordingly. The Chief General turned to his oarswain, and then pointed towards the nearest drakkar. Their craft veered slightly, with a handful of other neshorns quickly moving into formation around them. Ulfur shouted, "Attack!" The oarswain issued the same command in the Grhytan tongue, "Togrod!" Ulfur heard the cadence of the rowing call change. "Togrod! Togrod! Togrod!" The formation of neshorns was only moments from impact.

In force, Darkrrun warriors leaned over the gunwale shouting curses at the approaching Grhytans. Boom! Ulfur's neshorn pierced the hull with jarring force, lifting the stern out of the water, and throwing the rowers forward. The Chief General was ejected from his seat, and smashed into the sounder's back. The boat slammed back down into the water, twisting the ram beam upwards into the already splintered hull. Quickly gathering his wits, Ulfur commanded, "Pull back!" The Grhytans quickly reversed direction under a hail of Darkrrun spears. Enemy warriors began diving into the neshorn, swinging swords with unrestrained ferocity. Crack! Screech! The friction of ram beam against wood produced a piercing squeal as it was extracted from the hull. Sea water began pouring into the drakkar's gaping wound. The Grhytan rowers hurled the attacking Darkrruns out of the boat, but not before sustaining severe wounds. One soldier nearest the bow extracted a spear from his leg with one hand, while rowing with the other.

Ulfur shouted commands at the other neshorns, but they had already begun to disengage the enemy ship. Ulfur waved the oarswain towards another drakkar that was drifting nearby. The neshorns gathered back into formation and plowed towards their next target. Ulfur glanced back; the first drakkar was already listing to the port side. He then lifted his eyes towards the sky. The sun had completed its ascent over the tops of the peaks; the rays of light had just begun to gleam over shore and sea. Surveying the waters, he could see that his fleet was fully engaged with the enemy forces. The cacophony of battle surrounded him from all directions

Colonel Jakkur shouted to his oarswain, "Hard starboard!" Crash! The main mast of the capsizing drakkar ripped through the neshorn. Grhytan howls came from underneath the mass of twisted rigging. The knot of sail and rope had become a net of death for the trapped crew members. Jakkur scarcely had time to take in a chest full of air before being pulled under. He became disoriented in the dark water, but was able to focus his energy on the web of rigging that held him captive. He maneuvered his body into position and was able to remove the dagger he had stashed in his boot. That was all he needed. Cutting away the rope, he quickly shed the heavy armor that continued to pull him down towards the sea floor. He exploded up out of the water gasping for breath.

The neshorn had completely disappeared, and the drakkar was belly up. Darkrruns could be heard pounding the hull from inside their tomb. He slipped the dagger back down into his boot, and swam the short distance to the capsized drakkar. Digging the rock hard nails of his fingers into the wood, he clawed his way up towards the peak of the hull. Reaching the top, he encountered four Darkrruns moving in his direction. Now on his feet, he took hold of a long broken timber. The Darkrruns lunged towards him with swords slashing through the air. A wide forceful swing of the timber knocked two of the enemy into the sea. The remaining Darkrruns came at him from opposite sides. "Argh!" yelled Jakkur as a sword cut vertically through the flesh of his back. He spun around, grabbing the blade of the sword as the Darkrrun attempted another blow. There was no sensation of pain as the metal cut into his hand; his mind was completely consumed with the task of survival. He swung with his free hand, driving his fist into the Darkrrun's face. The enemy immediately dropped and slid down into the water. The remaining attacker charged. Jakkur skillfully flipped the captured sword in the air and grabbed the handle as it came back down. In an instant the Darkrrun was dispatched and no immediate threat remained.

The Colonel ran down the keel of the boat to the stern. He eyed a nearby neshorn and dove into the water. An oar was extended out towards him. He grabbed on and was pulled up into the boat. Once aboard the vessel, he looked about and pointed towards an untouched drakkar. "Togrod! Togrod!" Jakkur commanded. The oarswain leaned hard on the steering beam; the rowers burrowed their oars deep and pulled hard. Passing three other neshorns, Jakkur stood up and issued the same command. "Togrod! Togrod!" The crews of the other vessels needed no explanation and pulled into formation around Jakkur's neshorn. The sea waters across the line of battle were now filled with timber and carcasses. The Grhytans were unrelenting; the assaults continued, and the casualties being sustained only strengthened their resolve.

"Colonel Jakkur!" The Chief General's voice could barely be heard over the chaos. Ulfur motioned with a wave; Jakkur directed his group of neshorns in Ulfur's direction. As they approached, Ulfur yelled out, "Colonel, the Darkrrun's have brought a huendrak vessel into this battle. There are four hundred warriors on that ship! It approaches quickly. Turn back and command the captains of the two nearest drocmogs to move full sail and oar toward the tower ruin on the beach. They are to ram the huendrak and board the enemy vessel upon impact."

"As you command, Chief General!" Jakkur responded. Turning to his oarswain and rowers he pointed back towards the open sea. "Go! Now!"

Ulfur looked at the remaining oarswains. "You three now hold the rank of Sergeant! Gather all the neshorn crews in the vicinity and direct them to move towards the tower ruin with the greatest of haste. We need as many ram beams as possible to attack the huendrak. Fall out!" He then instructed his own crew, "We must do the same. There are two formations to our starboard side. Get me to them now!"

As Ulfur and the Grhytans assembled an assault group, the Darkrrun huendrak was quickly gaining speed. It moved towards the center of battle with Darkrrun warriors gathered on deck and poised for attack. Colonel Jakkur pushed his crew at remarkable speed and had already contacted one drocmog. He had driven his crew with such aggressiveness that three of the rowers had collapsed in their seats. Jakkur recruited a fresh crew of rowers and drove them with the same intensity to the second drocmog.

A large formation of neshorns now pushed hard and fast toward the huendrak. Chief General Ulfur knew the ship and its crew had to be destroyed, otherwise the landing would be in serious jeopardy. He also understood the consequences of the Grhytans boarding the enemy ship. The Grhytan military had no command for retreat. To take command of Grhytan forces, Ulfur only needed two commands, "Forward" and "Attack." The concept of retreat was beyond the comprehension of Grhytan soldiers. Once commanded to attack, they would pursue their objective unconditionally. In his former life Ulfur had battled the Grhytans and that is what he had feared most about them. Once engaged in battle, they would neither relent nor retreat. The Grhytan objectives had always remained the same; fight until victory or fight until death. Had the Grhytan military ever sustained sufficient numbers, they would have ruled Varrunas for ages past.

Boom! Boom! Boom! The formation of neshorns had begun impaling the huendrak's hull. Darkrrun warriors, with blades projected downward, began diving directly into the Grhytan vessels. They slammed into the crews with such force that their swords punctured the hulls of the boats. More thunderous crashing could be heard as another line of neshorns drove their ram beams deep into the wood of the huendrak. Many of them had become wedged in the hull and fierce combat was being waged aboard. The clashing of metal against metal, bloodcurdling Grhytan howls, and screams of pain now encircled the Darkrrun ship. The ram beams had caused some damage to the hull, but the punctures were not sufficient to bring down the massive vessel. Ulfur pulled himself out of the water and up onto a large timber that had broken loose. He looked back towards the sea and a spark of hope came to his heart. Two drocmogs were racing towards them just as he had ordered. The Grhytan captains would not veer from their course, nor would they be deterred by anything, or any living being, in their path. Ulfur realized he was in the direct line of sight with one of the ships. He yelled out commands to those around him, "Pull back! Pull back!" then dove into sea and swam as swiftly as he could away from the huendrak.

The impact of the drocmogs was thunderous. The three ships had melded as one; warrior's poured onto the decks of the Grhytan ships and the Grhytan soldiers scattered out onto the deck of the Darkrrun vessel. The fighting was the fiercest Ulfur had ever witnessed. The confined combat area was a horrific scene. Screams of excruciating pain coursed through the dense assemblage of Grhytan and Darkrrun combatants. Colonel Jakkur arrived with his crew moments after the impact. He spied Ulfur near the hull and moved close to pluck him from the water. Jakkur supplied the Chief General with a sword, and together they climbed up some damaged rigging to the deck. Setting foot on the deck of the huendrak, they were greeted with the swinging blades of angry Darkrruns. Fighting back to back, they held fast against a group of warriors that had surrounded them.

Suddenly, the ship listed heavily to the starboard side, causing a host of combatants to lose their footing and hit the deck. It was evident the huendrak was mortally wounded and going down. Ulfur regained his footing, looked about the deck, and considered his next command. "Jakkur, the drocmog wedged in the bow must be pried away. We must find a sounder and move to the bow. They fought their way to the bow with Ulfur sustaining a cut to the torso. A sounder was ordered to the deck of the wedged drocmog and Ulfur's plan was initiated.

The assembly call was issued. The horn blasts resonated over the combat area. The Grhytan soldiers were confused, but obedient. The fighting continued as the Grhytans moved aft. Colonel Jakkur pointed at the hull of the drocmog and boomed out the command, "Tog! Tog! Tog!" A mob of Grhytans drove their nails into the hull of the drocmog and began to push in rhythm with the Colonel's commands. "Tog! Tog! Tog!" There was a tremendous creaking and popping as the Grhytan ship was being extracted. The Colonel continued, "Tog! Tog! Tog!" Crack! Splash! The drocmog had been wrenched free. The Colonel nodded at the sounder and the boarding call was blasted out. The Grhytan soldiers were hesitant but began piling onto the ship. The deck of the drocmog was soon filled over capacity with both Grhytans and Darkrruns as they pursued one another's destruction. The ship drifted back away from the sinking huendrak. Soldiers and warriors clung to whatever they could. Many dropped into the sea while others were able to make it to the crowded deck and continue fighting. The combat persisted until the Grhytan soldiers presided over a deck littered with the bodies of fallen Darkrruns.

Ulfur pushed aside the Darkrrun that had collapsed on his chest. Rising to his feet, he cast his gaze over the carnage. Knowing the battle was not over; he quickly worked his way to the sterncastle to get a vantage point of the rest of the fleet. Scattered across the line of battle were numerous Varrun drakkars in various states of submersion. Only a handful of damaged ships remained afloat, and several of the drocmogs had already run aground. Along the length of the beach, a wave of Darkrruns emerged from their positions among the ruins and charged towards the advancing Grhytans. Flashes of intense light spread through the clusters of soldiers along the shore. They were igniting the flame spears. Ulfur yelled across the deck, "Captain! Are you with us? Captain!"

A deep, shaky voice responded, "Yes, Chief General. I remain."

Ulfur immediately issued new orders. "Captain, gather a pilot and crew and get this ship pointed towards the shore. Colonel Jakkur, command all available uninjured soldiers below deck until the rowing positions are full. The rest of you get the garbage removed from this deck. Fall out!"

The Chief General's commands were hastily executed. The Captain and crew were at their posts. Oarswains stood ready on the lower decks. "Colonel Jakkur, enlist assistance and cover every area of this ship to get the flame spears gathered and distributed."

Ulfur turned towards the captain. "Engage the rowers at full speed and run this vessel aground. Togrod!"

With great eagerness, the Captain issued the necessary commands to his crew. The drocmog cut through the sea towards the shore. Most of the Grhytans had been issued flame spears; torch bearers stood near the gangways, ready to ignite the spears as the soldiers disembarked. The rowers continued their aggressive assault on the water. The oars began to dig into the shoal, but the single-minded Grhytans continued to pull, snapping the oars like twigs. The keel hit the beach with jarring force. The few crew members not braced for the impact were thrown in all directions. A clamorous grinding underneath the hull was accompanied with pounding vibrations, and the drocmog came to a sudden halt. It was time for the rowers to be soldiers once again; they charged topside, eager to put their boots on the soil.

Pouring out of the gangways with flame spears ablaze, they greeted the Darkrruns with ear-splitting war howls. The wave of warriors came at them like a swarm of insects, encompassing the Grhytans from all sides. The soldiers pressed forward into the mass of darkness with their new weapons thrust forward. Flame spears pierced through the slits and crevices of the Darkrrun armor. The warriors writhed in pain as their bodies mutated into clouds of black haze that filled the air with the acrid odor of sulfur. A great number of Grhytans succumbed as hordes of

Darkrruns piled onto the soldiers, slashing their swords about with wild abandon. It seemed not to matter when one of their own was caught in the arc of the blades. The coastline had become blanketed with a web of combatants; the atmosphere grew dense with the fog of eradicated Darkrruns. Hurdroy's flame spears had given the Grhytans an advantage for their initial landing. However, pitch does not burn eternal and the fire of the spears began to diminish. Within a brief span, the soldiers held ordinary broadboar spears, which they quickly tossed aside in favor of their swords. The opposing forces had become evenly matched, and for a fleeting moment the Grhytans thought the battle would belong to them. Then the blast of Varrun merkhorns resounded over the expansive city ruins. A flood of Darkrruns emerged from behind the shattered stone walls along the entire line of battle.

Chief General Ulfur quickly tallied his officers among the horde that surrounded him. He shouted, "To the gorge! Issue the order!" Fighting his way through the mayhem, he reached a stunned sounder floundering about on the ground. Ulfur earnestly attempted to lift the soldier upright without success. In an act of desperation, he gave the Grhytan a hard kick in the center of his exposed rib cage. The sounder grunted and rose to his feet. "Assembly call now!" commanded Ulfur. The soldier snatched his horn from the ground and boomed out a series of calls. The Chief General engaged more officers across the field. "To the gorge! Issue the order!" The commands had begun to work their way across the length of the beach head. Grhytan soldiers began breaking off on a direct course towards the Balchdur Gorge. The Darkrruns pursued, and the center of battle shifted to the narrow gorge entrance.

Ulfur sought after Colonel Jakkur, pulling other officers to his side as he went. Finding Jakkur, he projected his orders over the pandemonium. "We must push forward to Ilkraador. Pull the troops together in column and lead a fast march up the gorge. Charge the Drok-Hund battalion to form a phalanx and follow up the rear. They must hold off the advance of the warriors. No Darkrruns must gain ground ahead of the column."

Jakkur pointed up the gorge and shouted, "Chief General! Some Darkrruns have already entered the gorge!"

Ulfur forcefully responded, "Execute your orders now!" He grabbed the arm of the officer closest to him. "You will come with me into the gorge. Call a sounder to assemble your platoon immediately."

The Lieutenant hastily enlisted a sounder. The powerful lungs behind the horn delivered several repetitions of the platoon's distinct assembly call across the battlefield. In short order, Chief General Ulfur charged up the neck of the gorge with the formation of mustered soldiers directly behind. They engaged a scattered assemblage of enemy infantry and Cuvaals, the mounted Darkrruns. The column had commenced formation and was already marching into the gorge. However, the Lieutenant's platoon of Grhytans proved more than enough to clear the trail. Though, unknown to the Grhytans, one enemy rider had slipped past them in the midst of combat.

The Cuvaal pushed his steed hard down the trail through the gorge. The animal's nostrils flared rapidly as it struggled to meet the demands of the heels that rammed into its haunches. A slather of foam covered its once well groomed coat. Unconcerned with the animal's distress, the rider sustained the painful jabs. Approaching an intersection in the trail, the rider veered right and continued to his destination, the Altar of Ehkkahn. The left arm of the trail led to the fortress of Ilkraador. It was there many generations of Varrun recruits had been trained. And it was there that three divisions of Varrun warriors were stationed and awaiting deployment. As a condition of the past season's truce, General Graeog also utilized the complex as a base for an equal number of Darkrrun forces.

The steed could no longer meet the rider's demands and its legs buckled, throwing the warrior onto the rocky trail. Understanding the importance of his task, the warrior immediately rebounded from the fall, discarded his armor, and began to run as swiftly as his feet would allow. Making his way around the final twist of the trail he felt as if his chest would explode. His destination was in sight; the Altar of Ehkkahn sat atop the high ridge before him. The sight of the Altar renewed his failing strength and he began to ascend the elevated plateau. He passed the stone cairns that marked the outer boundary of the Altar grounds. A wave of relief flowed through his bones, but there would be no rest until his task had been completed. Winding his way through the pedestals and columns he located the obscure, sunken vault that descended towards the arched tunnel entrance. He rushed down the slope, entered the tunnel, and stumbled down the stone staircase. At the end of the tunnel was a narrow timber door fastened together with forged metal straps and sturdy spikes. Straining, he heaved the heavy door open. "Elder! Elder Stolt!" he yelled down the passageway. The Elder approached him just as he reached the vestry entrance.

"Speak, Child. Speak!" Stolt insisted.

The exhausted warrior gasped for breath, "The Grhytans . . . The Grhytans have destroyed our fleet at Reitrius!"

"How is that possible? Our numbers were great!"

"Elder, they attacked our ships like monsters. The Grhytan vessels were fitted with stout ram beams; both troop ships and dory vessels such as I have never laid eyes on. Nor have I ever witnessed water craft moving with such speed! The strange dories attacked in small formations, and impaled our drakkars at water line. The brine burst through the ruptures, filled the hulls, and our vessels now lay on the floor of the sea. Many warriors lay with them, but many escaped and swam to shore."

Stolt attempted to interject, "Ram beams? On a dory!? I have never heard such—"

"Wait, Elder! I have not finished! They wielded spears of fire . . . flames of such intensity that the bodies of my warrior brothers were vanquished. They became as wisps of smoke and rose into the air. What of this Elder? You gave no warning of such a weapon!"

Stolt's demeanor grew solemn. "You are correct. I gave no warning, as I had no knowledge of such weapons. I do not understand-circumstances are not as they should be. The power of the darkness has become unsettled; my plans have come into disorder. Only one night prior, the Ehkkahn journeyed just beyond the Frellsari Channel. It was to visit destruction upon the other Grhytan fleet as they entered our waters. Upon the entities return I received no directives, no rewards, no admonishments-my presence was not even acknowledged. It merely plunged itself into the chasm and has remained there since. Still I do not know if the Grhytan fleet in the channel has been eliminated, or if it remains a force to contend with. Not in all my time with the Ehkkahn have I witnessed such an occurrence. Now, you bring me fanciful stories of flaming spears that decimate our brothers, and stories of little boats that sink our largest war vessels? The whole of these inexplicable and unimagined happenings bear evidence of the Ehkkahn's greatest enemy."

"Elder, I do not understand. Are not the Grhytans our greatest enemy?"

"You would not understand, my ignorant child!" Stolt gruffly replied. "The Ehkkahn is one of many manifestations of a spirit that has existed since before the language beings walked this temporal realm. It warred with the enemy I speak of even before the measure of time existed. The Frellsari call him Patayros; the Yonduts call him Theoas. This is the One we war against."

"Elder, I still do not understand."

"Enough of this talk! I do not have time to instruct you! What of Therak? What do you know of the Grhytan King? Is he with the fleet at Reitrius?"

Spent and barely able to continue the exchange, the Cuvaal slumped to the floor and leaned against the wall, "Elder, I know nothing of this Therak you speak of. The Grhytans were commanded by a Varrun!"

Stolt slammed his fist against the wall, "Ulfur! He is a curse! A damnable curse! Does the Varrun commander remain?"

"Elder Stolt, I do not know. I perceived the battle had turned. Reckoning it to be of utmost importance that you were informed, I fought my way past the Grhytans and made haste to the Altar."

"You have done well child-your actions are of great value. You will be rewarded accordingly. Now go. Fill your belly and quench your thirst; there will be further tasks for you."

Stolt's mind reeled with the news he had just received. Stolt spoke loudly to himself, "Ulfur and his Grhytans cannot stand against the power of Ehkkahn. I shall summon the entity, and its children will triumph." As if to convince himself, he proclaimed aloud a second time, "We shall triumph!" The Elder made his way directly to the precipice alcove that overlooked the chasm. He knelt down and began a fervent recitation of the 'Invocation of Wrath'. Within moments the awakening commenced. The choir of the dead filled the chasm with their haunting wails. Tremors shook the foundations of the Altar, and the Ehkkahn began its ascent. Stolt continued the invocation, "Master of the Blessed Darkness, arise in fury, arise in wrath, arise for your pleasure, arise for your servant. Arise . . . "

The last few groups of Grhytan soldiers fought their way through the ruins. They joined the trailing end of the column as it entered the mouth of the gorge. Darkrrun forces pursued close behind and began to amass in loose formation in preparation to enter the gorge. The enemy officers argued among themselves as to how they should organize the pursuit of the Grhytans. One particularly nasty disagreement was settled in a fashion typical of the island's inhabitants. A Field Major was bested during a squabble and summarily interred under a pile of stones collected from the city ruins. While the Darkrruns fought amongst their own kind, the Drok-Hund battalion formed a phalanx at the mouth of the gorge. The Drok-Hunds were renowned for the maneuver. The battalion had been credited with the victory of The Battle of The Plain, and these same soldiers were eager to confront the Darkrruns again to test some new tactical constructs they had only practiced during drills.

Farther up the gorge, the Grhytan column was fully engaged in its rapid march. The few oologs that had been brought ashore were mounted by the officers who led the formation. Ulfur, having appropriated one for himself and Colonel Jakkur, rode in front of the column. "Colonel, increase the cadence to double-time!" ordered Ulfur. Jakkur implemented his orders down the line and the soldiers responded with boots vigorously pounding the soil. The Chief General was pleased with the pace, and their progress brought him reassurance that his army would arrive at the Valley of Ilkraador in sufficient time to join with Therak's forces for the initial attack. He was even more invigorated when the column passed the junction of trails. "We're going to make it!" he thought to himself.

At first it seemed to the soldiers that a sea gale was moving inland. The low rumble seemed distant as the sound traveled up the gorge. The Grhytans gave it no other thought and persisted in their trek to the valley. The rumble grew progressively louder, reverberating up the stone trough that the soldiers traveled through. The trailing end of the column was still in sight of the junction behind them. Boom! Thunder issued out of the ancillary arm of the gorge. The amplified roar overwhelmed the marching Grhytans as they began to traverse a sharp bend in the trail. Several soldiers allowed themselves to be distracted by the noise and fell out of formation as they curiously gawked backwards down the trail. The gorge on the other side of the bend they had just passed through was cast fully in shadow. Not like a passing cloud, rather it was akin to the dark of a moonless night.

Boom! Boom! Boom! In rapid succession, dozens of dokkbolts carved into the high crags on either side of the column. Ancient stone formations exploded and broke apart into enormous boulders that bounced down the near vertical cliffs. The end of the column closest to the blast was caught unaware. The bedlam scattered the soldiers in all directions as they made every effort to avert the destruction bearing down on them. Massive serpentine arms emerged from the encroaching mass, reaching up the trail towards the disoriented Grhytans. The cyclonic gusts blasted up through the gorge all the way to the point of the column. The walls of the gorge now shuddered with the rage of the Ehkkahn.

Ulfur turned an ear back in the direction he had come from. In that same moment, a gale force wind drove bits of gravel into his face. His oolog roared with distress and bucked several times before the Chief General was able to regain control. "Jakkur! The Ehkkahn comes! Forward!" Colonel Jakkur looked at Ulfur as if he did not understand. "Colonel! The Not! It is The Not! Forward!" Jakkur needed no further orders; he drove his oolog to the front of the column, pointed at the lead sounder and shouted, "Togrod!" The lead sounder's signal echoed back down the column line with a volume that nearly matched that of the pursuing tempest. The roar of the Ehkkahn's wrath had become overpowering. The arms of the Ehkkhan burrowed into every crack, crevice and fissure in the stone walls of the gorge. The cyclonic pressure forced the rock to explode downward onto the Grhytans below. Back down the gorge, the trailing section of the column was encountering calamity. The incessant battery of dokkbolts had continued to carve into the canyon walls, and ship-sized slabs of stone crashed to the ground. The Ehkkahn's tactics were devastating as nearly half of Ulfur's army was crushed beneath the monoliths.

Chief General Ulfur pushed the forward segment of the column with muscle- wrenching intensity; keeping the remaining troops a breath ahead of the pursuing entity. A dense cloud of dust billowed up the gorge, obscuring the view of what lay behind them. The trail beneath them grew wider as they raced forward. Leading on point were Ulfur, Colonel Jakkur, and the lead sounder. They were the first to hear the scant horn blasts that filtered through the gorge from in front of the charging column. Ulfur and Jakkur shared a quick glance and the lead sounder turned to Ulfur anticipating an order for the engagement call. However, Ulfur only looked forward and the three sustained their bone jarring ride for a short span longer.

The haze of dust obscured the scene before them, yet they were able to discern a blue expanse of sky opening up before them. Another blast of horns was heard emanating from in front of them. The Chief General raised his arm to communicate the order; the lead sounder gave his oolog a hard kick in the haunches and raced pass Ulfur. Riding out of the gorge a short distance into the valley, he gave a hard pull on the reins and brought the oolog to a halt. He filled his lungs with air and with explosive force sounded the attack call using a repetitive series of short bursts. The Grhytan column exploded out of the gorge and into the valley, creating a wide arc of soldiers. With a thunderous roar, the amalgam of dust and Ehkkahn burst forth directly behind them. The Valley of Ilkraador was to become an arena of death.

Therak's fleet continued on their course with the moon lighting their way. In the dark of the morn they neared the landing shore. The smaller vessels moved into the shallow water. The soldiers disembarked and waded to the bank. The flagship lowered its neshorn vessels into the water and the troops began their way to the shore. Therak directed one of his soldiers to bring the oologs topside. The animals were forced off the deck into the water and instinctively swam towards dry land. Poodwah went below and came up dragging his pouch bag. Lohjji helped him load it into the neshorn. Climbing into the small vessel, the Yonduts were the last to disembark. It was a great undertaking but soon the entire invasion force made it ashore.

The oologs stood on the gravel, shaking wildly to dry their fur. Therak approached and mounted his oolog with the Yonduts following his example. As usual, Lohjji assisted Poodwah. Therak kicked his oolog to a trot, leading his friends to the front of the column. He commented, "You will ride with me in the position of honor."

Poodwah whispered to Lohjji, "I'm not certain I want to be honored in this manner."

It was still dark as they began their march, but Therak seemed to know exactly where to go. They continued their march as the sun began to peek over the coastline hills. The terrain had become steep and rocky as they came to the face of the mountains. Therak stopped and removed a map from underneath his garment. He studied it closely, made a slight change in his course, and continued on. He led the column into a narrow gorge.

Arunthal nudged his animal alongside Therak. "This gorge is perfectly suited for an ambush. Why do you lead us here?"

Therak replied, "You forget: I have guidance from Ulfur. He knows his general's thoughts and they could not perceive any invasion force using this route. I trust Ulfur's judgment and so we will continue."

The travel was difficult and the column moved slowly. They did not cease their travel until it became too dark to go any farther. Therak stopped the column and the weary soldiers settled as comfortably as they could among the stones and boulders. Therak gathered the Yonduts. "We will rise early and move to the valley perimeter. If all has gone as planned,

Ulfur's forces will be entering on the opposite side of the valley. Say your prayers, and try to rest your bones."

It was a fitful night; the imminent battle bore on the minds of all the soldiers. It seemed that they had only rested for a short while when Therak awoke and began walking through the ranks to rouse his troops. Returning to the front of the column, he mounted his oolog and began towards his destination. The gorge grew wider and the march a bit easier. After several lenads, Therak stopped his animal and dismounted. He approached Arunthal. "We are now in a position to begin the assault. I will inform the column. Wait for me here."

Shortly, Therak returned and gathered his friends close by. "Arunthal, honor us with an offering of petition to Theoas that we may be granted victory over our enemies."

Arunthal nodded and proceeded with a short, simple request. In agreement, each of the group responded quietly, "Amoda." Therak mounted his animal and moved forward with purpose. He called for his sounder to come close to his side.

The column entered the valley and the large fortress complex came into view. A concert of merkhorn blasts were heard coming from the watchtowers of the fortress wall. The Grhytan presence had not gone unnoticed. Therak motioned his sounder to the front of the column. He issued forth a loud series of blasts, and from the opposite side of the valley, similar blasts were heard. Therak yelled out, "Ulfur has arrived! Forward!"

He kicked his oolog in the haunches and charged directly towards the fortress. The column of soldiers sped past the Yonduts with swords drawn yelling out horrendous battle cries. Arunthal commanded, "Stay close and follow me." He led his group alongside the racing soldiers.

A fair distance away on the far side of the valley, Ulfur's army erupted out of Balchdur Gorge, falling into field formation as they ran. Directly behind them, billowing out the gorge, a tempest of soil, shattered stone, and Ehkkahn began to ascend above the valley floor. A fierce gale filled the valley and the sky became permeated with the entities darkness. The swirling arms of the Ehkkahn were centered on the Grhytans, but many of the opposing forces were also in its wake. Across the battlefield, the bodies of fallen Darkrruns dissipated as the Ehkkahn passed over them. When a Darkrrun was slain, its entire form became shadow and was absorbed into the dark mass. Yet the Darkrruns persisted. Their numbers poured out of the mountains like roaring rivers of melted snow. Ulfur's soldiers had scarcely begun to advance towards the fortress when they were engaged by a full regiment of Cuvaals riding as wildly as the wind around them.

A large group of Grhytans began to gather in loose formation in front of the main gates. The sound of the battle intensified as Therak dismounted his oolog and ran towards the gates. The formation of Grhytans followed their general and as one body heaved against the timbers which separated them from their enemies inside. The air above them grew cloudy with spears. Many Grhytans were struck by the weapons and fell to the ground. The gates splintered and swung open with a tremendous crash.

The inside of the complex was expansive and a combined force of Varruns and Darkrruns poured out endlessly from the barracks. Arunthal kept his group outside the wall and were soon engaging warriors passing through the gates. Staying as close to each other as possible, Jeddok and Lohjji wielded their swords with great effectiveness.

Poodwah dismounted his animal and found refuge in a hidden crevice of rocks near the timber bridge which approached the gates. He had managed to drag his pouch bag with him and built a small tinder fire. He soon had his lighting twigs smoldering and waited on the appropriate moment to roll out a skrugin. He had not waited long when he heard the battle cries come from behind his crevice. He peered through an opening and saw a group of Darkrruns charging towards the gate area. He picked up a skrugin and lit the fiber cord. Waiting on just the right moment, he rolled the object into their midst at the moment they passed by. His timing proved accurate.

Arunthal had been engaged by a Varrun and Darkrrun simultaneously and his skills with the sword became clearly evident to his foes. Inside the fortress walls, Therak and his soldiers were fighting ferociously, but the confines of the walls pressed the soldiers into extraordinarily close hand-to-hand combat. It was a predicament proving to be deadly for both sides. Ulfur's fight had moved closer to the fortress, and it did not appear to be going well. The ranks of the Cuvaals continued to swell and Ulfur's Grhytans succumbed to the onslaught of dark riders.

Poodwah remained in his crevice, tossing skrugins when he could. The center of the battle had moved to the outside the fortress walls. He gazed on the destruction before him; it was evident the Grhytan forces were losing. Their numbers were too few. As his heart filled with anger, determination, and fear, he spied a high outcropping of stone close to his hiding place. His heart directed him and he knew what he must do.

Leaving the safety of the rocks, he dashed toward the outcropping and scaled it. His friends were within viewing distance and Lohjji yelled to Jeddok, "Look at Poodwah! What is he doing?"

Jeddok immediately ran in Poodwah's direction and was passed as Therak charged by. Jeddok and Lohjji could not keep up with Therak and fell behind.

Just as Therak reached the base of the rock face, he was met by a group of warriors. Unexpectedly, the Chief General emerged from the dust of the battlefield with his sword at the ready. Ulfur and Therak established their stand and engaged the oncoming warriors, fighting side-by-side and then back to back. Just as Jeddok and Lohjji grew near their friend's position, they were struck by Poodwah's actions. He was kneeling down on the highest part of the outcropping. Lohjji turned to Jeddok. "He shouldn't be up there. We must fetch him down."

Jeddok responded, "It could be that Poodwah is the only one showing wisdom in this battle."

Then, all across the battlefield, something wondrous occurred. Each soldier bearing a Grhytan sword beheld something very unusual. The metal crafter's marks began to glow with a soft, warm light. It grew ever brighter as shafts of light enveloped the blades, and then explosively surged from the tips. The Darkrruns in the path of the beams burst into a dark mist while the same shafts of light pierced holes in the dark mass hovering above them. In response, the Ehkkahn roared with the collective voices of its entrapped spirits. Inadvertently, soldiers crossed the shafts of light and witnessed them merging. The merged shafts then converged with others. The Grhytans then began to combine the shafts of light and sweep the fused beams across the sky and battlefield as one. The Darkrruns were swept over by the waves of brilliance and disappeared in droves. Sensing victory, the soldiers adapted their sword skills to engage the Ehkkahn directly. As more beams were joined, the light completely enveloped the Ehkkahn. Its mass wrenched in all directions as it cried out with horrific unearthly shrieks. It began withdrawing into itself until it was reduced to a thin wisp of haze floating away with the wind. Across the valley, the remaining Varruns dropped their swords and raised their trembling hands in surrender.

The events had transpired so suddenly that all on the battlefield were shocked. After a moment of quietness across the valley, the reality of victory filled their bellies and the Grhytan's rejoiced for all the mountains to hear. However, as was the way of Grhytans, they promptly began to address the practical tasks at hand. The injured were triaged and treated, loose armament was gathered, and the collection of prisoners began. Still atop his rocky perch, Poodwah pulled off his helmet, and surveyed the valley. He yelled out "Theoas has delivered us victory!"

Arunthal, having just made his way back to Jeddok and Lohjji, hollered out in response, "And to Him be all glory and honor!"

The group of Yonduts then became aware of the absence of Therak's voice. He was not to be seen anywhere, nor Ulfur. Poodwah looked down from the top of the outcropping and pointed. Jeddok ran to its base. Underneath the bodies of Varruns, he saw a Grhytan arm and his heart sank. As the group began clearing away the fallen Varruns, grief fell upon them. There lay Therak and Ulfur, side by side. In life they were kings and enemies; in death they were soldiers and brothers. Arunthal wept silently as he knelt down beside his fallen friends. Jeddok laid a hand on his pap's shoulder, standing quietly beside him.

Poodwah, angry with grief, shook off his armor and threw it to the ground. He exclaimed, "I want no more of this. I am done." He walked a distance away to gather himself. Lohjji said nothing as tears formed in the corners of his eyes.

Arunthal stood up, and spoke. "We must build proper burial cairns. And find the next in command."

# CHAPTER 19

## YONDUSLAND

It was a somber moment as the group contemplated all which had transpired. Buried in the recesses of their minds, they knew that death could have come for any of them, but the reality of those thoughts had not been realized until they stood over the lifeless forms of Therak and Ulfur.

Arunthal composed himself and instructed the trio to wander about the battlefield and search out Colonel Jakkur. The trio went about their task with Arunthal staying behind to start construction of the cairns. It was a task which brought him both grief and honor. Never had he seen such valiant warriors as the ones he was about to lay at rest.

Jeddok came upon Jakkur a good distance away from the outcropping. He was injured but still able to function as the acting commander. He followed Jeddok back and they found that Arunthal had already laid out the first layer of stones. Jakkur and Jeddok took to placing stones for the second layer. Lohjji and Poodwah returned and joined in the work. With the foundations laid, they gently carried their friends to their final resting places. Other soldiers took notice of the fallen warriors and joined to complete the cairns. There was silence as the stones were carefully arranged by the hands of those who had fought with the ones they covered. Jakkur and

Arunthal set the last stones in place and then stepped back from the monuments.

Jakkur was the first to speak. "Rest, my brothers."

The Yonduts replied in unison, "Amoda."

Arunthal's mind turned towards the spectacle of destruction they had just witnessed. "What manner of providence came upon us? Never has any being beheld such a battle as this."

Jakkur replied, "What you say is true. I have partaken of many battles, but never have I seen an ally of light. From whence did it come?"

Jeddok spoke, "I believe Poodwah is the one responsible, but I do not know how."

Lohjji interjected, "Yes-it began when Poodwah ascended to the top of the outcropping. Poodwah, tell us what you have done."

Poodwah looked down at the ground and then lifted his head, "I merely asked Theoas to send The Helper. Those were the only words I could form."

Arunthal replied, "Warrior, your words were heard and honored. You were the only one among us to call upon the sole source of power that could bring us victory."

Jakkur commented, "I do not understand what you speak of. However, this I know: the Varruns and Darkrruns are defeated. And I must now task myself with housing the prisoners and gathering my troops. Yonduts, what of you?"

Arunthal replied, "I want to go home, nothing more."

The trio chimed in agreement. Jakkur responded, "You are very far from home. I do not know if the Balchdur Gorge remains passable. So allow me to offer you passage on Therak's flagship. My soldiers will guide you back through the gorge that brought you to Ilkraador. Therak's resident crew will be directed to take you as far as the land of the Luurds. That should shorten your journey by countless phases."

All but Lohjji was overjoyed with the Colonel's offer. He made certain the others had not forgotten about Leshti, who remained in Osrall with Ershrun. Jeddok asked, "I understand my friend, but what do you propose we do? Have you any idea how many lenads it is back to Osrall?"

"Yes, I do." Lohjji replied. "And that does not deter me. She faithfully ventured here with us and I will not abandon her."

Poodwah asked, "What are you saying?"

Lohjji said, "I'm going back for her, and we will make our way home across the mountains and by way of Hurshon's outpost."

Poodwah's eyes saddened, "My dear chum, what will I do without your presence?"

Jeddok echoed the same sentiment, "Yes, Lohjji. We have already lost friends. Are we to lose another?"

Lohjji chuckled. "You won't be losing me. It will only be a separation of a few phases and then we will be together again. And if I find favor in Theoas' eyes, maybe Leshti will accompany me all the way to the village. By then, I should have a much better knowledge of Untra."

Arunthal asked, "And you have no doubt in your decision?"

Lohjji looked directly at Arunthal. "Not a one."

The Yonduts did what they could to assist Jakkur in his tasks, then the General assigned escorts for the returning soldiers. After a heartfelt farewell, Lohjji separated from his companions and began the journey back to his Untra maiden. The remainder of the Yonduts worked their way back through the gorge to the landing beach.

They boarded the dory vessels and rowed their way to the awaiting flagship. The escorts relayed Jakkur's orders to the pilot and crew and then joined the rowers on the second level. The vessel was gently moved away from the shoal area to deeper water. The Yonduts were enlisted to assist in unfurling the sail and the wind filled the fabric. The pilot leaned heavy on the steering beam and the vessel turned sharply. It seemed a dream, but they were on their way to Yondusland. The combination of wind, sail, and oars wielded by Grhytans propelled the vessel sure and steady.

After only two phases of travel, they made their way around the Luurin Peninsula. One more phase brought them to the sparsely settled coast beyond the Luurd's capital. From their point of landing, they could see the mountains in the direction of the setting of sun. In the other direction was the great plain and beyond that, home. The Yonduts gave blessings and thanks to their Grhytan escorts and each party went their way. Arunthal and Jeddok made trade with the inhabitants of the coast and acquired two transport oologs.

Meals and slumber seemed unimportant and they moved along as quickly as the burdened oologs allowed. The pace was intense and their minds were focused on their destination. The great plain provided a relatively easy course of travel and the lenads passed quickly behind them. Foodstuffs were proving hard to come by, but water was plentiful. The gnawing in their stomachs proved only to feed their resolve and they were unrelenting in their trek.

After two phases, they reached the wide river and the oologs carried them across safely. On the opposite bank, it was realized the animals were showing signs of fatigue, possibly illness, and it was decided to allow them time for rest and recovery. It was difficult for the Yonduts to remain at the same campsite for two days. The thought of their village so close at hand made them restless. However, the rest did the oologs well and their strength was restored. Mounting the animals once again, they knew the boundary of Yondusland was close at hand.

The plain transformed into lowlands and the surroundings grew ever more familiar. One more phase of travel brought them through a grove of trees and within sight of the home they had been yearning for. They kicked the animals in the haunches and hollered loudly as they passed through the outlying hutches. The noise brought curious Yonduts out into the street, but many ran for the safety of their hutches. What were these massive six-legged animals doing their village? And why were scraggly, wild Yonduts mounted on their backs?

Halting the oologs at the edge of the Commons, Arunthal and Jeddok dismounted. They both dashed to Jeddok's hutch, their hearts pounding with anticipation as they went. The commotion had drawn Seeanna outside and her heart jumped. The moment seemed unreal to her, but the embrace of her husband filled her senses. Arunthal called out loudly, "Ceshona!"

His wife was in the garden patch behind the hutch but she quickly made her way to the front of the dwelling. The two stood motionless, gazing at each other in disbelief. Their surprise gave way to joy and they ran to meet each other. Their tight embrace was long in coming, as were the tears which flowed freely. No words were spoken, as none were needed. The two couples remained in embrace until Jeddok spoke up. "Where is Poodwah?"

Arunthal replied, "We left him atop the oolog. You should go fetch him, son."

Jeddok took Seeanna by the hand. "Come and greet Poodwah. He has returned also."

Seeanna responded with concern, "What of Lohjji? Please tell me he is with you!"

Jeddok stopped. "Lohjji is as hale and hearty as ever. However, his heart has led him another way home but he will be returning later this season."

Seeanna was comforted by the comments. "What are we waiting for? Let's go see Poodwah."

A few more paces through the hutches brought them to the edge of the Commons and there was Poodwah, still perched on top of the oolog. He seemed content reading his parchment while he waited. "Hello, dear chum! I knew you would not abandon me. Since this oolog is the tallest one I've seen yet, it seemed unwise to jump."

Jeddok moved close to the animal. "I am sorry my friend. Please allow me." With Poodwah safely on the ground, Seeanna approached. She leaned down and gave him a tight embrace and a loving kiss on the forehead. His cheeks turned the color of glowing rondra.

Poodwah exclaimed, "I must see Pap and Mum!" and then took off at a trot in the direction of his hutch.

Jeddok and Seeanna met Arunthal and Ceshona on the way back toward their home. Arunthal spoke, "Our old hutch needs work. We are off to begin some long overdue chores."

Jeddok replied, "Can we be of help?"

Arunthal grinned. "That is not necessary, my son. Spend time with your wife. I will enlist your assistance later."

The couples went their own ways as the sun began its descent. As night fell, there was a knock at Jeddok's door. There stood Poodwah. "The parchment? Do you still have it?"

Jeddok replied, "Yes, of course I do." as he lifted his jacket from the back of the chair.

Poodwah asked, "Would you mind if I took it home with me?"

Jeddok handed the roll to him. "Not at all, my friend. What do you have in mind?"

Poodwah unrolled the parchment and studied it momentarily. "It would be a wonderful gift for Lohjji to find a completed story upon his return."

Jeddok smiled. "Poodwah, you are always thinking of others. And it would be a wonderful gift. Theoas bless you." Poodwah bade his friend goodbye and headed home.

It was going to be a long night for Poodwah. He prepared the brew pot and made a batch of exceptionally strong beanbud. He lit the lanterns in his hutch, setting the largest one on top of the table.

He poured a large stein of the brew, settled himself on a chair, and unfurled the parchment. Dipping pen in ink, he began at the top of the first sheet, scribing the words, *Tale of The Not*.

# The End

# About the Author

**Scott E. Blades** resides in Wichita, KS with his lovely wife, Kelly, two cats and a fun-loving Shih Tzu. He is also the proud stepfather of two adult children, two grandchildren and another on the way.

Comments, suggestions, felicitations, adulations, critiques, admonitions, flattery, exaggerations, elucidations, observations, expositions, suppositions, delineations, acclamations, accolades, condemnations, commendations and other omnifarious miscellanea may be submitted to:
feedback@RadldPress.com